A DEAD GUY AT THE SUMMERHOUSE

Books and stories by Marian Allen

Novels

Eel's Reverence

Force of Habit

SAGE Book 1: The Fall of Onagros

SAGE Book 2: Bargain With Fate

SAGE Book 3: Silver and Iron

Sideshow in the Center Ring

A Dead Guy at the Summerhouse

Short Story Collections

Lonnie, Me and the Hound of Hell

Turtle Feathers

The King of Cherokee Creek

MA's Monthly Hot Flashes: 2002-2009

Visit the author at

http://MarianAllen.com

A DEAD GUY AT THE SUMMERHOUSE

MARIAN ALLEN

Per Bastet

A Dead Guy at the Summerhouse

Published by Per Bastet Publications LLC, P.O. Box 3023 Corydon, IN 47112

Cover art by Sara Marian

Cover Design by T. Lee Harris

ISBN 978-1-942166-08-5

This book is dedicated to my daughter Sara, and to the members of the Southern Indiana Writers Group, who devoted so much time and effort to helping me say what I meant.

A DEAD GUY AT THE SUMMERHOUSE

Chapter 1

It was 1968. Like a lot of seventeen-year-old males that summer, I was thinking about death. Not Bobby Kennedy's or Martin Luther King's. I was contemplating my own. I could feel my eighteenth birthday looming and I had to wonder if I'd spend my nineteenth in Vietnam, in Canada, in jail, or in the Great Hereafter. It was nearly the last mentioned, and not at the hands of the VC, either. I came *this* close to having my goozle slit right here at home in good old nothing-ever-happens Faelin, Indiana. But that was later.

I tried for a basket and missed, trotted half-heartedly after the ball, and caught it as it rolled to a stop against the fence. One good thing about playing alone on a day so hot the asphalt sucks at your sneakers: no razzing when you play like a stoned sloth.

The court ran along one side of the house, or Home or, as the Townies called it, The Orphanage. The official name was Faelin Municipal Children's Refuge, making me, I guess, a refugee.

The parking lot ran along the opposite side, which is why I didn't see the car that pulled in and parked. I wouldn't have supposed it had anything to do with me, even if I'd seen it; I'd long since given up any hope of adoption. As soon as I turned eighteen, I'd have to leave, anyway. Probably go into the Service. Probably try for the Navy.

With my dark skin, dark hair, and dark eyes, I always kind of thought I'd look sharp in a white uniform.

I thought about that, my last day at the Refuge, bouncing the ball across the court, not really practicing anything, just fooling around.

"Hey, Mitch!" I saw Jimmy Gassman's features pressed against the screen of our first-floor bedroom. Jimmy, my roommate, was ten, and a first-class pest. "Mrs. Brandt wants you to get cleaned up and go to her office. There's a lady in there!"

My heart did one of those flops like they talk about in True Romance comics. (Sometimes you get real desperate for reading material.) Like I said, I'd be leaving in a few months, and I'd been at the Refuge all my life; nobody had ever even taken me home for a month's free trial, but I'd never given up hope. Kids can be so dumb. I mean, the cops found me in a dumpster. With my coloring, there was some speculation that I might not be white. Nobody in small-town Middle America in those days was going to adopt a kid who might not even be white. Things were changing by 1968, but trust me to miss the benefit.

Anyway, I tossed the ball into the equipment shed and sprinted to the bathroom. No time for a shower. I slopped off the smell with a washcloth at the sink and darted into the bedroom for a change of clothes.

Jimmy still had his face smooshed against the screen, humming loudly. He said it tickled his lips.

"Cut it out," I said, pulling on a clean tee and buttoning my good Madras shirt over it. "You'll get lead poison or something. That screen's dirty."

"I washed it," he lied.

I hesitated between my pegged jeans or my new

bell-bottoms. I decided to go with the more conservative look, and squeezed my feet through the older jeans and into my loafers. Thank God, I thought, for Trinity Episcopal Sunday School's Dorcas Class, who had chosen the Refuge as their "mission" for the year. They tended to concentrate on the younger kids, but one of the members was a male clothes horse, and he'd passed me some pretty cool threads.

"Better hurry, before she changes her mind," Jimmy mumbled, without taking his mouth off the screen.

I shook some Barbasol onto my hair and combed it back. Mrs. Brandt was with-it enough to let me wear my hair as long as I wanted, even half-way down my ears, but she insisted I keep it neat. I could live with that.

I peered into the mirror. Did I need a shave? No, but maybe in a couple of days.

"Hope you like the taste of bug guts," I said, on my way out of the room. "Notice, if you will, the fly swatter on the floor under the window."

~*~

When I opened Mrs. Brandt's office door, the first thing I saw was that I wasn't going to be adopted, at least not by this lady. They were stricter, in those days, about who was "qualified" to adopt, and that was pretty well middle-class young couples, mostly white. This lady was white and, if her rings were real, she met the financial requirements, but she was old — like with white hair and wrinkles. I found out later that she was born in 1897, which was cool, so she was seventy-one that day in mid-July.

The second thing I noticed were the dogs. Two orange Pekingese dogs, to get technical about it. One was solid orange, and the other had a white patch on his chest and one white stocking. "Oh-oh," I said to myself. "Another mongrel. Pup, you and I are going to get along." I went down on one knee and held out my hand to the cautiously advancing dogs. They darted their noses toward my fingers, huffing and chuffing and waving feathery tails. At this delicate stage of diplomatic negotiations, I remembered there were grown-ups in the room and that I had been summoned for a purpose involving them.

"Mitch," Mrs. Brandt said, with a chuckle hidden under her voice, "this is Miss Amelia Hardesty of Willowbrook. Miss Hardesty, this is Mitch Franklin, the young man I was telling you about."

Willowbrook was the name of the town mansion on a hill outside of Faelin, too far off the state road to be seen in any detail. Also known as The Old Hardesty Place, and I guessed this must be The Old Hardesty.

The lady beamed at me. Apparently, making up to the dogs had put me on her good side.

"How do you do, Mitch?" She had a soft, sweet voice, a voice that sounded like the way talcum powder smells. "I'm glad to see you and my babies getting along so well."

I took my hands off the furry orange heads and stood up, wiping my palms on my jeans.

"I'm sorry," I said. "I'd shake hands, but—"

"Oh, I don't mind a little dog hair, especially from my own dogs." I guess she didn't: Her navy blue suit was covered with orange fuzz. She held out her little pink hand; it was soft, but cold. Her mild blue eyes darted from my face to the clock above Mrs. Brandt's head. "I'm looking for a young man to work for me, full-time, live-in. You'll have a room in the house, full board, and a salary, payable at the end of the week." She named a sum that was twice what

I made bagging groceries at the ShopWell. "You'll do some small household repair work — Mrs. Brandt tells me you're quite a handyman — but your main job will be to help me look after my babies."

I looked at the dogs, who were still sniffing at my pants legs.

"Their names are Chan—" the one with the white patches looked up at her expectantly — "and Wong." The other dog, solid orange, wagged his tail twice, vigorously. "How fortunate that they've taken to you already. That was my one worry. Will you take the job?"

Mrs. Brandt nodded when I looked at her, so I said, "Sure. I mean, thank you, Miss Hardesty."

The old lady laughed and said, "You must call me Aunt Missy. Will you?"

I looked down into those twinkly blue eyes, that white hair curling around those laugh-wrinkles, those dimples, and I knew I had my first case of Grandma-love. The Refuge traded visits once a month with the Oak Ridge Nursing Home, and the little kids always went nuts over some "Granny Ellen" or "Gran'pa Joe," but I never had. Now I knew what they felt: "This one is for ME."

"Sure, Aunt Missy. I, um, I need to give them two weeks' notice at the store, so I could start—"

Miss Hardesty sat forward and gripped the edge of Mrs. Brandt's desk. "Oh," she said, a gentle sound, full of dismay. "No, I need you now. I need you to start today. Can't you? Where do you work?"

I told her.

"Do you have the number? I'll call them. May I?"

Ten minutes later, I had a new job and a promise of a glowing reference from my former manager.

"There!" Aunt Missy folded her hands in her lap on top of her white gloves and black leather pocketbook. "We'll leave as soon as you're ready, Mitch, dear."

~*~

Mrs. Brandt came to help me pack. We stopped at the storage closet on the way, to collect an old black Samsonite suitcase and a brown canvas handbag.

"Just take what you need for overnight," she told me. "I'll send the rest out with Billy." Billy was the general workman for the Refuge. He'd taught me how to drive a nail and such.

"I'm really going to live up at Willowbrook?" Maybe that was a stupid question, but it was a little hard to picture.

"In the old days, the Hardestys had a lot of live-in employees. Lovely, clean rooms on the first floor, not 'servants' quarters' in the attic, or anything Victorian like that."

That's right, I said to myself. *I'm not a servant, I'm an independent contractor.*

~*~

As we came in, Jimmy looked up from the Batman bat he was drawing on the sole of one sneaker.

"Is Mitch in trouble?" Hard to tell from his voice if he was worried or hopeful.

"No." Mrs. Brandt stroked Jimmy's head. "He has a job. A live-away job."

I went through my two drawers and half-a-closet and separated all my worldly goods into a small pile and a smaller pile. The small pile, I put into the suitcase; the smaller one, I'd take with me. I stuffed a couple of my books into the handbag and left the others on the bed. My comic book collection was already in a brown paper bag. I put that on the bed, too, shooting a warning glare at Jimmy.

"Don't touch these."

"You're leaving?" This time, I heard an edge of almost-panic in the words. I knew how he felt. I'd been at the Refuge my whole life. Every kid who came through the Faelin system found me there and left me there; a kid, like them, but part of the process. Kind of a humanizing element, you might say. Like a camp mascot, only I could talk.

I pulled a dozen comics off the top of the stack. "Here, you can have my duplicates." I had planned to trade them, but I was feeling weirdly too-old-for-that-stuff right now. "You can have my *Enterprise* model, too, if you want it." I wasn't really into "Star Trek" anyway: the model had been under the Refuge tree in a box marked BOY 10+, and Mrs. Brandt's fat cousin in the Santa suit had just happened to give it to me. I had always planned to give it to Jimmy as soon as I thought he had drooled over it enough.

"S-sure!"

Mrs. Brandt's shoes clicked across the tile floor. "Come to the office when you've finished saying goodbye." Her voice sounded thick to me, like she was trying not to cry. Maybe I just thought that because it was what I was about to do.

"Where's everybody else?" I asked Jimmy. There were six of us at the Refuge just then, with room for two more.

"Movies." Jimmy went back to drawing on his shoe.

"Why didn't you go with them?"

"No money."

"Why didn't you ask me? I'd have given you—"

Jimmy stopped drawing and threw the pen at me.

"Go on and leave, then!" he shouted.

"Hey!" I used my deepest, hardest voice. His head snapped around to stare at me. I pointed at him. "Don't touch my comics. You do, and you die." I stepped over and ruffled his hair with my knuckles.

"Ow!"

And that was goodbye.

~*~

"Can you drive, Mitch, dear?" Miss Hardesty — Aunt Missy — asked, as we left the Refuge. "Do you have your license? Your permanent license?"

"Yes, ma'am."

"Would you drive, then? I may have overdone it; I'm feeling rather tired."

"Sure, Aunt Missy."

Chan and Wong trotted at her heels like a couple of perfect gentlemen. Ivy League obedience school, no doubt.

Aunt Missy pulled a set of keys out of her black bag and handed them to me. "This is it."

"It" was a deep green 1968 Mercedes Benz sedan. I'm not a gear head, but even I was impressed.

"It's an automatic," Aunt Missy said. "Can you drive an automatic?"

"Oh, yes." I let the dogs into the back seat, where they curled up on a plush white towel (now covered with orange fuzz). I settled Aunt Missy into the front. I couldn't suppress a grin as I slid behind the wheel and turned the key.

"It's a nice car, isn't it?" Aunt Missy asked.

"Yes," I said. "It's a nice car."

She leaned forward and worked some controls on the

console. I braced myself for 101 Strings playing Andy Williams' Greatest Hits, but what I got was a blast of cool air. Goosebumps in July. Who could ask for more?

I pulled out of the parking lot and turned right, toward the north edge of town.

"You know the way, dear?"

"Yes, ma'am."

"Good." She relaxed against the seat and closed her eyes. She gave a deep and shuddery sigh. "Such a relief," she said. "Such a burden off my shoulders."

"What, those little guys?" Chan and Wong were asleep in the back, each snoring in his own particular key.

"Yes and no. Somewhat indirectly, one might say. You see, dear, the real reason I need you, and needed you right away. . . . The dogs are in danger. Mortal danger. Someone is trying to kill my babies."

I glanced at Aunt Missy, long enough to see that she wasn't kidding me. Quit my job, left my home, trapped in a moving vehicle with a woman who thought somebody wanted to murder a couple of animated dust mops.

And I had thought it was tough just being an orphan.

Chapter 2

We drove in silence until I made the turn onto State Road 62. All the time, I could feel Aunt Missy's — Miss Hardesty's — eyes on me.

"You don't believe me." She sounded a little disappointed, but it was mostly just a statement. "You think I'm insane, or at least irrational, but I'm not. Truly, I'm not."

"No, I don't." And I didn't, exactly.

"Dotty, then." Well, yeah, that was more like it. "That's what they all think: everybody at home."

So this wasn't something she'd just come out with for my benefit. That helped, somehow. If they knew about this delusion at home and put up with it, it must not be too bad.

Miss Hardesty watched the highway for a while. "Next road on the right," she said, absently. "It's unmarked."

I slowed and made the turn onto the one-lane blacktop that curved back and forth up the hill to Willowbrook.

"Naturally, you don't believe me. Why should you? You don't know me, and you don't know that household. But would you do this for me?" She put a hand on my shoulder. I could feel its icy trembling through my shirt and tee. "Would you just reserve judgment until you've been with us for a few days? Can you do that for me, dear?"

Now, how could I resist an appeal like that? Needed. Trusted. Wanted. It made me light-headed, and it didn't matter that the appeal came from somebody who might be a little bit wacko. After all, who but a wacko would have chosen me?

"Okay, Aunt Missy. I will."

"Will you? Grand! Thank you!" She clasped her hands. "Now I don't care what anyone says!" She sat back, head raised and shoulders squared.

After a moment she said, "Do you smoke, dear?"

A lot of the kids at school sneaked smokes from their parents, but Mrs. Brandt wouldn't allow tobacco in the house or on the grounds. Billy had offered me a smoke a couple of years ago, when I'd gone to the hardware store with him. It had felt hot in my mouth and throat, and I hadn't even inhaled. Tasted nasty, too. I didn't care if it *would* make a man of me, I would have felt stupid forcing myself to pick up a habit I didn't even like. Same way with dope. A lot of the kids smoked it, but it tasted too nasty for me.

"No, ma'am," I said, feeling all clean-cut and upstanding. "I don't smoke."

"Do you mind if I do?"

Huh?

She had drawn a silver case and a silver lighter out of her pocketbook. The next time I glanced away from the curving road, she had taken a pink cigarette out of the case.

"Do you mind if I smoke?" she said again, just the least bit sharply.

"No, ma'am."

She lit up.

"I have these sent to me from Paris." She waggled the case at me before she stowed it away. "And don't tell me they aren't good for me, because I only smoke five a day, at most. I enjoy them, but I don't intend to become enslaved to them. That wouldn't suit me, at all."

"No, ma'am."

She seemed keyed up, like she was about to take a big test or something.

We crested the hill, and there stood Willowbrook. The drive, lined on both sides with some kind of drooping flowering bushes, curved across a flat lawn. The house rose against the blue summer sky, two stories of red brick. Smooth white columns supported a broad porch the width of the house.

"Pull up in front and bring in your bag." Aunt Missy stubbed out her cigarette in a spotless ashtray. "Leave the keys in the ignition."

"Yes, ma'am."

I was suffering from a minor shock, here, the kind you get when you realize that a paper-doll grown-up is a real person. I had labeled Aunt Missy "Grandmother doll" and she wasn't fitting my requirements for the label. Grandmother dolls don't smoke, and they don't give orders like Sergeant Rock in the war comics.

As we drew up to the house, one of the double doors opened and a woman ran out. I caught a glimpse of tan slacks and one of those green shirts with a blue alligator over the pocket. I pulled the car parallel to the porch and turned off the motor. The woman ran down the steps and stuck her face up to the passenger's window like a kid at a pet store. A thick black braid thunked against the glass as it fell over her shoulder. Her pale green eyes goggled in at us, and I wondered who was the fish-lover and who was the fish.

Aunt Missy turned to me, said, "Brace yourself," and opened the door.

"Oh, Aunt Amelia, oh, darling, oh, where have you *been*? Oh, we've been so *worried* about you, darling!"

I sat in the car, not liking it. In the first place, I didn't like the woman being there at all. I don't know why, but I'd assumed I'd have Aunt Missy to myself, and now this woman was not only claiming her, she was practically showing me her brand. In the second place, I didn't like the way she was talking — panic, with a little scolding, and all of it kind of phony-polite: Like she thought Aunt Missy was some doddery old crock who couldn't be trusted to drive to town by herself.

Chan and Wong woke up and scrabbled at the back of the front seat.

"Yes, yes, Lydia, it's quite all right," Aunt Missy said. "Mitch! Mitch, dear, bring your bag and come in with me."

"Bag?" the woman — Lydia — said. "A doctor brought you home?"

Then I stepped out of the car and opened the back door. Chan and Wong escaped and ran around the car, up the steps, and back down. I hauled out my canvas bag and went to Aunt Missy's side, feeling sullen.

"Lydia, dear, this is Mitch Franklin, from the Refuge. He was kind enough to drive us back. Mitch, this is Lydia Hardesty, my niece."

"How do you do, ma'am?" I said, not sure if I was supposed to shake hands or not.

Lydia stuck out her hand, though, so I shook it.

"Thank you so much for bringing her home," she said. "I'll give you a lift back to town."

"He won't be going back to town," Aunt Missy said. "Not quite yet, at any rate. I've hired him. He'll be staying here."

Lydia turned her gooseberry eyes on me and asked, "Hired him? For what, Aunt Amelia?"

Aunt Missy shrugged. "To keep me company."

Lydia smiled, as if Aunt Missy had just done something cute. "But that's marvelous, darling!" She hugged Aunt Missy, and kept an arm around her as she guided her up the steps. She gave me a smile, too, over her shoulder, as if I were part of the cuteness.

I followed, trying to figure out what was wrong with this lady. She was pretty enough, and I'm a sucker for a pretty girl, but this one wasn't having much effect; there just didn't seem to be enough wattage to her. I don't mean to say her bulb was dim or anything, but she should have been a dazzler and she wasn't; that's about as close as I can come.

When we went through the door, we left the heat and humidity outside. Between the air-conditioning and the decor, I felt like I'd stepped into the Palatial, Faelin's one and only movie theater. I mean, this was not a living room we were in, this was a foyer. Vast, with a black-and-white tiled floor, and I'm not talking linoleum. Across from the door, a marble staircase led to the second story, with what looked like miles of bannister up the stairs and across a sort of mezzanine to the side walls.

The walls were two stories high, and papered new-money green. Small bright chairs, tables of flower arrangements and what you call your bijou ornaments, and dark little oil paintings were scattered around to relieve monotony. A large round table stood a little off-center between us and the staircase, holding a cut-glass bowl of golden mums. I figured they needed a big table there to put the incoming checks on. The dogs settled in the table's shadow, taking shelter from a projected shower of pennies from heaven, maybe.

It was right about then that I saw Matthew Walton watching us from a door in the right-hand wall.

Matthew Walton was on the Board of Trustees for the Refuge, among other things. I'd seen him a couple of times; he was probably in his fifties, meaty but not fat, and his flat-brown eyes were a little on the beady side. He'd done a shoulder-grasping, "Are you a good boy?" job on me a couple of times when I was little. I still felt it when it rained.

What was he doing here?

Aunt Missy saw me staring and said, "This is Matthew Walton, whom *everyone* knows. He married my late niece Charlotte. And this," she announced, "is Mitch Franklin. I've hired him. I'll pay him out of my own money, of course; you've left me enough for that."

Mr. Walton's whole face pinched into a frown. He came toward us. "Hired him for what?"

"Protection from your insane rages, for one thing! I live in deadly fear of your foul temper!"

"I wish." He looked at me, still frowning. "Don't I know you?"

"I'm the good boy from the Refuge, sir," was all I could think of to say, but it clicked.

"Oh, yes. Mitch Franklin. James Michener Franklin; born, 1950. And you're still—" He stopped himself before he could say *still at the Refuge* or *still not adopted* or *still an orphan*, or whatever foot he'd been about to put in his mouth. As it was, he seemed to think he'd gotten a couple of toes past his molars, because his cheeks reddened and he turned away to Aunt Missy.

"Is that where you've b—" He stopped again and sniffed. "Smoke! You've been smoking in my car! In my new car!" He whirled around, eyes on the floor. I knew what he was looking for. "You took the dogs with you!" He pointed an accusing finger at them. "You didn't leave because they disappeared again! You *took* them! In my new car!"

"Contain yourself. I covered your precious upholstery with a towel." Then she smirked. "I did use the ashtray, though. Better send it to the shop." She lifted a shoulder as she turned away, sort of a shrug at Mr. Walton, sort of a "this way" to me as she said, "Come along, Mitch, I'm tired; I want to sit down."

Flickering a glance at the others, I followed Aunt Missy toward a nearer door than the one Mr. Walton had come out of. That glance showed me bafflement on Lydia's face, irritation and curiosity on Mr. Walton's. Myself, I was beginning to wonder if my new employer wasn't more than a little moldy in the cheese.

At the sound of feet on wooden stairs, Aunt Missy stopped and turned. A door opened in the side of the staircase, and a grim-looking man in a lab coat came out.

"Is she back?" he said.

"Andrew!" Aunt Missy opened her arms to the man, and I ground my teeth and asked myself what I had expected. It was a job, and it had been pitched as a job. I had accepted it as a job, so where did I get off resenting the lady's relatives because they weren't me?

The man came and hugged Aunt Missy while she said, "Andrew, they're acting as if I'm not to be allowed out of the house! It's intolerable! You mustn't let them bully me!"

"Oh, Aunt Amelia!" Lydia cried, and I had to admit, the

injustice of accusing that pastel person of being a bully was all but breathtaking.

Mr. Walton stuffed his hands into his pants pockets and sighed pointedly.

"My son," he said to me, by way of introduction.

I could see the resemblance: This Andrew guy was about twenty years younger, maybe in his thirties, a little taller and a lot slimmer, but he had the same limp black hair and brown eyes (clear, though, not smoky like Mr. Matthew's).

"Now, Aunt Amelia," Andrew said, "we've all been worried about you, that's all. We didn't know where you'd gone."

"And your driver's license has ex-pired," said Mr. Walton, pronouncing the word as if precision would clue her in to a meaning she had forgotten.

"Would any of you have taken me to the Refuge, if I had asked you? No questions asked? Or would you have quizzed me and argued with me and tried to jolly me out of it until I gave up? Well? Be honest."

I could see the answer in all their faces. Apparently, so could Aunt Missy. She left Andrew's side and came to me. I tried not to count it as a coup.

"Mitch, meet my nephew, Dr. Andrew Walton. He's a physicist." *Whatever that is.* "He has a lab in the basement. He studies the secrets of life."

Oh, really? Secrets of Life in the basement lab, eh? Okay. Yeah.

Dr. Walton laughed, and his thin fierce face sweetened like coffee with two spoons of sugar.

"This is Mitch Franklin," Mr. Walton told his son. "He's Amelia's new hire. Bodyguard, I gather."

Dr. Walton, looking understandably at a loss, shook my

hand. If he wanted an explanation from me, he was out of luck; I didn't have a clue what was going on here.

Aunt Missy tugged at my arm. "I want to sit down."

We all followed her into what I found out later they called "the sitting room." French windows opened onto a patio and the west lawn. The walls were lined with bookcases, except for the one the baby grand piano stood near. Two small sofas, a few chairs, some plants the size of teen-age trees, and the room still felt open and uncluttered.

Aunt Missy tucked herself into the corner of a sofa and, catching my eye, patted the seat next to her. I sat there, feeling out-of-place and very, very temporary.

Chapter 3

I never claimed to be a Whiz Kid, but I couldn't help noticing that I had met three people here, and none of them called Aunt Missy "Aunt Missy." They'd called her "Amelia" or "Aunt Amelia," but not "Aunt Missy." So why had she told *me* to call her that? No big thing, maybe, but it bothered me.

It bothered me, too, Mr. Walton saying, "You didn't leave because they disappeared *again*." It didn't take a Dick Tracy to figure out the dogs must have disappeared before. So maybe all that stuff Aunt Missy had been feeding me in the car about the dogs being in danger *wasn't* a bunch of malarkey.

I looked for my charges. They had followed us into the room and were snuffling around under the piano.

Aunt Missy raised her chin defiantly, although no one had said a word against her bringing me in like a new picture everyone would have to look at every day. No one had even questioned it. Maybe this was a regular thing with her.

"Where are Mary and Eleanor?" she asked. "I want to introduce them to Mitch."

More people? Is this a house or a commune?

"In Eleanor's room," Mr. Walton answered. "Eleanor didn't sleep well last night."

"She didn't?" Dr. Andrew sounded surprised, and I wondered why.

"Oh, poor dear," said Lydia. "I'll go see if I can help. If Mother feels she can leave Eleanor for a few minutes, should I send her down, Aunt Amelia?"

"If you would, please, dear. Thank you."

Lydia bustled out and I, for one, was just as glad. Lydia was a do-gooder, and I'd had plenty of them in my time. They just *ache* to do something for you, whether it's something you want done or not, and they grin in your face while they refuse to take "thanks but no thanks" for an answer.

"You missed the mail today," Mr. Walton told Aunt Missy. I felt like I had disappeared, and I was just as glad. "There was a letter for you."

I had another twinge of jealousy, especially when Aunt Missy smiled and said, "Really? From whom?"

Mr. Walton took a cream-colored envelope from the inside pocket of his suit-coat and handed it to her. "The name sounded familiar. After a while, it came to me." I craned my neck, trying to read the return address, as if it would mean something to me. "Grant Marsch. Do you recognize the name, Amelia? Remember Grant Marsch?"

"Who?" said Dr. Andrew. "The name does sound familiar."

Aunt Missy sat very still, holding the envelope by one corner. "I remember him." She put the envelope in her pocketbook and snapped the clasp.

"Aren't you going to open it?"

"Later. It is a piece of private correspondence. I'll read it privately."

"Aren't you going to accuse me of steaming it open and re-sealing it?"

"Did you?" Aunt Missy asked, but you could tell her heart wasn't in it.

"Grant Marsch was a friend of Albert's," Mr. Walton told his son. "A very dear friend of dear Albert's, as I recall. Surely you remember."

"Isn't he the one—" Dr. Andrew began, and Mr. Walton nodded.

"Albert," Mr. Walton told me, "was Aunt Amelia's last hire. He didn't work out."

Aunt Missy lowered her eyelids and turned her head away, as if she were watching the dogs, but I saw a glisten at the corner of her eye.

I didn't know what all this by-play was about, but if Aunt Missy had turned to me and said, "Mitch, dear, would you give Matthew Walton a pop in the nose?" I'd have said, "Sure," and done it.

Aunt Missy did turn to me, but all she said was, "No, he didn't work out." She smiled and patted my hand. "But Mitch will, won't you dear?"

Distracted by the soap-opera quality of genuine family life, I responded automatically with one of Mrs. Brandt's stock phrases: "Not knowing, I hesitate to say."

Mr. Walton grunted a laugh. Then he cleared his throat and said, "Amelia. I didn't mean to be hurtful. I've been — we've all been — terribly upset. When we realized you were gone, and couldn't find the dogs, we thought you'd—"

"'Flipped out,' as Lydia would say?" Aunt Missy's tone was probably supposed to be light, but the bitterness was sharp and audible. She had told me that everybody thought she was "dotty," and I could see now that she was right. They'd been chewing their nails to the elbow because they thought a crazy woman was running around loose. I resented it. I thought they might possibly have a point, but I resented it.

"And *my car* was gone," Mr. Walton went on, "and, since you haven't been in a car in five years, we hardly knew what to think. —Oh," he said to his son, "we'd better call the police and tell them she's back. Would you mind, Andrew?"

Dr. Andrew left with the air of a man making an escape.

"I suppose I should have left a note," Aunt Missy said grudgingly.

"And I suppose that's as close as you'll ever come to apologizing for throwing the whole house into an uproar. Well, I hadn't expected that much." Mr. Walton looked and sounded tired.

Maybe he really had been worried for Aunt Missy. I decided that, if I ever popped him in the nose, I'd maybe pull the punch a little.

We turned to the doorway at the sound of approaching footsteps. The woman who came in was tall and probably about Mr. Walton's age. Her hair was black, but it wouldn't have been if she hadn't worked at it, and she had it pulled back into one of those French twists. She was very pale, with frosty blue eyes looking down a length of straight nose, and lips pinched closed. Her makeup clung to her face like candle wax on a tablecloth. A dark blue sweater was draped around her shoulders and a pair of half-glasses hung from around her neck by a black cord. She looked like The Librarian from Hell.

"What is it, Matthew? Lydia and Corrie are sitting with Eleanor, but I don't like to leave her for long."

Dr. Andrew rejoined us. "Father says Eleanor didn't sleep well last night."

He seemed obsessed with sleep patterns. Maybe that was one of the Secrets of Life he was studying down in the basement lab.

"No," said the woman. "She didn't."

The subject was obviously closed, as far as she was concerned.

"Mary," said Aunt Missy, "*I* asked you to come down. I want you to meet Mitch Franklin, who will be helping me look after the dogs from now on."

Mr. Walton and I had stood up when the Dragon Lady came in, of course. Now she looked me up and down and said, "Will he, indeed?"

I felt intimidated and had an idea she wanted me to feel that way, so I said, "Yes, ma'am. I will, indeed."

"Mitch, this is Mary Seldon-Hardesty, who married my late brother Alain. Mary is Lydia's mother."

We had studied sex education my junior year, but I could not imagine this barracuda giving live birth. "Really?" I said, and wished I hadn't.

"Adoptive." Mrs. Seldon-Hardesty bit the word out, as if she resented sharing the information.

So there are worse things than spending your life in an orphanage.

"I just wanted you two to meet," Aunt Missy said.

"Yes, well, we've met." To me, Mrs. Seldon-Hardesty said, "I trust you can control those animals more efficiently than Amelia can. Animals have no business in the house in the first place; if they are allowed in the house, they should certainly not be allowed free range. I don't want to find them running loose upstairs. I don't want to find them running loose anywhere. Is that clear?"

I looked at Aunt Missy before I answered. She nodded,

so I said, "Yes, ma'am."

"Very good."

"Mary," Aunt Missy called, as Mrs. Seldon-Hardesty turned to go. "You will tell Eleanor, won't you?"

Mrs. Seldon-Hardesty glanced at me and said, "Of course."

"And ask Corrie to come down."

The Hyphenated One left, without a handshake, a goodbye, a kiss-my-foot, or anything. I stood there, afraid I'd soil the upholstery if I sat.

"Is this her house?" I asked, not particularly wanting to stay, if it was.

"It is not," said Aunt Missy. "Not entirely. My father left it to my late brothers and me. Alain's share passed to his widow, Mary. Jason's passed to his daughter, Eleanor. Frederick's passed to his daughter, Charlotte, and from her to Matthew."

Mr. Walton said, "And we all live here together: One big happy family."

There was an uncomfortable pause, while I stood there wondering what I had gotten myself into.

"Don't mind Aunt Mary." Dr. Andrew pressed a hand to my shoulder until my knees buckled and I sat. "She's a Seldon, and she takes it very seriously."

"She looks down on her mother," Aunt Missy said, "because she's only a Seldon by marriage." We both had a companionable little snicker over that one.

"Now, Amelia, Mary's a fine woman," Mr. Walton protested. He explained to me, as if he were Witness for the Defense: "She and her late husband — Amelia's brother Alain — adopted Lydia when she was five. She's been a wonderful mother to Lydia. Even you'll have to admit that, Amelia."

"I suppose so. Yes, I admit it."

"And she was a godsend, nursing the old folks through their last years."

"And with Mother," said Dr. Andrew.

Mr. Walton nodded. "I don't know what I would have done without her when Charlotte was diagnosed." He cleared his throat and blew his nose into a real cloth handkerchief. *A rich man puts in his pocket what a poor man throws on the ground*, I thought, quoting Billy.

Were all real families like this? Were they all full of pulls and pushes and irritations and deaths and conflicts, ritual unkindnesses and unexpected kindnesses? I supposed they must be. Not the cozy pink cushion I'd always sort of imagined.

"Yes, yes," said Aunt Missy, "Mary's a saint from heaven. Saint Mary Seldon-Hardesty, Our Lady of the Snobs."

I almost laughed, but I caught it in time and coughed it out.

"Amelia—" Mr. Walton rumbled, but stopped as someone else came into the room.

My jaw might have dropped. I wouldn't know. I could hardly see through the stars in my eyes. I hoped the breeze from all those little hearts swirling around my head wasn't messing up my hair, because I wanted to look my best right now.

She was an older woman. Twenty, if she was a day. Her red-gold hair curled softly around her face; her dove-gray eyes made her gray uniform look like something she had picked out on purpose. She was small (I estimated her head would rest nicely in the hollow of my shoulder) and delicate-looking, her rose-petal complexion a nice contrast to my darkness.

"Miss Mary said you wanted to see me," she said quietly, her gaze dropping before it met mine.

"I wanted you to meet Mitch," Aunt Missy said. "Mitch Franklin, this is Corina Crawley, who does maid-of-all-work for us. Corrie, Mitch is here to help me care for Chan and Wong. You know how worried I've been about them."

"Yes, ma'am." Corrie kept her eyes on the carpet and her hands clasped in front of her. She glanced at me. I hoped I didn't look as goofy as I felt.

"They'll be quite safe," Aunt Missy said, "with him around."

"Yes, ma'am. I'm right gl — I'm glad." She had the sweetest touch of a hick accent, like she came from way out in the sticks. I mean, Faelin isn't exactly Gay Paree, but it *is* the county seat.

"I'd like you to take Mitch backstairs and introduce him to Sandy and Ava, then show him to his room. — Oh! Mitch, I haven't arranged for a room for you!"

"No," said Mr. Walton, "you haven't. Typical."

"Matthew, don't you have some beans you want to count?" To Corrie, she said, "I want Ava to prepare the Honduras room for him." Corrie drew a sharp breath at that and shot me a brief, startled look. Maybe the Honduras room had mice or pygmies or something. Aunt Missy went on, "You can introduce him to Ava when you show him to his room."

"Yes, ma'am."

"I hardly think the Honduras room is appropriate, Amelia," said Mr. Walton.

"The Honduras room is next to mine," Aunt Missy told

me, as if Mr. Walton hadn't spoken. "Convenient, and I think you'll like it."

"Whatever you say, Aunt Missy." Rather pointedly, perhaps, I said, "You're the boss." I was already on my feet, ready to follow my vision anywhere: backstairs or to hell in a hand basket. "It was nice meeting you, Mr. Walton. Nice to meet you, Dr. Walton."

The men nodded to me. Aunt Missy twiddled her fingers in an impish wave.

I trailed Corrie across the foyer, trying to think of an ice-breaker.

She led me past the stairs and then turned right, through a door and into a sort of area or vestibule with a door in the opposite wall.

I closed the door behind us, expecting Corrie to open the other one, but she turned to me instead, raising her gray eyes to mine.

"Should I call you 'Mitch'?" she asked in a near-whisper.

I'd been asked before what I preferred to be called, but it had always been a casual request. "Sure. Everybody calls me Mitch."

She laughed, and I saw she had dimples on either side of her mouth. "Whatever you say, 'Mitch.'" She raised her hands and toyed with the collar of my shirt. "Mary said you were rude to her."

"Oh," I said, thinking about other things than conversation. "Did she?"

"Were you?"

Corrie's mouth was slightly open, as if she were breathless. I know I was.

"Maybe a little bit."

"I knew it!" She put her hands flat on my chest and

rubbed. I wondered dizzily what she'd do if I told her I'd spit in the old bat's eye.

Then, again, what was so stimulating about my being rude to The Dragon Lady? What was this chick, an anarchist or something? This didn't make sense. Much as I'd like to muffle it, a tiny little alarm bell started dinging in the far recesses of my mind.

"When she told me about that, I was so happy. A letter came from Grant today. It was to Miss Amelia, but I knew it was a Sign. And then Miss Amelia brings you home. And she's putting you in the Honduras Room."

"So?" This was some kind of gag, right? New kid at school, and all that. What else could it be?

Corrie laughed as if I'd made a sly joke. "Don't say anything to Sandy or Ava. They still don't believe, and they never would. We gave up on them."

"Right," I said. "Some people sure are stubborn." I was getting a chilly feeling at the base of my spine.

Funny thing about chemistry: One second it's running strong and the next, it just clicks off. I could feel the toggle switches flipping as we spoke.

Then Corrie did something that, two minutes earlier, I would have given my right eye for. She threw her arms around my neck and pressed herself against me. But now, I didn't like it as much as I might have. And the reason I didn't like it so much is what she whispered to me:

"You're back! Oh, Albert, you came back to me, just like you said!"

Well, *something* had broken the ice.

Chapter 4

"Get off! Get off!" I pushed at her arms as if they were snakes.

She backed away, though not nearly far enough to suit me. Her eyes shone with tears, and her soft mouth pursed in tender distress. The desire to comfort her stirred, but I shot it through the head and it subsided.

"What's wrong?" she asked. "Don't you love me no more?"

"You called me 'Albert,'" I explained.

"Oh." Relief washed over her features. "Yes, I forgot. I'm supposed to call you 'Mitch.'" She reached for me again.

I held out a cop-like hand of restraint. "And I *don't* love you any more," I said firmly. "I don't love you at all. I just met you." *Plus, you appear, dear girl, to be as crazy as a bird dog.*

"I thought it would be all right. Nobody can see us in here. But you're right. We have to be so careful."

"Safety first," I agreed heartily. "Could we go into the kitchen now?" If this "Sandy" chick turned out to be as flaky as Corrie Crawley, I'd just leave by the back door and keep on walking.

"Yes, of course. You have to 'meet' Sandy and Ava. I don't know why they're still here. They'd both be gone if I had my way, but She kept them on. Maybe so's you could get to them without any trouble."

I seemed to be having some trouble getting to them as it was. "I want to go into the kitchen now." I hoped a simple declarative sentence would have a beneficial effect on the conversation.

With a smile that would melt any heart but one frozen in panic, Corrie opened the door.

A long, wide, wooden island ran through the center of the kitchen; cooking utensils, pots, and pans hung from a rack above it. Two covered trays glistened on the near side and, on the far side, The Mighty Thor was cutting the crusts off sandwiches.

He looked up as we entered and pointed his knife at Corrie. "Beat it," he said, and held the pose while he waited to see if she would obey.

"Miss Amelia sent me," she replied stiffly, "to introduce a new member of the staff."

"Can he talk?"

"Yes."

"He can introduce himself. Make yourself scarce."

"I'm supposed to show him to his room after I introduce him."

"Go haunt the hall. I'll send him out when we're finished talking."

"I can't wait *that* long!"

"Ain't you funny? You oughta go on that 'Laugh-In' show, you know it?"

"Sandy—"

He leaned forward, still pointing the knife. "'Beat it,' I said and 'Beat it,' I meant. Now, beat it."

"This is Sandy Schneider, the cook," Corrie said defiantly, as she headed back for the passage door. "I'll let you introduce yourself." She winked at me and left.

I took a deep breath and let it out in a puff.

"Like she said, I'm Sandy Schneider," the cook said, putting down his knife. He wiped his hand on his apron and held it out to me.

I prepared to wince: He was a blue-eyed Nordic type, twice as big as I was, with muscles on his eyelids.

I didn't need the wince, after all; his grip was exactly as firm as I made mine. *A man who knows his own strength.*

"Mitch Franklin," I said.

"You a friend of hers?" he asked suspiciously, retrieving his cutlery.

"Of Corrie Crawley's? I most certainly am not." Of course, there was some difference of opinion about that.

"Good." He returned to cutting bread crusts off sandwiches. "She's nuts."

"I kind of got that impression." It was good to know that her — shall we say "eccentricities"? — were known and more-or-less tolerated.

"Miss Amelia dragged her in here about seven years ago. Little hick from the sticks. Sixteen, and the sweetest, shyest kid you'd ever want to meet. Now look at her. Mouthy, snotty goofball."

"Maybe it's some kind of late puberty or something."

Thor's chuckle was louder than most people's laughs. "You're okay, kid. Even if you *are* another one of Miss Amelia's."

I didn't exactly like the box he was building here, or the pigeonhole he was stuffing me into. Kind of ticked me off. "So you're saying she picks people up off the street like stray dogs and brings them home and then they piddle on the rug and I'm one of them, is that it?"

"No! God, no, kid, I didn't mean that! You're taking me wrong! I mean, maybe before, but, like I said, *you're* okay. She seems to be sticking to home now, so she'd be more careful who she brought here, wouldn't she? Before, she'd just breeze in from Tahiti or Venice or French Lick or someplace, dump somebody on us, and breeze off again. How they worked out was between them and us. Half the time she didn't even remember them the next time she buzzed through. Crazy old dame."

He must have seen something in my face, because he quickly added, "I don't mean that in any bad way. She's just, you know, kind of flighty. Spoiled little flapper girl who never grew up, if you ask me."

I could see that. I could imagine Aunt Missy, young and slim, in a mini-dress with fringe on the bottom, doing the Charleston with Bertie Wooster. "I think she's groovy," I said. "I think she's a gas."

"Well," he said, in a let's-be-reasonable tone, "if you want to put it that way. All's I'm saying is, she's no personnel manager, that's all. Corrie looked like she was going to work out fine, until Miss Amelia brought that Albert in here. Then, *kablooie!*"

While I was trying to figure out whether I'd be better off knowing as much or as little as possible about dear Albert, Sandy decided for me.

"She hauled him in from Paris, for the lova Mike. Paris, *France* — I'm asking you! Him and them two earmuffs she calls dogs. Said he was the dogs' valet. Now, ain't that a cute one? He strutted around here like he was the boss hog. Dr. Andy had just come home to work, and Albert razzed him up one side and down the other about that crazy stuff he's 'experimenting' with. I mean, sure Dr. Andy's a crackpot egghead, but he's a damn flat nice guy, just the same. And Albert just picked at him all the time. Matt Walton, too. Pick, pick, pick. Ask me, I think that's the real reason Miss Amelia brought him home: to aggravate Matt Walton. I don't think she knew her pet monkey was tormenting Dr. Andy, too, or she would have slapped him down but hard. And he made passes at all the girls. I mean, all of them."

ALL of them? Corrie? Lydia? THE DRAGON LADY?

"Ava, too. Ava's my wife. I came *this* close to giving him a royal shiner, but I was afraid Miss A would raise a stink over it. She probably would have thought he was funny, if she'd known about it."

The passage door opened and Corrie said, "'Mitch'."

"Will you get out of here?" Sandy demanded.

"I haven't got all day."

"Scram!"

Corrie retreated and closed the door.

"So, anyway. Six months after he comes here, the guy turns up dead."

"Dead?" So, back there in the passage, Corrie had snuggled up to a dead guy and whispered in his ear? Maybe I'd heard him wrong. "Albert is dead?"

"I'm talking doornail. And then Miss Amelia's two brothers — Well, Frederick died back in '52, two years before his daughter, Charlotte, the one that married Matt Walton, but Miss Amelia's *younger* brothers and a sister-in-law, they died in a car wreck on the way to the funeral. That was Alain, Miss Mary's husband, and Jason, and Jason's wife, Joan. Miss Eleanor ain't been the same since. Well, can you blame her?"

"I don't know anything about her." I was just as willing as not to leave it that way until my ears had time to cool down.

"Jason and Joan were her parents, didn't you know that?"

"I just got here," I pointed out.

"Oh, yeah. Well, Jason and Joan were Eleanor's parents, and it really hit her hard, losing them both at once like that."

I could imagine, because I'd seen kids who'd had it happen. Some of them acted like life was fine, and then they set fire to something or started poking their arms with pencils. Or they stopped talking and eating and washing; just turned themselves off as completely as they could. Or they managed to live with it, but they never lost this look, this hurt look, back behind their eyes, all the time, even when they were having fun.

Sandy went on. And on. "Miz Mary's been looking after her five years now. I'll have to give her that: she might treat the hired help like poor white trash, but she's good with sick people and old folks. And she was awful good to Lydia. You know about Lydia?"

"Adopted."

"Her old man, George Poston, and Alain and me was in the same unit together in dubya-dubya two." World War II, I realized he meant. "George and me was cooks, and Alain was the Looey for our unit, but we was all thick as thieves. Anyways, George and his wife died in '48, and George had it in his will that Alain was executor of his estate and Lydia's guardian. You'd think Miz Mary would raise all kinds of sand over that, wouldn't you? You met Mary yet?"

"Briefly."

"Yeah, well, wouldn't you think so?"

I nodded.

"Well, she didn't. You'd think that baby hung the moon.

She never had none of her own, see, but that don't soften some women toward other people's. Mary, though, she just about carried Lydia around on a silk pillow. You never seen anything like it."

I'd have had to see it to believe it. I could see her carrying a baby on a silver platter, maybe, but not on a silk pillow.

Sandy finished arranging his sandwiches and put a domed lid on the tray.

The passage door opened again, and Corrie said, "Mrs. Seldon-Hardesty wants to know 'if tea will be served at the regular hour or if you intend saving it for supper'."

"Tell her to keep her shirt on."

Amen!

"Well," he said, "I guess I better let you go. You're okay, kid."

Corrie stopped me in the passageway again. She giggled. "There's never been anyone like you! You're wonderful!"

"No, I'm not. I'm regular. Very normal and ordinary."

"But you've fooled them all! Nobody knows what's going on!"

Least of all, me.

She lunged for me again, but I sidestepped her. I mean, there's being embraced by a pretty girl, and there's being attacked by a raving lunatic. Gray eyes or no gray eyes.

"They're expecting me upstairs."

"Of course." Her dimples showed again. I couldn't blame Albert for making a pass at this girl, at least. *Wonder who she thought HE was.* Corrie looked up at me from under her eyelashes and said, "You always think of everything."

"Yeah, well, now I think you'd better show me to that room."

She blinked in surprise. "You know the way."

"I'm sorry, Miss Crawley, but I don't."

"Miss Crawley? It's Corrie. Don't you know me?"

"I just met you!"

She stared at me, speculation blurring the disappointment on her face.

Then she said, "Oh, I see."

She led me out of the passage and up the stairs. I followed, doing a little speculating myself. I was afraid this job was going to get old fast.

Chapter 5

Dr. Andrew sat at the top of the stairs, scribbling something in a small spiral notebook. He looked up as we neared him, a slight frown making his eyes look almost as beady as his old man's.

"What kept you? Ava had to leave." He looked at his watch.

"It was Sandy's fault," Corrie said. "You know how he talks and talks."

True enough, but at least the people he talks to are really there. I wasn't going to rat on the girl, though. I might say something to Aunt Missy later, but no way I was going to tattle to the doctor. Corrie probably had lots of men in clean white coats in her future as it was. He seemed to have his suspicions, anyway:

"Sandy's fault, was it?" He stood, stuffing his pen and notebook into a pocket of his lab coat. "Ava took tea to Mary and Eleanor. You'll have to take the sitting room tray."

"What about you and — and 'Mitch'?"

"I'll show him to his room, then take him down to the kitchen."

No tea in the sitting room for me? Boo-hoo. And I'd been surreptitiously practicing holding my pinkie in a delicate curve.

"But Miss Amelia told me—"

"If Aunt Amelia wants to know if you did as you were told, tell her I took over. Now please go on; she's had a very busy day, and I don't think she had any lunch, do you? It isn't kind to keep her waiting for her tea."

"You're right." With one last lingering look at me — or whoever — Corrie hurried down the stairs and away.

"Not that I think Aunt Amelia's feeling the want of food," Dr. Andrew said. He started down the hall, with me following. "She's in fine form this afternoon. She's probably down there, tucked into a corner of the davenport, taking big juicy bites out of my father's ego."

I felt myself flush with anger. "'Scuse me if I'm rude—" I stopped walking and hooked my thumbs through my belt loops to keep from making fists, "—but Aunt Missy isn't the only one taking bites out of people. Mr. Walton almost made her cry. I haven't known her long, but I happen to like her—"

"Like her? Of course you like her! You can't help liking her, unless you need to depend on her for something. She's a walking carnival — or used to be. If hiring you is going to bring my Aunt Missy back, I'm all for it."

"Your Aunt Missy?" This was the first time I'd heard anybody but me call her that. It surprised me.

Dr. Andrew nodded, and a tight little smile snuck onto his face. "When I was three, my nurse told me that Aunt Amelia was coming home for a visit. 'Your Aunt, Miss Amelia,' she called her. I heard it as, 'Your Aunt Missy Melia.' That's what I called her when we first met, and 'Aunt Missy' is what I called her until I turned ten and went away to school. I still call her that, sometimes. I assume she asked you to?"

I nodded, feeling an unexpected connection with the

doctor, just on the basis of our sharing that special "pet" name.

He took another step and threw open a door. "This is your room. Ava brought your things up."

I don't know what I pictured, but it wasn't this: deep-pile gold carpeting from wall to wall, heavy red and gold drapes pulled back from an oversized window, a four-poster bed, and three — no, four — wing chairs; two of the chairs stood, angled companionably toward each other, between the bed and the door. The furniture was all carved out of heavy, reddish-brown wood that Dr. Andrew said was Honduras mahogany — thus, the Honduras Room.

This was for *me*?

"Is it all right?" Dr. Andrew asked.

"It's too much," I said, in a hushed voice. "I mean, 'too much' as in 'far out.' Like, 'wow'."

"It's a museum piece." His face screwed into an expression of distaste. "I don't think the guest rooms have been redecorated since the Civil War."

"It isn't—" I laughed uncertainly, "—haunted, or anything like that?" And then I wished I hadn't put that particular notion into my own head. I mean, especially after Corrie's spooky act. What Dr. Andrew said next didn't help:

"Only by the memory of the last occupant. The 'Albert' we were talking about downstairs. But you'll take care of that, won't you?"

That is not in my job description. "I will?"

"Of course! Your being here will . . . will exorcise the spirit." Dr. Andrew glared around the room, as if daring "the spirit" to show itself. It was enough to make me wish I was Catholic, and had quart-jar of holy water in my bag.

"Nobody's been put in here since he died," Dr. Andrew went on. "I was beginning to think we'd have to place a gold rope across the door and declare it a shrine. But now she's brought you home and installed you in the 'sacred precincts'." he sneered. "It'll be good for — It'll be good for everybody."

He rubbed his hands together, as if satisfied that here was one thing taken care of. "Are you hungry?"

"Sort of." I was ravenous. Turmoil takes me that way, sometimes.

"Good. So am I." He turned to the right outside my room and led me past the stairs and toward the end of the hall. "This is the quickest way to the kitchen. There are more stairs at the other end; they go to the old servants' hall — nobody uses that but Corrie — and on down to the basement." We reached the bottom of the stairs and Dr. Andrew opened a door. "Sandy?"

The Mighty Thor got up from a square wooden table I'd missed on my first visit. "There you are," he said. "I was beginning to think they drug you in on that stuff I give 'em in the sitting room."

"I brought Mitch. Do you have enough?"

"I was expecting him."

Sandy plonked down a fistful of thick mugs and a plate of ham sandwiches layered with Swiss cheese, lettuce, dill pickles, and mustard.

"It ain't a san'wich without the crust," Sandy observed, pouring us each a mug of coffee. "I'm gonna have that put on one o' them little buttons everybody's wearing these days."

I had some of those buttons: *Question Authority, What if They Gave a War and Nobody Came?* The usual. *It Ain't a San'wich Without the Crust* would probably be popular. The coffeehouse groovesters could spend hours explaining its deeper meaning to each other.

Dr. Andrew, still standing, transferred a sandwich to a plate.

"Aw," Sandy said, "stick around for a change. Sit down and keep us company." He jogged me with his elbow. "Tell 'im, Mitch."

"Sure," I said, hoping I sounded more enthusiastic than I felt.

"He's afraid his particles are gonna get too excited without him," Sandy said to me with an exaggerated wink. "He's afraid they'll come swooping up here and take the joint apart."

Dr. Andrew smiled, his face sweetening as it had when he'd smiled at Aunt Missy.

"C'mon, Doc, nobody's gonna catch you unwound. And if they do, what of it?" He jogged me again.

"What of it?" I repeated.

"Well, I will, then."

Dr. Andrew sat down and bit into his sandwich shyly — you know, like the class geek when you invite him to sit with you in the cafeteria.

"Him and me go back to '45, when I mustered out of the army and come here to work for Alain Hardesty," Sandy said, waving a thumb in Dr. Andrew's direction. "You was what? Nine? Yeah, nine. — He used to hang around back here, him and that little Eleanor. Then he turned ten and They sent him off to school; like the regular school wasn't good enough for him."

"Oh, didn't they tell you?" said Dr. Andrew, with another tight smile. "I was a genius. I was wasted here."

"Yeah. Well. You spend too much time down in the basement. You're gonna start growing mushrooms between your toes if you don't come up for sun once in a while."

Dr. Andrew laughed out loud. He tried to smother it, but it came out in spite of him.

Sandy took the spotlight off the doctor by asking me what I thought about this year's World's Series. The two of us talked baseball for a while, then TV, then pop music. He liked the oldies, but he'd heard some Donovan that he liked, and a couple of songs off the *Sgt. Pepper's* album. We gave Dr. Andrew silences and looks, thinking he might join in, but he didn't.

Finally, Sandy said directly, "You ever listen to any music, Doc?"

"Jazz," said Dr. Andrew, picking at a crumb on his plate. He looked up, his face livelier than I'd seen it yet. "Dave Brubeck. Buddy Rich."

"Oh, yeah," I said. *Jazz, eh?* Somehow, Doc Walton hadn't struck me as the beatnik type.

"Buddy Rich?" said Sandy. "I saw him on the Sullivan show a couple of weeks ago."

"Did you? I wish I'd known. I'd have loved to see him." Dr. Andrew sat forward, relaxed . Elbows on the table and everything.

"I'll keep an eye on the *TV Guide* for you. Look out for the jazz guys, and let you know when they're on."

"Would you? That would be kind."

"Sure, sure. Can do." Sandy waved a hand, as if to show how easy it would be.

Corrie came in. The atmosphere cramped with tension.

She looked and spoke to me, as if I were the only person in the room. "Miss Amelia would like you to come take the dogs for a walk. She's in her room with them now."

"I'll be right there."

"I'll show you the way."

I didn't want to go with her. I mean, I *really* didn't want to go with her. Maybe Dr. Andrew sensed it, because he came to my rescue.

"Aunt Amelia's room is next to yours, Mitch," he said, his eyes back on his empty plate, "on the side closer to the foyer stairs. You can't miss it."

"Thanks." To Corrie, I said, "I'll find it. Thanks anyway."

"But—"

Sandy put his knuckles on the table and raised himself from his seat.

Corrie slammed the door as she left.

"Poor girl," said Dr. Andrew, as if the words had been squeezed out of him.

"Yeah?" said Sandy. "Yeah, I guess. She's just got a bad attitude. Little snot."

"I'd better get back to work." Dr. Andrew rose and smiled at us. "Thank you for the company."

"Our pleasure," said Sandy, and I echoed him. This time, I meant it.

When the doctor had left, Sandy and I cleared the table.

"That's the most I've seen of him since he come back," the cook said. "We used to be pals, when he was a kid. When they told him he was going away to that boarding school, he come back here to the kitchen and cried like his heart would break. Had to leave all of his friends at school, and he was a popular kid. Wiry, like one of them Scotch Terriers. Used to like baseball, but I guess that wasn't classy enough for 'em at school. Got him on the tennis team, for cryin' out loud. It did something to him, going away. Like it locked him up inside his head, you know what I mean? When he come back to visit, it was like he didn't know how to come out anymore, you know?"

I knew. I found out about wanting to fit in the day I started school. Like I could help it that I didn't have any parents. I tried inventing a family, I tried being invisible, and I tried pretending I was someplace else. Mrs. Brandt had a talk with me, about how I was as good as anybody and I shouldn't be ashamed of myself, that I had a lot to contribute to the world and all that. So I went back to school the next day and beat the holy living crap out of a couple of bigger kids, and that was that. But I remembered.

"Maybe you being here is going to be good for the Doc," Sandy said. "Somebody new to talk to, that isn't one of Them."

"You're not one of Them."

"Yeah, but I known him since he was knee-high to a bug. And I've been the only man around here the past five years, except Old Man Walton." Sandy made a sound that can't be spelled, but that means *big deal — forget about him*. "Maybe having another guy around is just what he needs. Show him what it's like, to be a regular guy, you know?"

That is not in my job description, I thought again but, considering my employer's telling me to call her by Dr. Andrew's "Aunt Missy," I wondered if that was entirely true.

Chapter 6

Aunt Missy's room was as big as mine and then some. It had more furniture in it than a lot of houses I knew of, and it still wasn't crowded. It had been decorated some time since the Civil War, too: Everything was slick, shiny, and angular. Wood was trimmed in metal, or inlaid with other colors of wood or maybe other material. The carpet was baby blue; the drapes were a little darker, with pink and gold geometric designs on them. I'd never seen anything like it. I know now the style was "Art Deco." It was a nostalgia thing in the Seventies, but Aunt Missy's was the original article.

Against the wall she had one of those "entertainment centers" you saw in Popular Science magazine, with a television, radio, record player, and tape player; she had a whole shelf of LP's, another one of 45's, another of old 78's, and boxes of tape reels. There were two speakers, one on either side of the center — Stereo! This was so cool! And it wasn't even a family system, it was private. I think Aunt Missy's entertainment center said "This is not the world you know" more than anything else had done so far. Suddenly, I felt shy.

Chan and Wong leaped at me.

"Down, you naughty boys!" Aunt Missy said. She sat in a low black chair with gold and pink cushions on it, a book drooping from her hand. According to the dust jacket, it was a Nero Wolfe mystery: *In the Best of Families*.

"Mitch, dear, how has your afternoon gone? Have you met everybody?"

Met some. Been some. "I met Sandy. I kept just missing his wife."

"Ava. And I don't suppose you met Eleanor. Well, you wouldn't, unless Mary introduced you, and I hardly think that's likely, knowing Mary. And given Eleanor's condition."

"Sandy told me something about that." I hesitated, not sure it was my place to say anything, but it would have felt wrong not to, so I said, "I'm sorry about your folks. And your friend."

"My friend? What friend?"

"What's his name." I knew his name. "Albert."

"Oh." Aunt Missy looked away into the past. "Albert. Well, I wouldn't exactly call Albert a friend, dear."

I had a sense of standing on quicksand; a feeling I got sometimes when I was talking to grown-ups. I mean, you never know when somebody else has laid a mine that you're going to walk straight into. The shop teacher had gone ape last year because a kid forgot to put a t-square back in the right place. They said his wife had left him, like that was supposed to explain it. I sensed, now, that Aunt Missy's blank face and bland talk was a kind of veil, but I couldn't guess what was behind it.

Maybe this wouldn't be a real good time to tell about Corrie's obsession. Maybe some other time.

"Well, I'm sorry about your brothers, anyway. And your sister-in-law."

Aunt Missy smiled up at me. "Thank you, dear. You're very kind. It was rather a dreadful shock to me, I'm afraid.

It's taken me longer than one might have predicted to recover from it."

Bits of information that had slid past me before suddenly lined up and meant something. "You haven't been out of the house since it happened," I said. "Until you came and hired me today."

"Until I came and *found* you, today." Aunt Missy looked away again, then gestured with her book to a nearby chair. "Sit down, dear."

I sat. Chan and Wong made a couple of dodges at me, maybe hoping I'd get up and chase them, then settled to the floor with mournful sighs.

"As my bringing you here seems to have raised the subject—" *Unfortunate choice of words.* "—perhaps I'd better tell you a little about that situation. I met Albert in Paris. Does that tell you anything about him?"

"He was French?"

Aunt Missy's laugh was surprised, silvery, youthful. "No, dear, he was American. I should have told you that."

When she'd said, "Paris," I had pictured him as "Ahl-BEAR," a European gigolo type, with a pencil-thin mustache and a black beret. Now I had to draw a new picture.

Aunt Missy went on, "Does his being in Paris tell you anything about him? No? Well, you are young. He was what we, in Paris, referred to as an expatriate. Do you know what that means?"

"No, ma'am."

"It means someone who prefers another country to his own. Like Gertrude Stein, and Ernest Hemingway, and dear Louis Bromfield. Albert kept company with that sort of crowd. He was very cynical, very amusing at other people's expense. Do you understand what I mean?"

If I did, he sounded like what we, in high school, referred to as "a jerk."

"He was short of money, so I gave him small sums and we pretended I was paying him to be kennel-master for the dogs, who were only puppies at the time. When the whim struck me to come home that year for a family Christmas, I invited Albert to join me. I was surprised when he agreed."

With the last sentence, Aunt Missy's voice took on a faintly pleading tone, as if she were entering a defense.

"I had only planned staying through New Year's, but Albert spent several days shadowing Matthew." Her lips twitched, probably remembering Mr. Walton's reaction to his shadow. "He — Albert — charmed the local officials and club-women he met those days, and I found he had been invited to speak to various groups through March. He suggested I leave, if I wanted to; if Matthew threw him out of Willowbrook he could find somewhere else to stay. I was still amused; I stayed to see what tricks he would get up to next."

Tricks. Like a dog. A pet monkey, like Sandy called him. And all the time, he was picking at her nephew and making passes at every woman who caught his eye and sweeping the hired help off her feet. Nice guy. I mean, since the draft, some of my best friends were expatriates up in Canada, but I hoped they knew how to behave in somebody else's house.

"He asked to stay for the Kentucky Derby, and I agreed. As each event passed, he found other sights and events he couldn't bear to miss, and I indulged him. Then he wanted to experience a real Indiana Fourth-of-July. Then he was dead."

Then her brothers and her sister-in-law were dead, and her niece Eleanor had to be "taken care of."

"Jason and Joan and Alain. . . . Their car went off the road on the way to the funeral. Albert's funeral. He was buried here. He had no next-of-kin that they could find."

Aunt Missy must have figured that, since she'd brought him home in the first place, it was her fault that four people were dead and another one was damaged inside. Two, counting Corrie. So she had sent herself to her room for five years.

"His will left his entire estate — and there was much more than he had ever disclosed — to a promising young poet. He was here for Albert's funeral. He spoke over the grave, at Albert's request, in lieu of a clergyman. Grant Marsch."

That name rang a bell. "The one you got the letter from today?"

"Letter? Oh! My letter! I completely forgot it. Where's my bag, dear?"

I found it on the floor by her bed and brought it to her. She took out the letter, handling it a little less gingerly than she had downstairs.

"Yes," she said. "I'll read it in a minute. Now, you'll need the dogs' leashes. Let me see, we haven't used them since Paris. I let them run free here. At any rate, I used to." One of her soft little hands formed a fist. The other one still held the Nero Wolfe murder mystery. "Look in the clothes press, dear, that little drawer at the bottom."

I had expected maybe red ribbons and collars with brass name-plates. I found harnesses and leashes made of blue leather, with flower-and-vine designs pressed into them; at the points where the leashes snapped onto the harnesses were smooth, fiery stones the size of my thumbnails.

"Moroccan leather," Aunt Missy said. "The opals are part of a set I bought in Tunisia." She held out her left hand, showing me a ring set with another of the stones. "I gave Albert cufflinks made of the other two. I wanted him buried in them, but they could find only one. I had it made into a pendant and gave it to Grant Marsch." She fingered her letter again; I knew she wanted me to go so she could read it in private.

Perversely, I wanted to stay so she couldn't. Whatever she had done, or thought she had done, whatever anybody else's opinion about her was, she had come and *found* me, and that made her mine. I didn't want to share her, not with Albert's memory, and not with his poetic friend's handwriting.

"What made you come out to the Home today?" *In the mind and out the mouth, as Mrs. Brandt says.*

Aunt Missy pulled her thoughts away from the envelope in her lap and gave me a large-eyed look that told me nothing. "It was a lovely day. I was fed to the teeth of this house and these people." That, I believed. "Matthew had been prosing on about finding work for a certain boy at the Refuge who's just turned sixteen."

That would be Sean Ryan, and you could find him work, but good luck getting him to do it.

Aunt Missy shifted in her chair. "I thought: Why not?"

Hold it. Skipped something. "Why not what?"

"I beg your pardon, dear?"

"You thought: 'Why not?' Why not what?"

"Why not go for a drive? Then I thought what fun it would be to interview that boy, and hire him to work for *me*.

Mrs. Brandt suggested you, instead, and I'm *so* glad she did!" She beamed at me, but I gave her the look I reserved for Jimmy when he tried to snow me. She held my gaze until I got the message: She had said all she intended to say. I could swallow my questions and keep things pleasant, or. . . . My mind didn't want to go there. I swallowed my questions.

~*~

I took the dogs down the back stairs Dr. Andrew had shown me and into the kitchen. I heard the faint creak of a rocker from behind a door to my right and, a second later, caught a whiff of cigar smoke.

"Sandy?" I wouldn't have been surprised if it was Corrie.

Sandy poked his head out and said, "Hiya, Mitch. — Hey, don't bring them dogs in here! They'll get hairs all over everything!"

"I'm sorry. I'm supposed to take them for a walk."

"Next time, take them down them other stairs." He gestured across the kitchen toward where Dr. Andrew had said the servants' hall would be. "There's a door outside over there."

"Okay."

"Go on through this time, but don't let them shed on nothing."

What am I supposed to do, shellac them? "I won't," I said, scooting across to the kitchen door as quickly as I could. Chan and Wong loved the speed. They didn't want to stop running when we got outside, but I had to bring them up short. I had to stop and stare.

A flagstone path led from the kitchen door to a terrace. Plants grew on either side of the path and all along the house. I didn't know the names but they smelled like food, so I figured they must be herbs. On the terrace, three round metal tables with green umbrellas shading them waited for company. Beyond, a flower garden spread back to the woods.

I've been razzed about it all my life, but I love flowers. In the last school yearbook, I was voted Most Likely to Marry a Girl Named Daisy. Now I drank in the colors and shades, the shapes of the flowers and of the plantings, the curves of the pebbled paths and the slanting afternoon sunlight on it all.

The dogs, in what must have been a rehearsed move, jerked their leashes out of my hand and took off like fuzzy bullets.

I took off after them, praying they'd keep to the paths: I might just have to kill them, if they tore through a flower bed. One leash or another snapped off a bloom here and there, but the destruction was minimal; the dogs themselves stayed on the pebbles until they reached the end of the garden.

They dove into the woods. I dove after them. The undergrowth had been cleared in an eight-foot swathe, making a sort of informal path. I followed it and the runaways into a clearing.

In the center of the open ground, a small, once-white building threw its shade across a bed of primroses. *Perfect. That was all this place needed, was a summerhouse or a gazebo or whatever you call these things.* But why was it all run-down, with yellowed paint peeling off its sides, shingles missing, lattices cracking from the weather? Behind it, a small stream gurgled past. I circled the summerhouse to get a better look at the water.

And saw the grave. The headstone read: ALBERT ALAISTER. 1916-1963. HE IS NOT DEAD, BUT SLEEPETH.

Gee, I missed the orphanage.

Chapter 7

Yeah. He hung around in Paris with the 1960's Hemingway-type crowd. Well I guess he did: Albert Alaister had been one of the greatest writers of the century, as far as I was concerned. We had studied some of his stuff in high school, and it blew my mind. I had read as many of his books and short stories as I could get hold of, and had bought as many as I could afford. I couldn't believe that *this* was the man Corrie thought she was talking to when she was talking to me.

And he had died *here* five years ago. Five years ago, I had been twelve, and the only writer I was conscious of was Walter R. Brooks, creator of Freddy the Pig. Albert Alaister had probably visited the high school. He had been all over town, according to Aunt Missy. He might have been to the Refuge, while he was "shadowing" Matthew Walton. And I never knew. *Dumb kid! Dumb, dumb kid!* I felt wild and dark and furious. At that instant, I would have done anything to turn back the clock, or to bring Albert Alaister back to life.

All of a sudden, Corrie kind of made sense to me. From what I'd read about Alaister (and I'd only read the "suitable for young people" textbook blurbs), he had been a pretty colorful and impressive character, and an uncomfortably vital personality. It was easy to see how an . . . er . . . impressionable mind might be so taken with him that his loss was absolutely unacceptable. She probably tried to talk every guy who came to visit into being Albert. I didn't doubt that she dropped it as soon as she got to know the guy in question — if anybody ever stayed long enough to get known.

But, wow! Albert Alaister. It told me maybe more than I wanted to know about the folks at Willowbrook: that they'd been stuffing "Albert" up my nose all afternoon, and nobody had thought to mention that he just happened to be a literary giant.

So what had he been doing, playing court jester to a little old lady?

I heard a whimper. Chan and Wong were curled up like eternal flames on either side of Albert's grave. Their floppy ears twitched and their eyes swiveled toward the woods. I heard the whimper again. It wasn't coming from the dogs; it came from the garden path.

A woman shrank from my gaze, trying to pull back into the shadows of the trees. Tears ran down her calm, pale face. Corrie held her arm, urging her into the clearing.

"I want to go back to the house," the woman said.

Corrie all but pushed her into the open.

The woman was even smaller than Corrie, though she looked a tad bit older, maybe close to thirty. Her old-lady clothes didn't look natural on her: a plaid housedress and a fuzzy green sweater. *Long-term residential patient*, was the phrase that came to mind.

"There he is," Corrie said, in a stage whisper. "What did I tell you?"

That made me madder than I believe I'd ever been in my life up to then. I went over and plucked Corrie's hand off the woman's arm and inserted myself between them, facing the weeping woman. *Poor little kid.* Ten years older than me, but she was hurt and she was helpless; I was here, and she was one of "my" kids.

"I'm James Michener Franklin, from down at the Refuge. You must be Miss Eleanor."

She looked up at me and said, "Albert?" *Oh, dear God, not another one.*

"You *do* see it!" Corrie breathed. I felt her hand run up my back.

"Cut it out!" I snarled at her, shrugging off her touch. To Miss Eleanor, I repeated, gently, "I'm one of the kids from the Refuge. They call me Mitch. I just got here this afternoon. Does your Aunt Mary know where you are?"

"Aunt Mary?" Eleanor smiled slyly, which was downright creepy, with the tears still trickling down her cheeks. "Aunt Mary and Lydia went to town for something. Ava's supposed to be watching me, but Aunt Amelia called her away. I took my chance. I had to see you again!"

"I'll be glad to see you any time, Miss Eleanor," I said, with firm subservience. "My name is Mitch Franklin." I wanted to reach back and slap Corrie so hard her teeth would rattle. I was ashamed of myself, even as I thought that: Corrie couldn't help how she was any more than Miss Eleanor could help *her*self. Two crazy girls up here, and nobody to keep them from feeding each other's nuttiness but The Dragon Lady. "Right now, why don't we go back to the house? Your Aunt Mary would worry, if she knew you were out here. This is a sad place."

Corrie went to Eleanor's other side. "Not anymore." Her eyes shone at me and I forgot to feel sorry for her.

"Will you shut up?" I snapped. "You told her I'm him, didn't you? You saw me come back here, and you brought her out to meet me, didn't you? Only not me, *him*."

Corrie's happiness crumpled; she seemed to draw into herself. "I'm sorry! I thought it would be all right. Eleanor has to know!"

Eleanor shook with sobs.

"*Now* look," I said to Corrie. "You've got her worse. Why don't you just lay off it for a while? — Miss Eleanor, come on back to the house with me."

"Oh, no!" said Eleanor. "She mustn't see you! She'd be so angry!"

"It's all right, Miss Eleanor," I said. "I'm not the person you think I am. Corrie is mixed up. I'm Mitch Franklin. I'm very pleased to meet you." I held out my hand, just as if she were a club lady bringing used crayons for the arts-and-crafts room. Eleanor's crying quietened and stopped. She wiped her face on the tail of her fuzzy sweater. Timidly, she took my hand.

"He's gone, isn't he?" she asked me, wistfully.

"Yes, ma'am. He's gone."

Corrie drew breath, but I glared her to silence. I gathered up the ends of the dogs' leashes and looped them around my wrist. If they got away from me again, they'd have to take my hand with them.

"Let's go on back, now," I said.

"Albert," Corrie said, from behind me. Whether she was talking at me or at the grave, I neither knew nor cared.

I had fond hopes of getting Miss Eleanor back to her cell — er, room — before anybody knew she was gone. I took her in through the door Sandy had told me to use. It opened into a "mud room," with a bench and a row of pegs.

There were two doors in one wall, probably one to the front hall and one to the stairs Sandy had told me about. Another door led to the servants' hall: it was open, and a woman scowled at us from the threshold.

"Ava!" said Corrie, her voice catching in surprise.

Ava was tall and thin, with short hair the color of my red-brown furniture. Her eyes were a rich, deep blue, like Cinderella's eyes in the picture book I used to read the kids to sleep with. If Cinderella had ever had an expression on her like Ava's, though, I don't think the Wicked Steps would have given her any grief. Even Chan and Wong sat without fuss or fidget.

When she spoke, her voice was soothing — on the surface, anyway. She put an arm around Eleanor and said, "Let's go back to your room, Miss Eleanor." In a sharper tone, she said, "Corrie, come help me. Then we will talk, you and I." Corrie hesitated, but she didn't hesitate for long. "Open the door for us," Ava ordered, and Corrie obeyed. "You, young man," Ava cut her eyes at me in a way I did not like, "Sandy wants to see. I'll speak to you when I come back down."

"Yes, ma'am," I barely overcame the urge to click my heels and throw my right arm up at a 45-degree angle.

Ava led Eleanor up the stairs, crooning, "Eleanora . . . Elena . . . My Lenora. . . ."

Whew! And I'd thought Mrs. Seldon-Hardesty had made my blood run cold.

I let the sound of footsteps fade, waited a little longer, and let the dogs tug me up to Aunt Missy's room.

"Come in," she called, in answer to my knock. "Oh, Mitch, dear! How were my babies?" I unsnapped their leashes; Chan and Wong flung themselves across the room and into Aunt Missy's lap, where they tumbled and flopped. "Were you good babies? Were you?" She put one hand on each of their furry heads and smiled at me in a way only Mrs. Brandt ever had before — a way that made me feel special and important. "Come and sit down," she said. "Where did you go? What did you see?"

I stared at my hands, at the carpet, at my shoes. Ava had given me the distinct impression that I was in hot water, but what I had done wasn't clear. I didn't want Aunt Missy mad at me, too, but I figured she was probably the safest person to ask.

"What is it, dear? What's happened?"

"Well, we went through the garden."

"Beautiful, isn't it? The Averys have kept the gardens here since Father built this house in 1890. I'm sorry, I interrupted you."

"We went back through the woods into that clearing. You know the one I mean."

"The one with the summerhouse."

"Among other things, yes."

"You went past the summerhouse?"

I snuck a look at her and saw compassion.

"Poor boy. You were surprised? Upset?"

"Well, yes, ma'am." *Not being used to stumbling across graves in the back yard.*

"I told you he was buried here. I'm sure I did."

"Yes, ma'am, but I didn't know you meant *here* here. I thought you meant here in Faelin. And I didn't know he was Him. I mean, Albert Alaister. THE Albert Alaister." I made a fist and punched my palm with it. "He was so great. I wish I'd had a chance to meet him. To know him."

"To meet him, yes," Aunt Missy said. "To know him,

perhaps not."

She was looking into the past again, and I gave her the point, based on what I'd been hearing.

"Then Miss Eleanor came."

"Eleanor!? Was Mary with her?"

"She said Mrs. Seldon-Hardesty was in town. Corrie was with her."

"Corrie." Aunt Missy's eyes grew wet and bright, but she blinked away the tears. "I'm responsible for that, too. I brought Corrie here. I exposed her to . . . to experiences she might otherwise have avoided."

"You didn't keep her here in chains," I said, although that was just a guess. "She could have left any time. You'd have given her a good reference, wouldn't you?"

"Yes, of course. She's a dear girl. A very hard worker, and so willing to please. A very sweet girl, really."

Crazy as a tree full of hoot-owls, but otherwise an ideal employee. Maybe this would be the time to unload everything.

"Corrie thinks I'm Albert," I said, before I could change my mind. "She thinks I'm Albert Alaister. She told Miss Eleanor that I'm Albert Alaister, and she brought her out to the grave to show me to her."

Aunt Missy's wide eyes and slack mouth showed her to be as startled as I had been, when the realization first hit me.

"Yes, ma'am."

"She thinks you're Albert? Because I brought you home with me. Because I linked you to the dogs. She actually told you she thinks you're Albert Alaister?"

"Ask for it by name," I said. "Accept no substitutes. I don't want to get Corrie in trouble, but I have to tell you what's happening. I think maybe. . . ." I choked on the words, but I cleared my throat and went on. "Maybe it would be better if I went back to the Refuge?" I made it a question, because I didn't want to make it a statement.

"No, dear." Aunt Missy bent forward and gathered my hands into hers. "That would be the very worst thing you could do. If you go before the illusion has a chance to break or fade, it would leave Eleanor and Corrie with the very worst impression."

"Well, yes, I can see that it might. But I didn't *mean* to do it! I didn't do *anything* to make them think I was him! Honest!"

"Of course you didn't! How could you? You never knew him; how could you deliberately imitate him, especially well enough to fool two women who — who lived in the same house with him for six months?"

Who was kidding who, here? Did she not know how Corrie felt about the dear departed, or did she think I didn't know and didn't need to know? Did she or didn't she mean to say that Eleanor had been as hooked on Albert as Corrie had been?

"Did anything else happen that you think you should tell me?" Aunt Missy asked.

"No, ma'am. I got Miss Eleanor to come in and Ava met us. I think she's mad at me."

"Oh, I doubt that. She's abrupt. That's just Ava's way. Don't be intimidated by it."

"No, ma'am." I had lost Aunt Missy's interest. Whatever she was thinking about now, it wasn't me or my problems. Typical. Grown-ups have no attention span.

Chapter 8

I stood up. "I guess I'd better go. Ava said Sandy wants to see me."

"Oh, yes." Aunt Missy played with the dogs' ears. "Yes. I'll just let Sandy tell you about that."

"About what, Aunt Missy?"

"About. . . . Let's just let Sandy tell you." She gave me one of her bright, closed looks, and I left.

Now what?

When I reached the kitchen, I found Sandy in front of the stove, gently stirring a cauldron of thick orange soup. I didn't spot anything in it, like vegetables or meat, just mushy broth. Other dishes, in various states of preparation, simmered or sizzled or drained or otherwise waited for the cook's attention.

"Hiya, Mitch," he said. "You're late."

"Late for what?"

"We eat at 5:30."

We always ate at 6:30 at the Refuge: that gave us time to do our homework and play outside a little before dinner.

"*They* eat at 7:00," Sandy said, "but you're supposed to eat with us."

Maybe that was what had Ava's nose out of joint: Late for supper. "I hope I didn't cause you any trouble."

"Naw, we figured out you probably didn't know. Thought maybe you thought you was supposed to eat in the dining room with Them."

At the same table as Matthew Walton, Lydia Do-Good, and The Dragon Lady? Not by choice.

"Hear about the fight?" Sandy put down the ladle and wiped his hands on his apron, a grin blazing across his heat-reddened face. "Miss Amelia wanted you to eat with the folks. Everybody expected you would; nobody was fussing about it. In fact, the Doc was actually going to come up to the table instead of having a tray in the basement, like he usually does." He shook his head. "Man, I don't know."

"Don't know what?"

He tasted the soup, opened a canning jar, took out a Sandy-sized pinch of dried something-or-other, and crushed the leaves over the bubbling liquid.

"I don't know exactly what's going on," he finally said, setting the jar aside. "What I do know is that this house is just a lit-tle bit strange."

Tell me about it.

"Corrie has been acting funny all afternoon. Not that she ain't peculiar anyways." His grin returned. "Then there was the fight. Lady Astor — by that I mean Mary Seldon-Hardesty — said she doesn't know what Miss Amelia's thinking about, wanting you to eat with the family. Said all you are is a common dog-keeper. Miss Amelia said her dogs are not common; besides, she likes you, she hired you, and she wants to see you. She said Miss Mary always eats in Eleanor's room anyway, so what the hell?"

I doubted Aunt Missy had used exactly those words. Then again, maybe she had.

"The Doc said he likes you, too, and he doesn't see what harm it'd be if you eat with them. Lydia said your feelings'll be hurt if they make you eat backstairs. Mr.

Matthew said the others could settle it among themselves. Well, nobody can stand up long against Lady Astor, so she won."

I couldn't say I was sorry, although I'd have liked to eat with Aunt Missy. And Dr. Andrew, if he really said he liked me. I couldn't imagine why he would, and I figured he had probably just said it to back Aunt Missy up, but that in itself made me feel all warm and fuzzy toward him.

"Then Miss Amelia dropped the bomb," Sandy went on. He poured the soup into a big tureen with trees and sheep painted all over it. He took a bunch of fresh leaves out of a glass and sprinkled them over the top, eased a ladle in under them, and put a lid on the tureen. "She pulls this letter out of her pocket," he said, "and who do you think it's from? Well, you wouldn't know."

"Grant Marsch," I said.

Sandy's jaw dropped, but it snapped closed when Ava came through a swinging door next to the hall passage. I caught a glimpse of The Forbidden Dining Room before the door swung shut.

Ava advanced, wagging a finger at her husband. "Gossiping again! Shame on you! Haven't I told you to keep out of what doesn't concern you?"

Sound advice, madam, sound advice. I planned to take it myself, as soon as anybody let me.

"It concerns *him*, though, Ava. Mitch."

Ava smiled at me and held out her hand. "We didn't introduce ourselves. I'm Ava Schneider, Sandy's wife. And you're Mitch Franklin, from Faelin. Everyone is telling me all about you." Her handshake was firm, which I would have expected. I didn't expect the shy warmth of her smile. "I'm sorry if I seemed brusque before," she said. "It upset me very much to find Eleanor had been out without Mary or me, especially with Corrie. We try never to leave Eleanor alone with Corrie."

Lucky Eleanor.

"I must take the soup in, now. They'll be down in a moment, and they like the soup to be waiting."

"I'll carry that for you," I offered, as she hefted the tureen by its gold-plated handles.

"I can manage," she said. "But thank you."

"I told ya he was okay," Sandy said to her back. To me, he said, "How'd you know about Grant Marsch?"

"I was there when Mr. Walton gave Aunt Missy the letter. Then she took it out to read later, and told me about his being here before, when. . . ."

"Yeah, 'when' is right." Sandy turned away and chopped a carrot into microscopic particles — *shoop, shoop, shoop, shoop, shoop* — just like that. Mrs. Brandt should have a knife like that, except that it would be dangerous, with kids around. The knives at the Refuge are more like blunt instruments. "Wait 'til you see this Grant Marsch," Sandy said. "He's a bird. I mean, this gink is the limit. Man, oh, man, he is the living end."

"When would I ever see him?" I eyed the unchopped carrots, wondering if Sandy would stand for my snagging one.

"That's the bombshell. He'll be here day after tomorrow."

That must have been a bombshell, all right. What had Mr. Walton called him? "A very dear friend of dear Albert." How was Corrie going to take this? How was Miss Eleanor going to take it? It bothered me a little that Aunt Missy hadn't told me. Then again, she hadn't told me I was supposed to eat with the other "service personnel" after she'd wanted me to eat with the family, either. Maybe she figured it would be less unpleasant for her to let Sandy tell me. That would fit in with Dr. Andrew's opinion of her.

Stop thinking like that! Aunt Missy isn't irresponsible. She wouldn't hire me, for instance, and then just go off and forget about me, like Sandy says she did some of her other hires.

"He hasn't been back since the funeral," Sandy said. "Well, why would he? He mighta written to one of Them; I wouldn't know about that. But he's coming back here. Five year anniversary, maybe. Betcha didn't know that: Saturday, it'll be five years to the day. July 13, 1963, Albert died. That was a Saturday, too, come to think of it. Two days later, Jason and Joan went to pick Alain up from the airport in Louisville, bring him back to the house for the 'service' — if you want to call it that — and went off the road on the way back and run into a tree. *Bam.* July 15, 1963."

"That's done," said Ava, bustling back into the kitchen. "Now, Mitch, I make you a sandwich, hmm? You may eat it upstairs on a tray, or you may eat in the servants' hall. Corrie will be helping me serve at table, but," Ava's smile faded as she finished, "she can keep you company between courses."

"I'll eat in my room, thanks."

Ava nodded approvingly. She took an uncut loaf out of a wooden box with "BREAD" stenciled on it and sliced off a couple of slabs. Home-baked, I bet. My stomach rumbled; I hoped nobody else heard it.

Ava reached into the refrigerator and pulled out sandwich ingredients, holding each up for my acceptance or rejection. "Just leave the tray in the hall when you've finished," she said. "If you have clothes you want washed, there's a hamper in your bathroom. We have breakfast backstairs at seven, lunch at noon, and dinner about 5:30. Except for Sundays and every other Saturday, either Sandy or I will always be in, so come back and see us any time you want company. Don't bring those animals with you, though. Sandy hates the hairs."

The animals. "Oh! Aunt Missy probably wants me to keep the dogs while she has dinner."

Ava shook her head, lips pursed. "The dogs sit in a corner in the dining room while she eats. I will say this much for them: they're well-mannered. She doesn't permit them to beg at the table. They are fed once, at 10:00 in the morning. I assume that will be your job, now, and not Sandy's. He has more than enough to do." She gave another satisfied nod.

"Yes, ma'am."

She loaded a tray and handed it to me. "Now, I must clear the soup."

~*~

In my room, I positioned one of the armchairs where I could see down the hall, past Aunt Missy's door to the head of the Grand Staircase.

The sandwich had been large and lush, the milk had been plentiful and cold. Ava had even given me a couple of carrots, a dill pickle, and a dish of hot bread-and-raisin pudding, which I normally don't like, but that was before I tasted Sandy's. She had offered me some of the soup, but I like my pumpkin in a pie, so I passed. I had put the tray in the hall, like Ava told me to do. Now I was settled in with a book of Bradbury stories, waiting for Aunt Missy.

I'm sure I would have heard her, especially if the dogs had been in good voice, but I was deep enough into my book that the tense whisper, "Mitch!" nearly took me out of my chair.

It was Corrie. At least she'd got my name right.

"Hello, Miss Crawley." I rose, trying to keep things formal.

"Call me Corrie."

I didn't invite her in, but she came anyway, and closed the door and leaned on it.

"Uh, look, Miss Crawley. . . ."

"They can't hear us now, Albert."

"Miss Crawley, I'm not—"

She raised a hand and placed it on my lips. "Hush! You are Albert. I feel it. You feel it, too. You'll feel it more, the longer you stay here. It'll help when Grant Marsch comes. You'll see. It won't be long now, and Mitch will be gone!"

"Mitch will be what? Now, wait a minute!"

"I could tell this afternoon, Albert wasn't completely in control. But you aren't fighting him, and that makes all the difference! You want to be Albert. Of course you do."

Buy time. The family should be coming up from dinner, or Ava will come to get the tray.

"Uh, yeah, I, uh, I bet that would be really neat. About how much longer will it be, do you think?"

"I don't know." She smiled at me from beneath her lashes. "I'm not the expert."

"Albert is, right?"

"Right. Now, what I came to tell you is this: Dr. Walton managed to give Eleanor a sleeping powder tonight, so we won't be able to meet."

"Oh, darn it!" Dr. Andrew was really hepped on Eleanor getting her rest.

"Does Eleanor have to be awake before we can meet?"

"She wouldn't be much use if she wasn't—" Corrie

suddenly lost all her color. She pressed herself against the door, as if she couldn't get far enough away from me — from Albert. "You don't mean. . . . You don't mean what I think you mean."

"What do you think I mean?" Not that I really wanted to hear the answer to that question.

"You always said it was the idea that was important! You said we didn't need to really. . . ."

I had not the slightest inkling what she was talking about, but there are some things I'd rather keep in the dark, and I had a strong notion that whatever this was, it was one of those things. So, I said:

"Relax. I just thought maybe we could get along without her, that's all."

Corrie's terror seemed to collapse, leaving it flat, but still there. "Oh. Oh, I see. Of course. I'm sorry I didn't understand. I've been so confused, without you." She tried a smile. "Yes, Eleanor has to be there. At least, Mary says so. If you think we can do without her, though—"

Mary says so? "Mary who?"

Corrie laughed and colored up like I'd just said something flirty. "I'd better go now." She slipped out and away.

Well, so much for reading.

Chapter 9

I wondered if Corrie's little friends (if she had ever had any little friends) had called her "Creepy" Crawley. It might account for a lot.

I sank back into my armchair and thought in a way I had never had to think before. Oh, sure, I'd had to ask myself if Eileen Timberlake meant I should or shouldn't ask her out when she said she really ought to stay home and study. Now, I had to ask myself if Corrie was or was not hallucinating when she said she and Miss Eleanor and The Dragon Lady had plans to meet me by moonlight. That was kind of the same thing, but kind of different.

Of course, Mary is a pretty common name; maybe Corrie had a friend named Mary who had been dragged into whatever tar pit Corrie and Eleanor seemed to be stuck in. Aunt Missy had said that Albert got around while he was here; he could have met any number of Marys.

I heard voices in the hall and, when I looked up, the first thing I saw was Mrs. Seldon-Hardesty. That set my mind at rest on one point at least: This Mary did not look like a Mary who would hob-nob with the help, not even to raise the dead. In fact, I would have dismissed the whole "meeting" business altogether if it weren't for Dr. Andrew's concern about Eleanor's sleeping habits.

Aunt Missy came into view and I went out to meet her. Chan and Wong pulled their leashes out of her hand and she said something I didn't think well-bred ladies knew how to say.

"I hate those tethers!" she said then, massaging her fingers, where the soft leather had rubbed them. "Ridiculous!"

I picked up the dogs, letting the leashes dangle. "They'd stay with you, wouldn't they? You don't have to have them on the leashes all the time."

Aunt Missy's frown didn't fade as she closed us into her room. "It's safer this way."

Ah, yes, I had forgotten: The dogs were in danger. And I was possessed by the spirit of a dead novelist. *Who needs dope when there's Willowbrook?*

I could see Aunt Missy didn't feel like socializing. She had a tiredness, a did-I-do-the-right-thing air; a kind of attitude you see in a couple who have really had to struggle to adopt. At the last minute, they wonder. So I just passed a few minutes, soaking up whatever it was I soaked up when I was with her, and offered to take the dogs to my room for the night.

"No, I think it would be better if you get used to things here before you start caring for them full-time."

I made a private vow that, if I ever got used to some things at Willowbrook, I'd shoot myself.

Dr. Andrew was waiting for me in the hall.

Aunt Missy called after me, "Close the door, dear," in a tone that said I shouldn't have had to be told.

"We keep our doors shut," Dr. Andrew said. He tapped my door frame with one finger. "Yours is open."

We kept our doors open at the Refuge, most of the time. Of course, the only people at the Refuge who needed treatment were *getting* treatment.

"I'll try to remember," I said.

"May I come in?"

"Sure." I swept an arm toward the open door. "Be my guest."

He stepped inside and let out a quiet sigh.

It may have been that more than anything else — his not letting out that sigh until he was inside my room — but I closed my door firmly after us, and did it feeling I just had to.

"Do you mind if I sit with you for a while?"

"No, sir. Of course not."

He took one of the chairs by the bed, and I took the other.

Well, here we are. Sitting. Now what?

Dr. Andrew looked around the room, eyes narrow, lips pressed tight. In a way, I wished he'd say something; then, again, with the kind of thoughts that might go with that expression, I'd rather he didn't let them out.

Maybe I could divert his attention. What could I say? *Any progress in the lab, Doctor?*

"I saw you did get something to eat," he said at last. "I saw your tray in the hall." His thinnish face twisted into a cold bitterness. "Sometimes Aunt Mary . . . Aunt Mary can be. . . ."

"Sandy told me about the argument. And I really don't mind eating backstairs or anything. I mean, that is where I belong and all."

"Possibly. But Aunt Amelia wanted you to eat with her. Lydia and I are happy to please Aunt Amelia whenever we can. And Father would've welcomed the change of audience."

He seemed so certain I'd been deprived of what was rightfully mine, I started to resent the matter a little, myself.

"We wanted you in the dining room," he said. "But Aunt Mary, for some reason known only to God, didn't. As usual, she got her way. We just sat back, as usual, and let her have things as they pleased her. Why did we do it? Why do we always do it?"

He looked at me as if he wanted a real answer and believed I could give him one.

I took a shot, based on my vast experience of life. "She's pushy. You aren't."

Dr. Andrew chuckled. "You don't know my father. Why doesn't he stand up to her?"

It couldn't be because he thought it would be rude to talk back to a lady — look at the way he talked to Aunt Missy.

"There, you got me," I said.

We were both silent for a while. Then Dr. Andrew sighed again and stood up. "You don't have to sit up here twenty-four hours a day waiting on the dogs. Aunt Amelia seldom gets up before nine and she invariably goes to bed at eleven. Lydia works at the mission in Faelin in the mornings, so she won't be here then, but Father has an office behind the sitting room — behind the room we were in this afternoon — and I'm almost always in the lab. The Schneiders have rooms off the kitchen, and Corrie has rooms off the servants' hall." His face went blank when he mentioned Corrie. I wondered if she had ever pulled the "Let's play like you're Albert" routine on him.

I hated to ask, but Aunt Missy had one, so I thought it might not be too lower-class. "Is there a television I could watch sometimes?"

"A television? Of course. Across the foyer from the sitting room. Just close the door and don't play it too loudly. Lydia and Father keep the television listings for the week in there, with the shows they want to watch circled; other than those times, watch whatever you like."

Hello, *Hawaii 5-0*! I usually watched *Dark Shadows*, the day-time "spook opera," too, but that would be coals to Newcastle.

"Thank you, sir," I said.

"Don't 'sir' me, please. Aunt Mary has some Victorian notions about people having 'places,' but the rest of us live in the twentieth century." Dr. Andrew stood and stretched. "Back to work." He sighed again and left.

So I had the run of the house. *But who wants the run of* this *house?*

I did wish I didn't feel so comfortable in Albert's room. There was something eerily familiar about it, and I started drifting slowly toward the willies.

Then I realized what it was: the floodlights under the eaves. I went to a window and pulled the curtain back all the way. I was bathed in the same white light I knew from the street lights in Faelin. Florescent reassurance, courtesy of your local electric co-operative.

The garden was as bright as a night-game, washed in a blue solution of light and shadow. I wanted to go to the TV room so much, I thought I might cry from the pain — the TV room at the Refuge, that is. I was homesick, and how.

A telephone rang in the hall. It rang again, then stopped mid-way through the third ring. A moment later, there was a tap at my door.

"Just a minute," I called, closing the curtains and rounding the bed. I had nearly said, "Come in," but I'm a quick learner: Instead, I opened the door wide enough to see out, bracing it with my foot.

It was Lydia. With a slight frown, she said, "It's for you. It's Mrs. Brandt."

"Am I not supposed to get calls?"

"Oh, no, no! No, of course you may have calls — and make them, too — Certainly! It's just that. . . . Well, you're away from that place, now. You're part of our big family." She made a "cute and squishy" face to welcome me in. "Don't cling to the past, Mitch."

"I'll try not to, Miss Lydia," I said, and went to the phone.

"Hi, Mrs. Brandt!"

"How are you doing, Mitchy — I mean Mitch?" She chuckled. "How long has it been since I called you 'Mitchy'?"

"Long time." I'd started asking her not to call me that "baby" name when I entered kindergarten. By about fifth grade, she had pretty well stopped. I liked hearing it again, now.

"How are things going up there? Are they being nice to you? Did you have enough to eat?"

This was my chance to tell her I'd traded one institution for another. She'd send Billy after me in the morning; maybe call him up and have him come bring me back right away. Back to the Refuge. Back to Jimmy Gassman and the other kids who came and went. Back to waiting for my advancing age to throw me into the arms of the Viet Cong, with nobody to get the flag they shipped me home under. Mrs. Brandt would mourn me, but she'd always have a houseful of kids to manage, and I'd fade before too long. I wanted to cause some real pain when I died.

Like Albert? I asked myself.

Not that much pain, I answered.

"Mitch? Are you still there?"

"Still here, Mrs. Brandt. They're real nice up here." *Some of them*. "Had plenty to eat. Food's great."

Mrs. Brandt laughed. "Bound to be better than mine."

"No, no. Good, but not better than yours."

"So you think things are going to work out?"

If I can keep this crazy woman from turning me into some dead guy she used to know. Sounded pretty stupid, even to me.

"Yeah," I said. "I think everything's going to work out." Before I could help it, I said, "Tell you the truth, I'm kind of homesick."

She gave a sympathetic cluck. "Bless your sweet heart. We miss you, too." After a brief pause, she said, "Billy will bring the rest of your things up tomorrow, then. Right?"

"Right. Thanks."

"If you change your mind before he gets there, you come on back with him."

"All right."

A series of crashes and shouts came through the telephone.

"Ohh! I have to go, Mitch. Good night. Don't let the bedbugs bite."

"G'night. Tell the kids—"

She disconnected.

I guess some pasts are easier to cling to than others.

I went back to my Bradbury book, but I couldn't concentrate on it. In a lifetime without a family, I had never felt as alone as I did that night.

This sounds like a job for Brains Brannigan. I toyed

with the idea of calling him. Brains Brannigan wasn't his real name, of course. His real name was Scott Coulson. His adopted name was Scott Masters. He had also been known as "Killer" Spike Cokebottle, the Mad Boxer.

This "Cokebottle" thing started with me and three of my friends. We drank so much Coca Cola, Mrs. Brandt called us "The Cokebottle Quads". We liked it, and made up first names. (I was Squire Cornelius Cokebottle.) It had caught on. Within days, everybody over the age of five either had a Cokebottle name or was thinking of one. We had a Captain Horatio Cokebottle, a Big Duke Cokebottle, a Sister Mary Francis Cokebottle, and so on. It made us feel like more of a family. Jimmy Gassman was Viktor von Cokebottle, after Viktor von Doom, his favorite comic book villain. We also called him Gollum, when we wanted to yank his chain.

We even chipped in together and bought a scrapbook to commemorate the retiring Cokebottles as they were adopted or grew up and moved out. Retiring Cokebottles signed their Cokebottle names and legal names in the scrapbook next to their fictitious autobiographies.

Scott got adopted at eleven by Mr. and Mrs. Masters, one of the history teachers and his wife. They lived in Faelin, and Scott came back to see us so often it didn't seem right to cut him out of Cokebottlism entirely, so we made him Brains Brannigan, two-fisted private eye and friend of the family. If anybody might understand how I felt now, it would be Scott.

I didn't call, though. For one thing, I didn't want to use their phone, even though Miss Lydia had said it was okay. For another thing, what if he didn't understand? That would make things much, much worse, and they were bad enough already.

At 10:30, I gave it up. Wearing a pair of pajamas which, I reflected, might have been donated to the Refuge by Mr. Walton himself, I went to bed.

But first, I locked my door.

Chapter 10

I woke about six, as usual, ready to rise and shine. Back at the Refuge, I was called "The Beast of the Morning," because of my hideous cheerfulness before breakfast.

Ravenous, in jeans and a t-shirt, I left my room in search of food. And who should stand between me and the kitchen stairs but Mrs. Seldon-Hardesty, dressed in a navy blue skirt and jacket and a white blouse buttoned up to her chin.

She smiled ever-so-slightly, and said, very softly, "Another early riser."

"We have breakfast backstairs at 7:00," I said, innocuously.

With a gracious gesture, she indicated the west end of the hall and said, "Please take those stairs. Your footsteps are unfamiliar; they disturb my niece."

If she thought my footsteps disturbed Eleanor, she should have seen what my presence at Albert's graveside had done. I could only assume no one had told her, and I could only hope that no one would.

Obediently, I took the stairs to the mud-room.

A small window in the right-hand wall was open, making the air chillingly fresh. It surprised me, how cool the morning air was; in town, in the summer, it was stuffy and dusty-smelling 'round the clock.

It was "blowing up a storm," as we said in Faelin. I looked out at the overcast landscape, whistling a sprightly little tune I'd had in my mind since yesterday afternoon.

In the woods that curved in a crescent around three sides of the grounds, the beeches showed the silver side of their leaves and rustled like rice-paper wind chimes. "The trees are showing their petticoats," Mrs. Brandt would have said.

"What are you looking at?"

I started at the unexpected voice, but recognized it: Corrie. Without turning, in as discouraging a tone as I could manage, I said, "I'm looking out of the window."

She giggled. "Well, I can see that." She moved forward, so I scooted over to give her room. "But why are you looking out of the window?"

I sighed. "Just checking the weather. Gonna storm today." Automatically, I followed this prediction, as I did all such down-home wisdom, with the unfortunate phrase, "I am blessed with the gift of prophecy."

"I know you are." Corrie tucked an arm around mine. "I remember."

"Corrie," I said firmly. It was time to be firm. "I want you to listen." I looked her straight in the eye and said, "I am not now, nor have I ever been, Albert Alaister. I will never be Albert Alaister. Never."

"Oh, Mitch." She patted my arm. "This weather's just got you down. Come into the Hall and I'll get you some breakfast." She let me go and crossed to the servants' hall door. "Come on, now."

She led me into a large room. A long wooden table filled the middle of the floor, eight straight-backed chairs tucked around it. A refrigerator, a pantry cabinet, and a stove — all old stuff, cast-offs from remodeling the "real" kitchen, I guessed — lined up along one wall. There was a window in the back wall, above a sink, and a door that must have led to the kitchen.

"Sit down," Corrie said. "I remember what you like."

Of course she didn't, so I said, "I'll help."

"You'll do no such thing. Sit down. Go on."

I sat down.

Corrie fluttered around busily, throwing me warm looks now and again.

"Where's Ava and Sandy?" I asked.

"They eat in the kitchen. They don't like me. Nobody does, much. Miss Amelia. You."

Me? Where did she get the notion I like her?

"Wait a minute," I said. "Do you mean me or Albert?"

Corrie regarded me searchingly. Some part of the search seemed directed toward herself, and she answered slowly, "I don't know. You change so quick."

"I never change. Believe it."

A weak smile played across Corrie's mouth. "I always believed you."

"Him," I said, icily.

After a moment, Corrie said, in a melancholy tone, "Him."

It came home to me very strongly, then, that we were talking about ALBERT ALAISTER — the incomparable Albert Alaister — and that Corrie was speaking from personal knowledge. I said something then that I wouldn't have dreamed of saying before I knew who "dear Albert" really was: "Tell me about Him."

Corrie smiled sweetly, her dimples showing and her eyes alight. "He was a very attractive man." She actually blushed — not a mottled red, but a beautiful, soft rose. It was enough to make me wish she wasn't a lunatic. "He was kind of short, for a man, but strong. Like you."

I refused to be flattered.

"He had your coloring. Dark hair and eyes, kind of Hawaiian looking."

That was the first time I'd been placed in that particular category, and I'd made the rounds, depending on the racial prejudices of the person who happened to be attacking me. No wonder Kono was my favorite character on *Hawaii 5-0*.

"And his face was broad and handsome, like yours. His features weren't like yours at all, though. But I guess you mean what was he like Spiritually."

If there was one thing I did not want to hear about, it was Albert's Spirit. "Uh, never mind." I had a notion that Corrie wasn't likely to be brim-full of literary anecdotes, which is what I guess I was after.

Corrie misunderstood my reluctance. "You don't need me to tell you, do you?" She stopped what she was doing to beam approvingly at me. "I knew he was getting stronger when I saw you standing at that open window, whistling His tune."

His tune? I tried to remember where I'd picked up that piece of melody, but I couldn't even remember how it went.

"He always stood there," Corrie said, "every morning, in all kinds of weather, and waited for me. Then we would stand together for a minute, and I would come in and get his breakfast. Just like today."

She had paused in the act of slicing ham and, since this involved a knife, I didn't protest that this morning was pure chance.

"He always got up early, too," Corrie continued. "He didn't need much sleep, he said. Always up and doing. You never could rest long."

"He, Corrie. *He* never could rest long." I realized that this wasn't really an improvement.

"Why did you lock your door last night?"

That one took me on my blind side.

"Why shouldn't I?" I silently congratulated myself on having done so.

"I came back after everybody was in bed." Her voice was puzzled and hurt. "Your door was locked."

"It was night time. You said good night, yourself."

"I didn't! I jus' know I didn't!" Her accent went farther back into the woods the more agitated she got. "Oh, don't torment me, Albert. Please tell me if I done somethin' wrong."

"No, no, not that I know of." Obviously, she was not yet ready to realize that I was me and that she would have to look for Albert elsewhere. I decided to go for a laugh, to lighten things up. "What's the matter? Got a guilty conscience?"

She didn't laugh. Her face went white and she fell to her knees beside my chair. Clasping her arms around my waist, she cried, "No, Albert! I swear!"

"Okay! I believe you!" I put a protective arm around her. Protecting her from what? From the man who was supposed to be inside of me. My scalp prickled and I gritted my teeth in rage. My hero, Albert Alaister, had worked on her so that a word from somebody she thought was partly him threw her to her knees. I didn't like it. People shouldn't do things like that to people.

"I never even thought of another man in all these years," she went on desperately, quietly. "How could I, after . . . after what we was to each other?"

Oh, Lord, I should have guessed. Not just a girlish crush,

not just a city-slicker flirting with a good-looking hick. That stinking rat.

"Now, don't cry, Corrie, please don't." She wasn't listening to poor old Mitch. There was only one thing I could do for her, and I did it: "I've. . . . This whole business . . . the possession and all . . . is very tiring. And . . . I have to concentrate a lot. And besides, Mitch is a growing boy. He needs his rest. If I'm going to live in this body, I have to take care of it. So I locked my door. That's all there was to it."

Now, was it going to work? Yes, there it was again: the dove-gray glow.

"Of course," she said, and palmed away her tears. "I wasn't thinking." She stood, holding my arm around her waist as if she were afraid of my letting her go. She touched my shoulder, and I had to turn away from the gratitude in her face.

"Eleanor was in such a good mood last night," she said. "Seeing you yesterday done her — *did* her a world of good. After your accident, she just fell apart. And then her Momma and Daddy, and her Uncle Alain, right after."

I hadn't asked, and nobody had told me. How did Albert die? What kind of accident? Then it struck me: After *Albert's* accident, Eleanor fell apart?

"They took her to a doctor," Corrie went on, "but all he said was 'rest,' so they decided to bring her home." Corrie took my hand. "She isn't always sad, like she was yesterday afternoon. Like I said, she was real good last night. She was back to cutting bride pictures out of the catalogs and planning another wedding. She's got about eight for you to pick from."

Whoa — time out. Eight weddings for me — for Albert — to pick from?

Corrie chattered on with that nervous energy you get after a scare. "That's what she does when she's happy. Cuts out pictures of brides and flower girls and churches and writes out the invitations and all. Once you're really back for good, she'll be all right. You and me, we'll help her."

The door to the kitchen opened and I snatched my hand out of Corrie's clutch. Ava came in, carrying a covered tray.

"Morning," I said.

Ava nodded, but there was no answering pleasantry. Because I was with Corrie? "Mr. Andrew is ready for breakfast," she said, putting the tray on the table.

"I'll take it right down," Corrie said, barely civil.

"I was not speaking to you. Mrs. Hardesty needs you upstairs. Mr. Andrew wants Mitch to bring down his tray. He's in the laboratory. Through that door and down the stairs."

She returned to the kitchen without another word.

"You see?" Corrie said. "She don't like me at all. I don't like her, neither." But her eyes were more hurt than hateful. It was a line I'd heard — and used — many a time in the schoolyard, when someone who used to be a friend turned away.

Chapter 11

The carpet on the mud room stairs was completely different below the landing than above it: newer, and in a blue and green paisley print with yellow and red bits. Very with-it, very Now. I wondered if Dr. Andrew had chosen it himself. I wouldn't have thought so, but you never can tell with jazz men.

The stairs led down to a corridor. The door to my right was open, so I went in. The room was small, but comfortably furnished with a cot-like bed, a square table, three wooden chairs, a floor lamp, and Dr. Andrew.

"Good morning," he said, sounding like he wanted to be brisk but wasn't quite up to it. "When I called upstairs on the house phone, Ava told me she heard you and Corrie talking in the ser MARIAN ALLEN vants' hall. She didn't approve. Ava seems to have taken a dislike to Corrie, for some reason."

Maybe Ava caught Corrie trying to Albertize Sandy. That would just about do it for most wives, I would think.

"I hope you don't mind my asking her to have you bring this down." He took the tray from me and put it on the table.

"No, sir. Why should I mind?"

"It isn't what you were hired to do. I don't know." He shrugged. "You're Aunt Amelia's—" he gestured vaguely and finished with an uncertain "—hire. You might feel above tray-bringing."

"I'm just a poor little orphan-child on my first full-time job. I don't feel I'm above much of anything."

Dr. Walton smiled wearily. I wondered if he'd been up all night working, or if he was worried about something. He was certainly in the right house for it.

"Have you had breakfast?" he asked.

"I tried, sir."

He chuckled. "Ava told me you were eating with Corrie. I expressed doubts."

"She's kind of emotional, isn't she?"

"Aunt Amelia is very fond of her."

I thought about telling him that she thought she and Miss Eleanor and an unspecified Mary were going to insert spirit A into body M, and then I decided not to. Couple of days, and Corrie would transfer her obsession to somebody else, or pack it up for another five years, or however it worked. I'd be off the hook, and I didn't see any point in putting Corrie on one.

Dr. Andrew uncovered his tray. It held four heaped serving plates filled with toast, eggs, bacon, hash browns, plus a pot of butter and one of jelly, a coffee pot, a small sugar bowl and creamer and two place settings.

"Germanic efficiency," said Dr. Andrew. "Will you join me?"

As Mrs. Brandt would say, I fell upon the food like a swarm of locusts. While we ate, we talked about the weather, sandlot baseball, school social politics (works pretty much the same in a fancy private school as it does in nasty old public school) and other relatively normal subjects.

"Oh," he said, when we were nearly done, "before I forget: Father wants to see you today, in his office. There are some forms you need to fill out and things like that. I don't know much about the red tape."

"Well, you don't need to, do you?"

"No." Dr. Andrew's face grew bitter. "Albert once told me I knew nothing about anything except what went on in my lab, and that even that, I largely misunderstood."

"Creep!" I growled. Dr. Andrew looked at me in surprise. Young people did not criticize grown-ups to other grown-ups. I went on, "He used to be my favorite writer. I mean, I guess he's still my favorite *writer* but, as a person. . . . I mean, based on what I've been hearing around here, he was a creep."

Dr. Andrew nodded. "He was a good writer. Almost a great writer, I'd say. Of course, we saw very little of that in him, here. He was playing the court jester, playing the impudent underling, the wicked servant. It was some sort of role he'd written for himself, and he seemed determined to stick to it. After a week or so, we — Lydia and Aunt Mary and I — gave up trying to engage him in sensible conversation."

"Maybe he was on something."

With a startled laugh, Dr. Andrew said, "Now that's a thought. He may have been, but he was also, as you so pithily put it, a creep."

The doctor checked his watch. "Father should be in his office now. I'll show you the quicker way up. Leave the tray. Corrie or Ava will come down for it."

He took me back into the hall. We turned to the right, turned left at the end of a wall, and were at the foot of another set of steps.

"These come out at the side of the main staircase, just opposite Father's office, where I came up and met you yesterday. I have to get back now. See you later, I hope."

"Thank you, sir."

He tried another small and weary smile. "My name is Andrew."

"Thank you, Dr. Andrew."

He chuckled. "Good enough. We'll work on it."

~*~

The door to Mr. Walton's office was ajar. I knocked gently and the door swung open. Mr. Walton looked up with such a swift, convulsive movement, I retreated a step. His hands fluttered, concealing some papers he had been studying.

"Oh, Mitch," he said. It might have been my imagination, but he seemed relieved.

Now, who had he thought I was, coming up from the basement?

The red tape didn't take long. It would have taken even less, but I read everything before I signed it. I once signed a petition for a friend without reading it, and later found out that I had helped swing the decision for band uniforms to day-glo orange. Since then, I have always read everything before I signed it. I was afraid Mr. Walton would get irritated by the delay, but he was just surprised for a moment, then seemed to approve.

Barking — nervous and loud, a bark with a lot of whine in it — came from somewhere in the house. A terrified howl ended with a solid, sickening thud and a hideous yelp.

I knocked my chair over, getting up and out. The half of the foyer I could see from the door was clear, so I circled the staircase, my stomach in an iron knot.

Mr. Walton was behind me at first, but he stopped at the

staircase, gripping the bannister.

From where he stood, he couldn't see what I saw: Chan, twitching on the tile floor, looking like a rag that had been crumpled up and thrown away. His fur bristled, his glazed eyes showed white all around the rim. His sides heaved. As I came toward him, he tried to stand, but he fell back with a soft, wet whimper. There was blood on his face; I could see where it had gotten into the ridges in the tile near his head.

I took a couple of deep breaths and forced myself to think clearly. I went back to Mr. Walton, who still clenched the bannister. His face looked like it had been put on with greasepaint.

"It's Chan," I said.

"Oh, God!" Mr. Walton leaned against the post. "Is he—"

"He's hurt. I'm going to take him to a vet. You go upstairs and tell Aunt Missy."

A door opened upstairs. *What were they waiting for?* I wondered, then realized that only seconds had passed since that first burst of barking, not the forever it seemed.

Aunt Missy peeped around the edge of the wall, her face so white it was almost blue. Wong tugged at the end of his leash, trying to get to his wounded buddy.

"Mitch." Her voice quavered. "I told you. Didn't I tell you? Nobody believed me. Maybe now they will."

Mr. Walton started up the stairs, saying, "He's all right, Amelia. Chan had a bad fall, but he's all right." Half-way up, he turned to me and said, "Ava has the spare keys. I'd like to speak to you again, when you get back."

"Yes, sir." I'd consider the implications of that, later. Now, I had Chan to worry about.

I remembered seeing a green afghan folded over the back

of a sofa to the left of Mr. Walton's desk. I ran and grabbed it to wrap Chan in while I drove him to Dr. Aaronson, who took care of the orphanage pets.

On my way out of the office I almost crashed into Dr. Andrew.

"I thought I heard something," he said. "What's happened?"

"Chan." Dr. Andrew followed me around the staircase. "He fell off the balcony. Mr. Walton went up to Aunt Missy."

Dr. Andrew turned almost as pale as his father. "How bad is it?"

I wrapped the afghan around the dog, who snapped in pain but didn't really try to connect. "He has a bloody nose, and I think maybe a broken leg. I was going to take him to our vet, but I guess he has his own?"

"Dr. Aaronson. I've driven Aunt Missy there with the dogs before. Come on." Dr. Andrew trotted to the door, pulling a set keys out of his pocket.

"I know the way. Mr. Walton told me to ask Ava for keys."

"This is faster. Meet me out front." He left the door open.

Sandy stuck his head out of the kitchen passage. "What the hell?"

"It's Chan. He fell off the balcony."

Sandy cocked his head to look up. "You mean he fell down the stairs?"

"Off the balcony." I pointed an elbow at the bloodstain. "There's where he. . . ," I couldn't bring myself to say, "landed." I could still hear that yelp, that thump.

"Okay," Sandy said, dubiously. "I'll tell Ava she was right. She said she heard something. Gotta clean that up before Miss A sees it. Need a lift to the vet's?"

"Dr. Andrew's getting the car."

Sandy retreated with a nod and a shout of: "Ava? Whaddya think?"

I waited on the porch, murmuring what were meant to be calming phrases to Chan. Dr. Andrew pulled around in a brand-new, candy-apple red Corvette. Not what I would have expected. Then again . . . jazz. . . .

It couldn't have taken fifteen minutes to reach the vet's but, by the time we got there, Chan's whines and yelps had both of us sweating with the strain of keeping within the speed limit.

The nurse took one look at Chan and one at Dr. Andrew. "Oh, Dr. Walton, how dreadful!" She took the dog, no questions asked. When she came out of the examining complex to fill out the appropriate blanks, she told us that the doctor was with Chan already.

I wondered how that would sit with the lady in the three-piece suit who had been waiting when we came in, but she rose to the occasion.

"Was that your little dog?" she asked me.

"No, ma'am. My employer's." Funny: I had almost said, "My aunt's."

"Oh," she said. "I had a—" Her eyes flicked to my right arm. She paused and swallowed. "I had a dog once, who—"

I looked down and saw what was bothering her: My arm was smeared, bicep to wrist, with a wide, bright ribbon of Chan's blood.

I excused myself. In the men's room, I splashed the blood off and scrubbed my arm with a paper towel, then wet another towel with cold water and pressed it to the back of my neck.

I found I was faced with one great hope: that Chan had fallen. I mean, where had Wong been, when Chan was taking a flying lesson? What had the barking been about? and that howl? I remembered Dr. Andrew saying Lydia spent the mornings at the Mission, but where had The Dragon Lady been? Where had Corrie been? And then there was Sandy's questioning my accuracy. It made me wonder: Was there enough space between the bannister posts for Chan to go through by accident? Or would someone have had to help him over?

Aunt Missy kept insisting the dogs were in danger. Yesterday, Mr. Walton said they had disappeared before.

So I was left hoping that Chan had fallen, because I didn't want to think about a person who would pick up a friendly little dog and toss him over a 15-foot drop.

Chapter 12

It took me a few minutes to get control of myself. When I got back to the waiting room, Dr. Andrew was gone.

"The man who brought you," the suit-lady said, "got a phone call and had to leave."

I had an *abandoned* rush. "Phone call?"

"He asked me to tell you he had to leave. Oh, and somebody's coming to pick you up. Linda or something?"

Lydia. That would make it a perfect morning. I thanked the lady and sat down, twisting in my seat until I could look out into the parking lot. The promise of early morning fulfilled itself by pouring down rain.

"Radio says it's going to storm," the lady remarked. "Thunder and lightning and everything. All over the state. An electrical storm. It's raining now. It's supposed to get worse."

That pretty well covered the subject, so she patted my hand a couple times and started reading a magazine.

The phone call would probably have been from the house. I considered calling to find out what was up, but decided that, if it had been something drastic, Dr. Andrew would've left word. But, if it hadn't been drastic, why had he left without rapping on the men's room door or something? Maybe it had been personal, or maybe I wasn't as much a buddy as Dr. Andrew made me feel. Maybe he'd heard about the electrical storm and rushed home to plug in the monster.

Dr. Aaronson's nurse, Janet, came out of the back carrying a covered bird cage.

"My bird," the lady said. She took the cage, chirped to it, smiled at me, and left.

Dr. Aaronson came into the waiting room. He was carrying the green afghan, folded so the blood didn't show.

"How is he?" I asked, rising.

"Well, Mitch!" Dr. Aaronson came over to shake my hand. "How's who?"

"Chan. Amelia Hardesty's dog."

"How do you know Chan? Where's Andrew?"

Of course: Dr. Aaronson knew me only as one of the kids from the Refuge.

Janet said, "He came with Dr. Walton."

"I work for Miss Hardesty," I said. "Dr. Walton had to leave; Miss Lydia is picking me up."

"Ah, yes. Fine girl."

"How's Chan?" I said, determined to hack through the small talk, if I had to use a machete to do it.

"He'll be all right. I'd like to keep him here for a few days."

"Sure." I tried not to feel relieved, not to say to myself, *At least one of them will be safe.*

"He broke his left foreleg and a couple of ribs. Gave himself a bloody nose. Slight concussion. He seems awfully shaken up, and those particular dogs are hard to shake. What happened to him?"

"He fell off the balcony." I wished I didn't feel like I was establishing a convenient fiction in repeating that.

Dr. Aaronson nodded. "Well," he said. "So you work for Matt Walton."

"No," I said, "I work for Amelia Hardesty." Score one for Aunt Missy.

I realized that I had never cared for Dr. Aaronson: It was typical that he should vet Aunt Missy's dogs but think of her in terms of Mr. Walton, the community mover and shaker. I also realized that, Dr. Aaronson being vet to people like Aunt Missy and the Three-Piece Suit, he didn't need the Refuge business. He had always told us the Refuge paid him for doctoring our animals, but now I realized he was probably one of Matthew Walton's charitable donations. It was nice of Mr. Walton — not something just anybody would have thought of. But, if I'd known Dr. Aaronson's heart wasn't in his work for us, I'd have taken my late turtle elsewhere.

~*~

Lydia wasn't long coming. She looked like a Power to the People Barbie: crisp new blue jeans with a slight bell flare, a white t-shirt under a tunic-length brocade vest, and mushroom-colored Earth shoes. Her shining black hair was held back in a red and white paisley bandanna.

"Oh, Mitch, you poor boy!" She threw her arms around my neck and patted me with implacable sympathy.

"I'm all right, Miss Lydia. Thank you. I'm fine."

"I can't imagine how that must have been! Were you right there? Did you actually see it?"

"No, ma'am, just heard it."

"Andy said you took charge." She let me go and thumped me admiringly on the biceps. "I really appreciate that. Chan was so lucky you were there."

She must have taken a course in "Building Self-esteem in Staff and Volunteers."

I resisted the cartoon impulse to say, "Aw, shucks,

ma'am; 'tweren't nothin'." She probably would have just told me not to be so modest.

"I think I'd better get back to Aunt Missy," I said, instead. "She's probably upset; might want me to help her with Wong."

"Yes, of course. Suppose I take you to lunch first? Would you like that? A hamburger and a shake? Sound good?"

I didn't want to tell her it sounded like a fish for the performing seal — it was so obvious she meant well.

"That's nice of you, Miss Lydia, but I'd just as soon get back."

"I really admire your sense of responsibility. All right; let's go."

~*~

On the way back to the house, Lydia drove the black and silver 1963 Ford Fairlaine 500 — a decent car, but nothing flashy, doubtless bought so as not to make the Mission's beneficiaries too jealous. She told me about the Mission: it was a sort of catch-all agency cobbled together out of the Red Cross, Salvation Army, local churches, and what-not. It handled homeless people, transients (car broke down, no money, no food), abused women and children, elderly, shut-ins, military families, and disaster victims. It had a food pantry and a clothes closet. Sometimes they sent stuff over to the Refuge, Lydia said, but she'd never made the run.

She asked me about what life in the Refuge was like, "if you don't mind talking about it." I didn't mind, exactly, but it was weird. I mean, you grow up in a place, and that's the way things are. What is it like? What does that mean? It's like . . . it's like it is, that's all.

I got off onto the subject of Jimmy Gassman, and had

her laughing before we turned off the highway. She looked better when she was laughing: not so phony. Less like she was made out of industrial plastic.

"You have a great laugh," I told her. "Or should I say, 'I like the way you laugh'? Isn't that right? An 'I' statement, not a 'you' statement?"

She pushed playfully at my shoulder with her fingertips. "You're terrible!" She cut her eyes at me and said, "I suppose you've had enough social workers to last a lifetime."

"Yes, ma'am. I'd just as soon you stopped treating me like a client. I savvy the lingo, if you know what I mean."

"You mean you know what message I'm trying to send when I say certain things in certain ways. I can't boost your self-image unobtrusively, because you recognize the technique."

"Give the little lady a cigar." To be honest, I was surprised she'd got it. I revised my opinion of her: not stupid, not completely dense. That's kind of scary, when somebody who's usually thick as a brick flashes bright. Takes your breath away, and reminds you not to take what you think you know about people for granted.

"I'll make a deal with you," Lydia said. "I'll stop trying to snow you if you'll stop 'ma'am'ing me. Deal?"

"I don't think your mother would like that much, Miss Lydia."

She smiled ruefully. "No, you're right, she wouldn't. Poor mother's been through so much. I try to give her her way in as much as I can. I think I owe her that — and more. I miss her so much."

"Miss her? But—"

"We used to go shopping together in New York,

Atlanta, West Palm Beach . . . gossiped together. . . . She's very active in volunteer work, did you know that?"

I shook my head. I tried to visualize The Dragon Lady driving the van for the Mothers' Day Out, and failed.

"Well, she is. But she's different, since Papa Alain died." She shook her head and gave a fake laugh. "But why am I bothering you with this?"

"People do. — Tell me things, I mean. Somebody gave Mrs. Brandt two tickets to the orchestra in Louisville and we took the Greyhound over. We had to sit in different rows on the bus; by the time we got across the bridge, the guy next to me had told me things he wouldn't have told his mama."

"Yes." Lydia stared thoughtfully at me. "You have a kind face."

Just what every teen-aged boy wants to hear from a well-built young woman. Lucky it was just Lydia, or I might have broken down and cried.

We found Aunt Missy, Dr. Andrew, Mr. Walton and Mrs. Seldon-Hardesty in the sitting room.

"Oh, Aunt Amelia!" Lydia lunged for her.

Aunt Missy dodged and came to me for a hug. She clutched my shirt with trembling fingers. I dropped the afghan and put my arms around her, but I felt like I was the one being embraced.

"I told you!" she said. "I told you they were in danger! I told you they had enemies!"

"Nonsense!" Mr. Walton said abruptly.

"Chan is all right, Aunt Missy. He'll be home in a couple of days. He has a few broken bones from his *fall*—"

"I knew it would happen some day! Something like this."
She glared across her shoulder. "I hold *you* responsible,
Matt Walton!"

Mr. Walton's frown looked like it had a headache
behind it. "Amelia. . . ."

Mrs. Seldon-Hardesty looked at her watch and said, "Is
this going to go on much longer? I don't like to leave Eleanor
alone."

I had almost forgotten about Eleanor. Now that I
remembered her, I remembered that she hadn't come
running at the sound of a dog in distress, and neither had
Mary. Neither had Corrie.

"Where's Wong?" I asked.

Aunt Missy said, "Sandy and Ava have him in their
quarters. Will you go get him, Mitch?"

It seemed to me she wasn't standing as straight as she
usually did. She looked old and frightened, and that scared
me.

"You want me to bring him to your room?"

"No." She sighed deeply and shook her head. "No, I'm
going to lie down for an hour or so. Bring him in at about
one and we'll have lunch together, you and he and I."

"Yes, ma'am."

Lydia touched Aunt Missy's arm. "I'll take you up. I
know how to make you comfortable, don't I, Aunt Amelia?"

Aunt Missy transferred her weight to Lydia and rather
vacantly allowed herself to be escorted away.

"You," Mrs. Seldon-Hardesty pointed out to me, "are
supposed to be getting the dog."

"Yes, ma'am," I said, not moving. "Mr. Walton, you
said you wanted to see me when I got back?"

"Later. Drop by my office later this afternoon."

Dr. Andrew swept up the bloody dog-wrapper. "I'll take care of this."

Mrs. Seldon-Hardesty stood and, if looks could kill, I'd have been dead in three languages. She was chalk white except for her rouge.

"Can't you do what you're told?" Her voice grated through her teeth.

"Yes, ma'am," I said simply, and left as fast as I could without actually scuttling.

Chapter 13

Wong was unusually subdued. When I picked him up, he sniffed the front of my t-shirt until it was wet, probably smelling Chan. But, when I let him down on my carpet, he just wandered around the room, looking lost and confused.

"Ava's up with Eleanor," was all Sandy had said, when I had gone to fetch the dog. "Miss Amelia wants you to eat in her room with her at one." Just the facts.

This wasn't like the Sandy I had come to know. It unnerved me, like when a guy in a jungle movie says it's quiet and the other guy says, "Yes. *Too* quiet."

I could still feel Chan's blood on my arm, so I would have wanted to shower and change my shirt even if Wong hadn't wiped his nose all over me. I wasn't going to get in under running water during a thunderstorm, though, so I had to wait for a lull and make it quick. I locked my door. And the bathroom door. I hadn't seen *Psycho* for nothing.

Wong followed me into the bathroom, which was lucky for both of us; I wasn't about to leave him alone, but I didn't relish a bout of dog-wrestling before lunch.

I went back to my Bradbury stories while I waited for one o'clock to roll around. Wong lay at my feet, opening his reddish-brown eyes every so often to be sure I was still there.

This was probably the first time in his life he'd ever been without Chan, and he probably didn't know what to do with himself alone, not to mention trying to figure out, with his little doggie brain, where in the world his brother had disappeared to.

Somebody knocked at my door. I asked who it was.

"It's Andrew."

I stepped back to let him pass and closed the door behind him.

"I wanted to explain why I left Dr. Aaronson's," he said. "Father called. Aunt Amelia insisted on seeing me. She was in the kitchen with Wong and wouldn't talk to anyone but Sandy and Ava. She was asking for you, too, but one of us had to stay at Dr. Aaronson's, and you were unavailable. I suppose I should have waited, or come and told you. It was an impulse, to come home as quickly as I could."

"I would have done the same thing. But you don't have to explain anything to me."

Wong raised his head at the sharp tone of Dr. Andrew's voice: "I know I don't have to. I want to."

"I'm sorry, sir," I said, baffled. What had I done to bring that on?

"No, no, no." Dr. Andrew rubbed a hand over his eyes. "I'm sorry I snapped at you. It's just. . . ." He exploded: "This house has never been what one might call a haven of peace and rest, but ever since Albert Alaister came, we've been falling apart! It's been five years since he died, and we're still deteriorating. Sometimes I almost forget he's dead. Sometimes I wonder if he is."

I said nothing.

"What I mean is," he went on more calmly, "he's alive in Eleanor's mind, Corrie thinks he's coming back — Oh, yes, I know all about that — the atmosphere around here is . . . less than relaxed. I seem to feel. . . . Something's wrong.

Very wrong. It's been five years, and the sick, tense feeling Albert gave me is still here." He put a hand to his stomach. "I felt better for a brief while, after he died, but the feeling keeps coming back. It's back now, and it's as strong as ever."

This is not good. This is not good, at all.

The door opened, and Corrie walked in.

"I put a door there," I said nastily. "If I'd wanted you to walk right in, I would have left the door open. I put a door there, see, for you to knock on it first."

Corrie apologized with off-hand familiarity, so I knew she knew I was me and not Him, and told me that Aunt Missy was ready for lunch and I was to go down to the kitchen and help bring up the trays. She and Dr. Andrew seemed oblivious to each other.

I excused myself from Dr. Andrew, who volunteered to deliver Wong to his aunt.

Partway down the kitchen stairs, Corrie turned on me.

"You and him seem to be pretty chummy," she said.

"So?"

"It just seems awful funny, is all. You always despised him, before."

"I just *met* him!" Be she dangerous maniac or moonstruck victim, enough was enough. "Now, listen close, 'cause I don't want to tell you again: I am not Albert Alaister. He's dead. I'm Mitch Franklin." I patted myself on the chest, as if looking for something. "Nobody in here but me. Unpossessed. Period."

I passed her and heard her following me.

"What do you two have so much to talk about?" She still sounded snitty.

"That's none of your business, is it?"

Her footsteps stopped, and I heard a smothered sob.

I turned back and looked up at her. Her red-gold hair was slightly tumbled, and her lower lip stuck out like a sad little kid's.

"Well, it isn't." I went back up to her. "Corrie," I said, reasonably, "we don't talk about anything in particular. We just . . . talk. Why?"

"What are you planning to do?" She almost whispered it.

"What am I —" She was talking to Albert. I continued to the kitchen without another word.

Music filtered through the closed door to Sandy and Ava's rooms. Two covered trays sat on the counter in the empty kitchen.

Neither Corrie nor I spoke as we took the trays back upstairs. Just before I knocked at Aunt Missy's door, Corrie said, softly,

"I didn't do that, you know. I didn't do that to the dog. You know that, don't you?"

"I never thought you did," I lied. "It was an accident."

"Oh, yes, that's the story, but we know better, don't we?"

"Do we? What happened, then?" I was suddenly cold, right to my fingertips.

"It was an enemy, of course."

"An enemy. Of the dogs." Now she was starting to sound like Aunt Missy.

"No, of yours. No dogs, no boy. No boy, no Albert. You'd find another host body, but that would take time. Maybe what your enemy wants is time."

"Time for what?"

"Time to get stronger, maybe. Time to finish some kind of project."

That had a schoolroom tone to it, like building a model of Stonehenge or mapping a gerbil's family tree. I doubted that was the kind of thing she meant.

"But I didn't do it," she insisted. "I didn't. I even like the dogs. Please believe me, Albert! I wouldn't try to stop you!"

The spell broke, and I sighed. "I said I didn't want to tell you again. Now, who am I?"

"You're Albert."

"Who am I?" I asked again, prepared to repeat the question until she got the answer right.

"You're. . . ." She peered at me intently, shuddered, and said, "You're Mitch."

"Thank you."

". . .Now."

~*~

Aunt Missy looked more like herself, upright and brisk, but it seemed forced, I thought. She smiled and indicated a door in the wall to her left. "There's a table in the closet."

By golly, there was. Not a plastic-and-chrome card table, either, but a heavy wooden one with fold-away wooden legs. I set it up and spread out our lunch: milk and sandwiches for us, dog food and water for Wong.

"He missed his meal this morning, didn't he?" Aunt Missy cooed to the dog.

I wasn't sure whether to touch on the subject of what had broken up the routine. Aunt Missy took the conversational ball out of my hands.

"Andrew tells me the two of you are becoming good

friends," she said, with delight. "I'm so glad. He's been simply lost since the accident. Not Albert's, of course. The Other One. Andrew worshiped his Uncles Jason and Alain, and dear Joan was a second mother to him. Since the accident, he's had only me. And now you."

"He has his father," I said. I'd meant it as a filler, one of those things you say to show you're still awake, but Aunt Missy affirmed it.

She gave an irritable shrug but agreed. "Always his father. He and his father have always been able to depend on one another. That goes without saying."

I bet it had, too — gone without saying. Mr. Walton didn't strike me as the Ward Cleaver type. Couldn't see many cozy heart-to-hearts between those two.

"And now all I have is little Andrew and my dogs," Aunt Missy said. "And now you, of course," she repeated.

Seventeen years an orphan and all at once everybody needs me.

"You have Lydia," I said.

"Oh, Lydia's a sweet girl, but she's too emotional. I can't depend on her in a crisis. That horrible Matthew's the same way. Running up here and leaving you to take care of Chan. Why? Because when he heard Chan fall, he thought it was Eleanor or me. If it had been, we'd be down there still for all the good his delicate feelings would do for us. Stupid man!"

Mr. Walton wasn't my favorite person in the whole wide world, but he didn't have that coming. "Why do you hate him? Because he yells at you?"

"I don't hate him. I wouldn't waste the emotion. He's very rude to me. He owns my house and most of what used to be my assets and *allows* me to live here. He's infatuated up to his beady little eyes with Mary Seldon-Hardesty—"

"Oh, YUCK!" I clapped both hands over my mouth.

Aunt Missy either didn't hear me or ignored it. "He destroyed Albert right before my eyes — showed me the truth about him and made him loathsome to me — and Albert was very dear to me before that. Albert's death, as far as I was concerned, was an anti-climax." She drew a deep breath and said, "I was going to order him to leave, but he died the same day."

The thunder, which had begun rumbling some time before, now swelled to a series of ear-splitting cracks. Wong leaped into Aunt Missy's lap. The noise sent me into a sullen, humorless temper. I hate thunder. Hate it!

"Oh, dear," Aunt Missy said, "Wong won't be able to eat until this is over. Why don't you run along and amuse yourself while I try to comfort him?"

And who would comfort *me*? At least at the Refuge, everybody knew how I felt about thunder. They might rag me about it, but they knew and cared, one way or another. Mrs. Brandt would have hunted me out and asked if I was okay, and I would have laughed and acted like it was a goofy question, and she would have smiled and I would have felt better. Here, I just got sent from the room.

I paused in the hall, undoubtedly doing my Brooding Young Man imitation. I'm not a bundle of nerve-endings, each one delicately attuned to the moods of those around me; sometimes I'm an imperceptive clod. But there had been a sense of something suppressed behind Aunt Missy's attitude that disturbed me even more than the weather.

And it was going to be a bad Corrie day, because she had been very bad already, and she had looked like she was getting tired. Tired people don't listen very well.

From the top of the staircase, I could see a little into Mr. Walton's office. His light was on, and I could see the pale fluttering shadows of papers. I decided to risk interrupting something to see what it was he had wanted to talk to me about. Since he had made the demand on the tail-end of being told what to do by the dog-boy, I had a pretty good idea, but it had to be done.

"Albert's tune" came back to me, and I whistled it down the stairs. It kept coming out minor this time, no doubt part of my reaction to the constant thunder.

Mr. Walton wasn't in his office. Mary Seldon-Hardesty was.

Chapter 14

I tried to back out, but she stopped me with a look. Speared against the door, like John Wayne at the end of THE ALAMO.

She smiled the same slight smile she'd shown that morning. She raised one eyebrow, and the smile grew a bit. She looked almost pleasant. I could see that, for an old lady, maybe if she did her makeup different, and her hair, and wasn't so pale, and improved her personality, she wouldn't be bad-looking to a man as old as Mr. Walton. Maybe she hadn't always been a Dragon Lady, and his "infatuation" was left over from the old days.

"You've come to see Matt?" she asked.

I nodded.

"What do you suppose he wants of you?" Her voice had a touch of playfulness in it that was completely at odds with any tone she had ever used toward me before. I wondered if she'd been drinking, but I didn't smell anything. —Sure, I knew what it smelled like: I wasn't a booze-hound, but boys will be boys.

I glanced at the desk and said, "Maybe he wants me to find out who's been going through his papers while he's out."

I couldn't believe I said that to her. "I'm sorry, Mrs. Seldon-Hardesty. It must be the thunder. It gets to me."

"I know," she said.

Mr. Walton came up behind me. He brushed me aside and strode to his desk, leaning over it, his fists on his papers. "Were you looking for something, Mary?" he asked sharply.

Mrs. Seldon-Hardesty became aloof and impassive. "What would I be looking for, Matt? Do you think I'm an industrial spy?"

"No, of course not." He straightened, but his eyes still scanned the desk, checking on what she'd moved and seen. "Was there something you wanted to see me about?"

"No." She passed Mr. Walton without a glance, but she looked directly into my eyes. I turned away, and she left with a breath of laughter too soft for Mr. Walton to hear.

Corrie was right. Corrie wasn't nuts — or, at least, she wasn't alone. The Dragon Lady had the Alberts.

No. Surely not. Oh, man, did I ever hope not. If there really was a Mary who wanted a secret meeting with my special guest spirit, I did not want Mary Seldon-Hardesty to be her.

"What is it?" Mr. Walton moved around his desk, sorting his papers, riffling through them. He sat and rubbed his fingers along the edge of his blotter, frowning impatiently. "Mitch? What is it? You wanted to see me?"

"*You* wanted to see *me*."

His frown deepened. "Yes. Another time. I've changed my mind. I'll speak to you another time. Uh, close the door as you leave. No, I'll do it."

I think he would have pushed me out if I'd hesitated to go, but I didn't. As I walked away, I heard the click of a lock.

~*~

At least Sandy was back to normal — if that's the word
I want.

"Over here," he called from behind the central island.
"You're a handy-man, aren't you?"

I circled to where he crouched rummaging under the
sink. "Sort of. Junior Grade."

"I'm trying. . . . This disposal, this garbage disposal. . . .
It hasn't been working right the last two-three days." He
pulled out of the recess. "You reckon you can fix it?"

"Probably. I'd just as soon wait for the storm to pass,
though, before I fool with anything electric."

"Oh, sure." He stood up quickly and closed the
recess door.

"Anything else I can do?"

"Yeah, a coupla things." He meant many things.

"I tell you," he said, shaking his head, "this place is
falling apart. But it goes in cycles, don't it?" He twirled a
finger, to indicate the cyclical nature of maintenance. "A long
run of nothing, then everything goes at once."

Trust me to come in on the "everything goes" end.

Book shelves, loose cabinet door, sticking drawer —
Sandy kept me occupied, and I was glad of it.

After a while, Lydia joined us.

"I just came back to spend some time with you," she
said to Sandy. "Corrie and Aunt Amelia are playing cards,
and Uncle Matt is in his office. Andy is down in his lab, of
course, and Ava is busy. Mother is with Eleanor. I'd like to
help her, but she won't let me in."

"She's right," Sandy said. "It would just upset you. You
oughtn't to have to think about sad things like that, Little
Girl."

Lydia chuckled. "I'm not a child any more, Sander. I

work at the Mission: I see sad things every day. I always hold up."

She turned her black-fringed eyes on me. "Uncle Matt told me he found Mother taking you to task about something today."

She seemed to want a reply, so I said, "Oh?"

"I want to apologize to you for it. You must understand about Mother. She has a lot on her mind. Taking care of Eleanor is a very great strain. But she regards it as a sacred duty."

"Good with sick people and she was always crazy about you," Sandy told Lydia. "I said it before, and I'll say it again."

No doubt.

"Try not to be hurt or angry with her, please?"

"I'll try, Miss Lydia." *Of course, the first time she calls me "Albert," I plan to run screaming into the night.*

The storm passed, I unclogged the garbage disposal and washed up, and Sandy threw us out so he could concentrate on something special for the Quality's tea. Lydia asked me to walk with her to the west garden.

The sun had come out. The garden's gravel walks were well-drained and dry. The gravel glittered and the flowers looked as if they had just sprung into fresh bloom.

"Are you adjusting?" Lydia asked, when the screen door had closed behind us.

"Adjusting to what, Miss Lydia?"

"To. . . ." She waved a hand in a gesture which was apparently meant to explain, but didn't. When I didn't answer, she tried again: "To life with a family. To belonging somewhere. Not that you didn't belong in the orphanage. Not that you *belonged* in the orphanage. . . ."

"It's okay, Miss Lydia, I get you now. I guess I'm adjusting as well as could be expected. I mean, it's not like I'm adopted, or anything. I just work here. It's not the same."

"Yes that's true. And, then again, it isn't. 'Just work here'? I don't think that's quite so. You've slipped into place, Mitch. I know you have no point of comparison, so you can't know how unusual that is, to just slip into place as if you had always been a part of us. Andrew and I have brought friends home from school, Mother and Papa Alain have had friends come to stay. They were all guests, no more."

"That's diff—"

Lydia raised a hand. "Hear me out. We've had live-in staff as long as I can remember, and they were never more than staff. Oh, Sander and Ava are 'family' for Andy and me, because we grew up with them, but they aren't 'family' for anyone else here. Sander and Ava like it that way, too. And Corrie. . . ." Lydia folded her arms, as if she were suddenly chilled. "She's an odd little duck, as Papa Alain used to say. She used to talk to me, the summer after she came, before I went to college."

We had reached the west garden, which was just wide gravel paths bordered by waist-high squared-edge hedges. I found out later that the ground covers underneath the hedges were vinca and creeping phlox. The French doors of the sitting room centered on a sunny wooden deck. There were stone benches here and there along the garden paths, but most of them were in the hedges' afternoon shadows. Lydia sat on the deck's edge and patted the warm wood beside her. Warily, with an eye out for "Mother," I sat.

Lydia glanced at me, but looked away as she said, "Corrie came from a strict Fundamentalist background. I hope that doesn't offend you."

It puzzled me why she thought it might. Maybe she thought I looked Fundamentalist, or maybe that I didn't, but I simply said, "No."

"They were also very poor. Corrie had to quit high school and go to work as a maid for one of the better-off people in. . . ." She flapped a hand. "I forget the name of the little town she came from. At any rate, the young man of the family . . . he . . . he took advantage of her. She told her employers and they fired her. When she told her father, he said that it was probably her fault, that she was probably 'in the family way,' and he threw her out of the house. This was just before she came here; must have been around 1960, I suppose. Can you imagine? In this day and age?"

She looked at me, now, her gooseberry eyes wide with indignation.

I hoped I didn't look as sick as I felt. I hoped I wasn't going to heave all over the lawn. Did something like that happen to my mother? Is that why I was dumped on the state? I'd thought about it some before, of course, but it's one thing to invent possibilities in the privacy of your own head; it's another thing to have one of the possibilities shoved in your face.

"She wasn't expecting, as it turns out, but she didn't know that until she'd come to Faelin. Aunt Amelia was 'rubbing elbows,' as she calls it, in the Star Diner."

"Oh, yeah, I know the Star."

"Corrie walked in and all but collapsed. Nerves, Aunt Amelia thought."

Probably a safe guess, with Corrie.

"Aunt Amelia brought her home and installed her in the maid's quarters and canceled the cleaning service. That was really all the help Ava needed, but now she has Corrie."

Some help.

"And . . . then . . . there was . . . Albert."

Dear God, not Lydia, too!

She broke a twig off the nearest hedge and picked the leaves off it, one by one, as she said, without apparent passion, "He was here for some months, and he never fit in. I don't believe he wanted to. He played at following Aunt Amelia's 'orders,' but he was here for some reason of his own. Just freeloading, maybe, but I don't know. He kept himself at a distance."

Only if you were lucky. Poor Corrie. It was enough to break your heart: Tossed out of her own home because of a man and she walked straight into Albert. I studied Lydia's face to see if she knew about Albert and Corrie, but she showed no sign of it.

"Of course," Lydia said, still casually, "he did court Eleanor. And I haven't made up my mind about that: if he ever really meant to marry her, or if that was another pose. He might have meant to. Then, again, there was Grant. I haven't made up my mind about him, either."

"Grant Marsch? The poet?"

She looked at me in surprise, and I explained what little I knew about dear Albert's dear friend. I said, "I thought he just came for the funeral."

"Aunt Amelia invited him down for the Derby, at Albert's request. She invited him several times after that, but he never came back until. . . . I don't know if someone made him feel unwelcome, or we were too provincial for his tastes, or what. I always wondered if he were jealous of Eleanor."

"Of Eleanor?"

"You know. . . . Eleanor and Albert."

"Why would Grant be jealous —" Finally, I got it.

"I don't have anything against Them," Lydia assured me. "I think what two consenting people do behind closed doors is nobody's business but theirs. I'm not shocking you, am I?"

In 1968? In Indiana? Of course she was, but I wasn't about to be uncool enough to admit it. I shook my head.

Lydia continued: "I just never could decide whether Grant and Albert were . . . you know . . . that way. Grant was very flirty, but he was flirty with men as well as women, especially Albert. Sander hated them both."

"Still does."

Lydia nodded. "Grant wept openly many times while he was here then. That's understandable, of course, even if he and Albert weren't . . . that way. Then, when we heard about Papa Alain and Aunt Joan and Uncle Jason, he was as shocked and upset as any of us. He asked to stay for their funeral, and really was quite a help. Still, he was . . . let's say, more courteous than kind. And curious. He was very curious. Always turning up somewhere in the house one wouldn't expect to come across him, always asking questions — Did Albert ever use this room? — that kind of thing. I suppose that's understandable, too, wanting to know everything he could about his friend's last months."

The French doors of the sitting room opened and I jumped up like I'd been given a hot-foot.

Mary stood looking out at us, with a cold not-quite-a-frown.

Lydia rose more gracefully than I had. "Tea ready?" she asked. She put a hand on my shoulder to boost herself onto the deck.

Mrs. Seldon-Hardesty stepped out to give her room to pass.

Lydia turned in the doorway and waved to me. "It was nice talking to you, Mitch. Be good."

Mary held my gaze as she pulled the door closed, shutting the family inside and leaving me in the encroaching shade.

Chapter 15

Sandy and I had our snack alone: Ava was in Eleanor's room, Dr. Andrew stayed in his lab, and God only knew where Corrie was lurking. Lydia popped in just as we finished.

"Aunt Amelia and Uncle Matt want to see Mitch in the sitting room," she said, with a merry wink at me. I hoped whatever they wanted to see me about would buck me up as much as it had her.

Aunt Missy sat on the couch, with Wong draped across her legs. Mr. Walton stood, sipping something clear and yellowish out of a wine glass — wine, perhaps? — and inspecting one of the bookcases. He swiveled to face me. Lydia sank into one of the overstuffed chairs and beamed.

"Mitch, dear, come and sit down." Aunt Missy held out a hand and tugged me gently down beside her. "We were just talking about you."

"Oh?" From her manner and Lydia's, I assumed I wasn't about to get the ax — to be fired, rather.

"You don't have enough to do around here," Mr. Walton said, fidgeting with his wine glass. "A young man needs more to occupy his time than walking a couple of dogs and keeping Aunt Amelia company. Don't you agree?"

I looked to Aunt Missy for some guidance, but she toyed with Wong's ears, leaving me to answer on my own.

In all honesty. . . . "Yes, sir."

"Now, Lydia tells me that you've been a great help to Sandy, and that's fine. But Sandy won't need your help every day."

"Oh, Matthew, for heaven's sake!" Aunt Missy said. "Don't be so pompous! The child's accomplished more today than *you* have."

Mr. Walton clamped his mouth into a thin line and swirled the wine left in his glass.

"I'm open to suggestions, sir," I said, trying not to bite my nails right there in front of him. "I could go back to the grocery and ask if I can work part-time."

"By no means!" Aunt Missy hid her clenched hands within Wong's coat, but I saw them. "I need you here. I need you to *be* here."

"Amelia, would you let me finish?" To me, he said, "I was about to suggest that you do some work for me. Writing up reports, filling out forms, typing, filing, and so on."

"Oh, Mitch," Lydia cried, "this is a marvelous opportunity for you! That's how Uncle Matt started out, isn't it, Uncle Matt?"

"It's how Uncle Matt is going to end up," Aunt Missy said, "if he doesn't stop falling apart at the seams."

"I do not 'fall apart at the seams'." Mr. Walton clinked his glass down on the end-table; I half expected the stem to break. "I didn't make a very good showing this morning, but I was extremely upset."

"That's right, Aunt Amelia," Lydia said, as if they had come to her for a judgment. "Uncle Matt has been very tense lately, and when he thought you might've been hurt, it threw him off balance."

Mr. Walton looked grateful for her defense — a pitiful

sight, to my mind, although nobody else seemed to take notice. Mr. Walton turned his attention to me. "What do you say? Like to help me out?"

"Cheap," Aunt Missy said, very Old Lady. "Cheap, cheap, cheap. He thinks if he can get you to work for him, he won't have to hire a secretary. That's his psychology. Besides, I'm paying your salary. Clear profit for him. That's his idea of heaven: clear profit."

The surface came off Mr. Walton's voice, and his flat-brown eyes flashed. "I could remind you, Aunt Amelia, that part of his salary is his bed and board, which I finance."

"I am not impressed by your high-handed posturing, Matthew Walton, you pretentious upstart. And don't call me 'Aunt' Amelia. — Come, Mitch."

She rose and exited, grand and dramatic. When I stood up to follow her, Mr. Walton reached out and grasped my shoulder with his familiar iron grip.

"Come to my office in about an hour."

"If Aunt Missy says it's all right," I said, embarrassed. "She *is* the one who hired me, sir."

He nodded. "Go along, then."

"They eat backstairs at 5:30, Uncle Matt," Lydia said, in a tone of quiet reproach.

"6:30, then," he said. "My office, 6:30."

When I joined Aunt Missy in the foyer, she laughed under her breath. "Mitch, dear," she whispered, "of course I don't mind if you work for Matthew as well as for me. I shall insist he pay you something, if only to watch him suffer. Do as you please about it, but I don't mind. It is a lovely opportunity for you. That insignificant boob can work miracles for you, if you want a career in business."

I didn't know that I did. I didn't know that I didn't. I might. At any rate, it was a new sensation, to be in a position to have someone work miracles for me. I just hoped he wouldn't change his mind again about our talking. The suspense was getting to me. I also hoped he'd be in the office when I got there. I didn't need any more nasty surprises.

~*~

A little before 6:30, I knocked on Mr. Walton's office door.

Mr. Walton let me in and carefully closed and locked the door behind me. By that time — what was it, about 36 hours I'd been in the house? — closing and locking doors had ceased to strike me as sinister.

"Sit down." He waved me toward a padded chair in front of his desk while he settled into his own businessman's swivel rocker. He stared at me, drumming his fingers on his desk blotter. "Mitch, I need your help."

"Yes, sir. I've discussed it with Aunt Missy, and she doesn't have any objection."

"That's fine, but that isn't what I meant. I do need your help in that capacity, but not . . . not just with those duties I mentioned earlier. The filing and so on. Something else. Something more important."

I didn't want to hear this. This was what he'd been tap-dancing around all day, and I just knew I didn't want to hear it.

"I want you to . . . I want you to start spending a good deal of time with my son." Perspiration dewed up on the ridges across his forehead and in the hollows under his eyes. He clenched both hands into fists, rubbing his thumbs across the other fingers with a faint scratching noise, very clear in the silence that followed his request. Then, just as if I had said, "Sure," he said, "Go down to the lab at irregular times during the day. Look in on him unexpectedly. If you ever find yourself alone in the lab, look around you. See if . . . if you see anything which seems . . . odd or unusual to you . . . and report to me. But be careful. Be very, very careful. If you think he's the least bit suspicious of you—"

"Are you kidding?!" I could hardly talk. "You want me to spy on Dr. Andrew? Your own son?" I remembered Mrs. Seldon-Hardesty's question and said, "Do you think he's an industrial spy?" And I had started out thinking Aunt Missy was paranoid.

"No, of course not. I—"

"Well, I won't do it." I tried to force-feed some respect into my voice, but I couldn't hear any, and I didn't really care.

"Please, you aren't—"

"I won't spy on anybody, least of all on Dr. Andrew. He's been. . . . He's been, like, friendly to me; more than anybody else in this whole house—"

"But that's just it!" Mr. Walton exclaimed, having found a place to grip his argument. "Andrew does not make friends easily. He would never take anyone into his confidence so quickly."

"Well, he has," I said, more than a little insulted. "So maybe you don't know your son as well as you think you do."

"That's what I'm afraid of. And that's why I need your help."

"I won't spy on Dr. Andrew. That's final. Sir."

Mr. Walton sighed deeply. "I want to make it quite clear

that this in no way affects the job offer. That is still yours. Understood?"

"Yes, sir."

We stood, me looking at him and him looking at the floor, until I decided the interview was over and moved to leave.

"Mitch, wait." Mr. Walton reached out a hand, as if to hold me in place. "I want your opinion of something."

"Sure." He wanted *my* opinion of something? That was almost flattering but, in my experience, whenever somebody you hardly know asks for your opinion, they really mean they want to sell you something.

One wall of his office was a bookcase; he went to it and pulled out a large and heavy leather-bound volume.

"Take this up with you. Don't even open it until you're alone. Let me know what you think."

I backed away from him, holding the book as if it were a snake I'd gripped just behind the head: I didn't want the damn thing, but I was afraid to let it go. What was this book, pornography or something? Mr. Walton was acting just too weird about it.

"Will you look at it for me?"

"Sure," I said, heading for the door. I'd look at it so I'd know what to be creeped about, then I'd call Mrs. Brandt and get the hell out of Dodge. Would I tell Aunt Missy what I saw in the book? I would tell Mrs. Brandt, and she could take it from there. Thank God I was still a minor, and could leave the nastiest jobs to the grown-ups.

Back in my room, I dumped the book on a chair, locked my door, and checked the bathroom, closets, and under the bed for unwanted household pests like, say, red-headed maids. Certain I was alone, I sat cross-legged on the floor and opened the book.

It was printed in German, in large, Middle-Englishy type. On close inspection, even a yap like me could tell that the rough, yellowed paper the book was printed on had been artificially aged, and that the thing was nothing but a modern rip-off imitating a rare work.

Why had Mr. Walton been so hipped on my looking at it? Was I being tested for artistic discrimination? For German?

I flipped over a section of pages and discovered what Mr. Walton had wanted me to find: A rectangle of the paper, about nine-by-twelve and two inches thick, had been cut out of the middle of the pages; tucked into the hollow were two black-and-white speckled composition books, with the white parts felt-tipped scarlet.

I lifted them out. One of the books was filled with symbols — stars and pentagrams and horoscope signs — and drawings of skulls, upside-down crucifixes, horned men with fangs, and knives dripping blood. I closed it and wiped my hands on my shirt. The other book was almost filled with small, clear writing in what looked like Latin, but wasn't anything I recognized from high school.

Well, at least it wasn't pornography. I turned over the pages of one book, then the other, and asked myself *Why? Why did Mr. Walton want me to see these books*? It had to have something to do with Albert — everything weird I'd come across at Willowbrook (with the possible exception of pumpkin soup) had something to do with Albert.

Surely Mr. Walton wasn't. . . . Corrie hadn't mentioned him in her membership list of the Meet-By-Night club. There couldn't be *two* groups. They'd be tripping over each other in the dark. Could it have to do with Mary? She *was* in his office, looking for something. Did Mr. Walton know or suspect that Mary and Corrie and Eleanor had this sick fixation? Did these books belong to The Dragon Lady? And what in the name of God did he expect *me* to do about it?

~*~

The door to Mr. Walton's office was ajar but his light was off. Dinner time, of course. I thumped the book in the middle of Mr. Walton's desk and sat in his big, padded swivel chair. It felt good. I thought how funny it would be if he came in and found me there.

No sooner had I thought it than I heard someone coming. Mr. Walton opened the door wide and snapped on the light. He looked startled, then his glance dropped to the book.

"You've looked at it?"

"You mean 'them'."

He closed the door and locked it. "'Them', yes."

"Was there a point?"

Mr. Walton gave me a peculiar look, and said, "When I first came in and saw you sitting behind my desk — it was just for a second. . . ."

As if I only then realized where I was, I stood and joined Mr. Walton near the door. I made a feeble gesture, indicating that he should claim his seat, but he didn't respond to it.

He said, "Albert used to come in here sometimes when I'd just stepped out. I'd come back and he'd be lounging in my chair, smoking one of my cigars. I don't think he bought one cigar in all the time he was in this house. Between the two of us, I don't believe he *smoked* until he came to this house."

I could understand his taking up the habit. I was on the

verge of thumb-sucking, myself.

"So," he said. "The books. You looked at them; do you have any idea what they are?"

"Some idea," I said, edging closer to the door. "I'm not into that stuff, though. Not into it, don't want to be."

"That's why I told you to be careful. I'd rather not have shown you those books, but you wouldn't listen to me." His voice was harsh. I thought he was accusing me of yet another thing that wasn't my fault, and it almost ticked me off, but when I glared into his eyes I saw they were sick with worry. He still sounded mad when he spoke again, but this time it didn't make me mad. This time, it kind of hurt. "If you hadn't been so damned loyal, I never would have shown them to you, but you had to see for yourself."

"This doesn't — They don't — Those books don't have anything to do with Dr. Andrew."

"They are my son's notebooks." Mr. Walton sat in one of his visitor's chairs, as if it was either sit or collapse. "I found them on a book shelf in one of his rooms downstairs. Now you see why I need your help."

Chapter 16

"Mr. Walton. . . ." I swallowed. "I can't believe for one minute that these are Dr. Andrew's. These are . . . they're *evil*. Crazy, mean stuff." Why was I so sure of that? Little kids draw bloody daggers and monsters with horns and fangs, but kids draw them on their binders or the backs of their hands and show them around and laugh at the people who go, "Ewwww!". They don't hide them, and they don't put them together with pages and pages in a secret language and then hide that, too. And, besides, they're kids. Grown-ups are supposed to be the ones going, "Ewwww!". No, this was different. This was bad — I was certain of it. "Dr. Andrew would never be involved in anything like this."

"How would you know?"

Good question.

"You've only known my son one — two — days; you're hardly qualified to speak as an expert. I've known him all his life and, God help me, I don't know him much better than you do."

So this was what had The Great Man strung out. This was what had worn his nerves until he wasn't good for anything but worry. No wonder he'd been so touchy about Aunt Missy's teasing.

His thin lips were dead grim; his small eyes, screwed even smaller.

"I found these last week when I was down seeing Andrew's latest line of experiments. He left the room. I puttered around the book shelves while I waited. All technical stuff, of course. Pulled a couple of volumes out, and saw these wedged back behind them. I took them out by the hall door while Andrew was still gone and locked them in a drawer. Later, I put them into this trick book. I should have left them where they were — now he knows I have them. At least, he knows they're gone, and he can make a pretty good guess about who took them."

He was afraid of Dr. Andrew! I couldn't imagine. Then I thought of the savagely bitter look on Dr. Andrew's face whenever Albert was mentioned, and I could. Then I thought of Dr. Andrew popping into my room — Albert's old room — at odd hours, and I wondered. Then I thought of his interest in how Eleanor was sleeping, and I wondered some more.

"I ask you to reconsider, Mitch. I have to know if there are any more of these books. I have to know how deeply my son is into this. If I know, I may be able to help him get out. I know it's unspeakable, asking you to do this, but who else could do it? He certainly doesn't confide in me, or in anyone, anymore." He actually wrung his hands. "But how can I ask you —" He slumped in his seat and pressed his palms against his eyes. "How can I *not* ask you?"

"Have you tried to translate the book with all the writing in it?"

He nodded. "I found an old Latin grammar in the attic and had several tries, but I can't figure it out. I think it's not only in Latin, it's in code, as well." He stood and slid the "trick" book back in place. Standing there, body rigid, not looking at the spines of his books, he asked, "Will you do it?"

"Yes, sir. But I just don't believe those notebooks are Dr. Andrew's."

"They were in his rooms."

"And now they're in your office, but that doesn't mean they're yours."

That swept him around. His eyes were as large as they ever got as he said, "I'd give the world to believe Andrew isn't involved in this abomination. But I'm afraid I can't. He had these books hidden down in his lab, where he spends most of his time; all the writing's in some sort of Latin, Andrew's second language. They almost have to be his. But, if they aren't. . . ?"

"Whose are they, right?"

"Right."

I thought about The Dragon Lady, searching through the papers on Mr. Walton's desk.

"I'll do what I can. Whatever that may be."

Mr. Walton grasped my hand and pumped it. "Thank you. Thank you, Mitch. I won't forget this — by God, I won't. Thank you."

~*~

I felt a strong urge for quiet contemplation, a need I was certain would go unfulfilled if I remained within shrieking distance of the house. I crept out the nearest rear door and into the woods.

I refused to believe Dr. Andrew was into devil stuff, even as an experiment. He just didn't seem like that. I knew kids in my high school who were into that stuff. Most of them were just cases of arrested development, just played at it to freak people out. The other ones, the ones who would say something and then clam up — they had a kind of glaze behind their eyes, a looseness in their smiles and a tightness across their cheekbones. It's hard to explain, but I could spot them. Dr. Andrew didn't fit the bill.

Did Mary Seldon-Hardesty? Did Corrie? Well, Corrie was a loony, so she didn't count. Miss Mary, though? She radiated too much general and specific hostility for anything else to get through.

But if I couldn't read Corrie and I couldn't read Miss Mary, what made me think I could read Dr. Andrew? Maybe grown-ups were different. Maybe Mr. Walton was right about the doctor not making friends easily, and this whole friendship routine was just a warm-up for the pitch.

But that didn't feel like the truth, and I couldn't shake a feeling that those notebooks were Albert Alaister's. I didn't know they were, of course. I couldn't know it. Unless. . . .

That really bugged me: I knew I wasn't being possessed, but reinforced conditioning had already got me to the point where I would call myself Albert if nobody else was around to do it.

I didn't realize I had come into the summerhouse clearing until I nearly stepped in the water. The creek was about four feet wide and just over six inches deep. The bottom was covered by little round pebbles.

Okay, and there was the grave. I stopped trying to resist, and looked at the stone again.

He is not dead, but sleepeth. Made me wish I could install an Eternal Tape-player with an endless loop of lullabies. I did not linger.

By my watch, the family should still be at dinner. I would

go to my room and wait, then spend some time with Aunt Missy, then take Wong for a walk, then lock myself in for the night. Not even *Hawaii 5-0* would lure me out; to hell with Jack Lord and the surfboard he rode in on.

Ava met me at the kitchen door. Billy had been and gone while I was outside.

"I called you," Ava said. "Sandy saw you go out, but the man said he couldn't stay. Here are your things; I would have taken them to your room, but we are just at dessert."

I thanked her and picked up the suitcase and the brown bag of comics. "Did Billy say anything? Leave a message for me, I mean?"

Ava's lips twitched and she answered, "He said, 'Be cool, my man.'"

~*~

It was turning into a tradition for me: sitting in my room with my door open, waiting for Aunt Missy. I had put my clothes away, and a pretty pitiful showing they made, too, in that double-wide closet and that high-boy chest-of-drawers. I'd separated the comics by publisher and put them into the drawers of the writing desk. Now I was sitting with the Bradbury book in my hands, pretending I was reading.

I wished I could have seen Billy. I could have gone back to the Refuge with him. I didn't know that I *would* have, but I *could* have, and I hated to have missed the chance, whether I would have taken it or not. And why not take it? When things kept getting weirder and weirder, why not bail out?

Aunt Missy, for one thing. I knew now that some sicko *was* doing ugly things to Aunt Missy's dogs, and she had come to town for help and I was what Lady Luck had handed her. I had to stick: as this girl I had dated twice would have said, it was my karma, man.

Then there was Dr. Andrew. He needed a friend, and he seemed to have chosen me. What was I going to do, say, "Sorry, bud, get yourself another pal"?

Corrie. Like Aunt Missy said, what would Corrie do if I left? She wasn't hurting me, calling me Albert. She was hurting herself, and maybe Miss Eleanor, but I could help more by being on the spot than by cutting the poor kook loose. Especially with dear Mr. Marsch coming tomorrow.

Mr. Walton? Who cared about that grump? I did. It irritated me to realize that he had turned into another one of my kids. At least all he needed was a pat on the back, because Dr. Andrew had nothing to do with those notebooks.

While all this was running through my mind, I tried to place "Albert's tune," but I couldn't. I kept getting odd flashes from it, and kept thinking it had words, but I couldn't get any more than that.

"Mitch." Corrie had crept up on me again and was standing in the doorway. For one wild moment I entertained the thought of kicking the door shut, but the Corrie who cross-examined me on the stairs merged into the Corrie who had been thrown away by her own family, and I stood up and told her to come in.

She entered more slowly than usual, and didn't leap into either my arms or conversation with Albert. She had been tired at lunch; she was dead-tired now. Rock-washed, wrung-out, and shrub-dried. Her prison-gray uniform was wilted and she had sweated her curls into dull brownish kinks.

She sat down, closed her eyes, and sighed convulsively. "We finally got her calmed down. I've never seen her this bad. Naturally, Andrew was in his lab all day with the doors locked and a machine on and the phone off the hook. And Mary refused to give her a sleeping powder. Andrew left some." She started slightly, gave me a quick look, then leaned back again. "Dr. Walton, I mean. I've been with Mary and Eleanor all day; they always call him Andrew."

I didn't care if she called him Andrew behind his back. I used to have a teacher I called Flatface behind his back. So what?

"Look at me," she said, standing. "Let me see your eyes."

"The hell I will." I walked to the window. "What are they, limpid pools of beauty or something?" I knew what she wanted, of course: she wanted to see who was looking at her from inside my skull: me or Albert.

"Listen." Corrie started around the bed, but stopped halfway between the chair and the window where I stood.

I turned to face her. "I guess you came in here to remind me of whatever it is we're supposed to do tonight, you and me and Mary and Eleanor. Well, I'm not coming, do you get that? Are you listening? Am I getting through to you, Corrie?"

She closed her eyes again and two tears broke loose and quivered down her bloodless cheeks.

I melted. "Corrie, please. Please. I'm Mitch Franklin. I keep hoping you'll remember that from one hour to the next. Aren't you ever going to?" When she didn't answer, I flapped a hand in disgust. "Ah, I give up."

"No, Mitch, no!" She threw herself against me with a force that almost sent both of us out the window. "Don't! Don't! Oh, you don't know!" Her hick accent thickened, a sure sign of genuine distress. "It was awful when he died. I thought all I wanted in the world was for him to come back."

Her voice trembled, and she had double fist-fulls of my t-shirt. "But when I saw him usin' you, makin' his words come out of your mouth, it made me sick. It scared me. He's got so much power!"

"Corrie," I said, de-fisting my shirt, "he hasn't been using me. He hasn't got any power. Albert Alaister is dead. Dead."

Corrie shuddered. "You poor lamb. You don't even realize it."

"Oh, for crying out loud!"

I held her gently for a minute while she tried to control her shudders. *Poor Corrie. Poor, poor little Corrie.*

"Mitch?" She stopped crying, but her voice was still tense. "You won't give up, will you? If you give up, he'll just take over somebody else. Grant — Grant Marsch is coming tomorrow. I'm so scared! What if Albert decides to take Grant instead of you? Grant might like it. He might help him. Please don't give up!" Her voice dropped to a whisper, as if she thought Albert was in the next room rather than inside my personal body. "I'll help you. If he wins, he'll punish me, but he'll punish me anyway, so I really got nothing to lose."

I was surprised and moved. Even if all this was hogwash — which, of course, it was — Corrie believed it, and her offer was the bravest thing I'd ever heard.

"You win," I said. "We'll beat him together, okay?" Convincing her Albert had tried for me and been driven off might turn out to be easier than convincing her he'd never tried at all.

Corrie hugged me tightly. "You won't be sorry."

I wish I'd given her odds on that.

Chapter 17

"Did you tell the Fortune 500 poster boy you'd work for him?" Aunt Missy asked, when we were closed in her room.

I had to grin, in spite of everything. "Yes, ma'am. I guess I start tomorrow." Now I came to think of it, my clerical duties had been given short shrift. *File this under D for Demon, and throw a little holy water on my son.*

"Dinner tonight was appalling," Aunt Missy said. "Not the food, of course. One thing I will say for Matt Walton, he knew a good cook when he saw one. I was afraid he would let Sandy and Ava go, after the accidents, since Mary was so set on it, but he stood firm for once. The way to Matthew Walton's backbone, apparently, is through his stomach."

Wong snorted meaningfully at me and trotted to the clothes press, snuffling at the drawer where his and Chan's leashes were kept.

"Oh, he's a clever boy!" Aunt Missy cooed.

You couldn't say the same for me: It had taken me until now to see with my mind what I'd seen with my eyes that morning.

"You had Wong on a leash. Why not Chan?"

"I beg your pardon, dear?" Aunt Missy looked up at me with figurative cookie crumbs all over her.

"This morning. Why was Chan loose? Wong wasn't."

Her little fists opened and closed, and I saw that one

had a purple band across it and down her first finger. She turned her head away and *thump-thump-thump*ed her fists on the arms of her chair.

Softly, I said, "He got away from you, didn't he?"

She nodded. After an attempt at a light laugh, she said, "The wages of a life of frivolity. I'm a feeble old woman at seventy-one."

Seventy-one sounded like a respectable age for being feeble to me, at seventeen. What did she expect at seventy-one?

"Why didn't you come tell me he got away? Ava knew where I was, or Dr. Andrew."

"I was ashamed." She held her hands in her lap and looked at them: soft and rounded, pink and clean. "Useless," she said. I sat in the chair next to her and took her bruised hand. It was clammy and it shook.

She blinked rapidly, then said, "I had them ready for their morning walk; I thought you and I could go together, after your breakfast and before mine. I opened the door to look for you, and they lunged. I held Wong, but Chan pulled away and ran down the kitchen stairs. I brought Wong back in and closed the door. I thought Chan would run into the kitchen and Sandy would bring him back, or send you back with him. When that didn't happen, I began to worry. I didn't know what to do; I was afraid to go out again, afraid Wong would run away, as well. I had just decided to tie his leash to a piece of furniture when . . . when I heard. . . ." She bit her lip.

"Sandy was backstairs," I said. "So was Ava. So was Corrie, for a while, I know. Mr. Walton was with me. Dr. Andrew was in the lab." But was Corrie backstairs during The Time in Question? Come to that, was Dr. Andrew in his lab? The joint was crawling with staircases; what with that and the closed-door policy around there, anybody could play tag with a pet and not worry too much about being seen. Of course, Corrie had assured me — more important, maybe, she had assured Albert — that she hadn't hurt the dog. And Dr. Andrew. . . . I was officially declaring Dr. Andrew off the list of suspects.

"Mary," Aunt Missy said. "Eleanor."

My traitor mind asked, *And where were you? Nobody believed you when you said the dogs were in danger. Now we do.* I imagined myself punching myself in the nose, and firmly crossed Aunt Missy off the list, too.

She pulled a linen handkerchief from the pocketbook at her side. Delicately, she wiped her eyes and blew her nose. Then she said, "You remember that letter I received from Grant Marsch?"

"Yes, ma'am."

"He's coming here tomorrow." She dropped her gaze to the table by her side, opened a carved wooden box, and took out one of her pastel cigarettes.

"I know. Sandy told me."

She lit up, taking a most unladylike drag. "Matthew thought he was going to be manly and domineering and insist that Grant stay elsewhere. Surprisingly, Mary supported me in maintaining Grant's welcome. That's what made the meal so appalling: Mary detested Grant when he was here before — both times before, which, of course, was the appeal, to me, of his coming. Now she can't wait to see him again. She's even borrowed poetry books and magazines from the library with his work in them; one can only assume she's reading them. One wonders why."

One sure does. Had The Dragon Lady developed a

secret softness for literature? Or could it be because dear Grant was a friend of dear Albert?

"Now," Aunt Missy said, "let's have that walk."

I opened the drawer for Wong's leash.

"They're both there," I said.

"I don't understand."

"The harnesses and leashes. They're both in the drawer."

Aunt Missy looked blank. "I removed Wong's gear when I left him in Sandy and Ava's quarters. I remember clutching it, while Andrew escorted me back here. I remember putting it away in the drawer. Chan's wasn't there, of course. I supposed you had it. I supposed it was on him when . . . when you found him."

I shook my head.

"Mitch, where was it? Who put it back?"

Those were good questions. I had some more, but I didn't say them out loud: Why take off a dog's gear, if you're just going to chuck him off a balcony? What would it matter, if he's leashed or unleashed? Why do something awful like that and keep the evidence of it — for a while, at least?

We harnessed Wong and took him out for a stroll along the edge of the woods, and talked a little about poetry — Yes, I've read some, in school, and even liked some. E.A. Robinson, A.E. Houseman, Robert Browning's weirder stuff and, if you must know, Emily Dickinson. Aunt Missy preferred limericks, and the "naughtier" the better. She told me this but, when she saw through my I'm-so-cool indifference to how shocked I was, she refrained from quoting me any examples. Dr. Andrew had called her a walking carnival, and I was beginning to see why.

The sun sank toward the trees and the light turned rosy

gold. We rambled back to the house.

"Wong can bunk in with me," I said, when we got to Aunt Missy's room. "He might keep you awake."

"No, it's all right. I couldn't sleep without my baby. It'll be difficult enough without Chan. I won't open my door until you come by in the morning. About nine-thirty?"

"Okay. If you're sure?"

"I'm sure. Good night, Mitch dear. And don't worry."

I slept heavily, dreaming one of those eternal, senseless, deeply-colored confusions that wake you up more tired than you were when you went to bed. I came awake with heart-thudding suddenness — in the middle of the dream, I remembered that I had forgotten to lock my door. I knew as soon as I woke, gasping, that it was too late.

Someone was in bed with me. I couldn't see much in the darkness, but a weight pressed on the mattress where no weight belonged, and I could hear breathing, ragged but quiet. Whoever-it-was raised on one elbow and leaned over me. Even in the dim light, I could now see that, for the first time in my life, I was in bed with a woman. Somehow, it wasn't as pleasant as I'd always hoped it would be.

Straining to make out her features, I prayed, *Please, God, if it has to be anybody in this house, let it be Corrie. Not that I want it to be Corrie but, if it has to be anybody. . . .*

"Albert," she whispered. "Are you awake?" She ran a hand through my hair. "Dearest?"

It was Eleanor.

She moved closer to me and kissed me quickly on the mouth.

"Miss Eleanor," I said, and tried to scoot away.

She scooted after me, put an arm around my neck and leaned on me. She leaned all over me. She kissed me again.

I kissed her back. I didn't want to — I mean, I *didn't want* to — but I did. I wanted to push her away and get out of that bed, but it seemed like I couldn't. And I started to like it. I mean, I'm a gentleman and all that, but I'm only human.

A thud at the base of my door took Miss Eleanor's attention, and I could breathe again. The thud was followed by a series of bone-chilling growls.

"It's just the dog," Eleanor said. "The other one." She leaned toward me again.

I threw off her arm and slid out from under, out of the bed and onto my feet.

"Albert?" She sounded puzzled.

I got into my institution-issue robe and switched on the light.

Miss Eleanor reclined on my — on Albert's — bed, wearing a long silky yellow nightgown. She shielded her eyes from the sudden light and laughed. Her short hair was tousled. She looked relaxed and happy, and much younger than she had by the grave.

"What are you doing?" she asked easily.

"I'm not Albert," I said.

"Don't be silly, Dearest."

"I'm not Albert. Do I look like Albert? I mean, really?"

Eleanor shook her head slowly. "But you *are* Albert. I know you are. I could feel it. I would know."

"Maybe I was," I said, taking the simple way out, "but I'm not Albert now. Listen to the dog."

Wong was silent.

Eleanor left the bed and I backed up as far as the door. She reached for me and I fumbled for the doorknob. Before I could find it, the door opened and The Dragon Lady joined us. Wong didn't come in with her, so I assumed she had put him back in Aunt Missy's room.

"It's true, Aunt Mary! Albert was back." With one hand, Eleanor massaged my chest; with the other, she stroked my neck. I thought I was going to scream.

Mary spoke so tenderly, I cut my eyes at her to see if her lips were moving: "Are you sure you weren't dreaming, dear? Or mistaken? Are you sure the young man wasn't just teasing you?"

Eleanor kept her hands on me, but at least they stopped moving.

"I was asleep, ma'am," I said. "And I don't tease about stuff like that." In what I hoped was a compelling plea, I whispered, "Could you please get her off me?"

Mrs. Seldon-Hardesty took Eleanor's wrists and folded the thin hands within her own. "Why don't you go back to your room now, Eleanor?"

Eleanor pulled away and shrank towards me — towards Albert. "No! I want to stay here! I want to be with Albert! I want to help him come back for good!"

"Eleanor." It was all Miss Mary said, and she said it quietly, but Eleanor went to her room without another word.

"Mrs. Seldon-Hardesty, I swear, I was sound asleep. I forgot to lock my door, and that's the truth." I had been a sport about this long enough. "If you want to come down on somebody with both feet about this, go find Corrie. She's the one who put this notion in Miss Eleanor's head about me being Albert, and helping him come back and all that. I keep telling Corrie to knock it off, but she won't do it. I'm telling you, it's getting on my nerves."

"As for you," she said, ignoring my tirade, "Eleanor is lost. I can see that. But I want you to stay away from my daughter." Her stony blue eyes were frostier than ever. Her face, without its daytime paint, was a floury white, with splashes of dull red across her cheekbones and forehead. "Do you understand me? Stay away from her. I warned you before; I won't warn you again."

She left, closing the door silently behind her. I locked it. I braced one of the chairs under the doorknob. I left the light on and I slept, sitting up, in the other chair, but I can't say I slept at all well.

For one thing, I couldn't remember: When had she warned me before?

Chapter 18

When I woke the next morning, with cramps in my neck and back, it was quarter past seven. I threw on some clothes and scurried guiltily to the servants' hall.

Corrie was there, pacing. When she saw me, her eyes lit up, the way they had when she'd first greeted me as Albert, and her drained face flushed to its normal color.

I braced myself.

"Mitch!" Corrie cried. She flew into my arms and hugged me in a wholesome, sisterly way.

"I'm not — Hey, you got it right!"

"Oh, Mitch, I knew you were strong enough to fight him. You're winning! You're winning!"

"I am?"

"Eleanor told me about last night — About how she went to Albert and almost brought him back, and how you broke loose of him—"

Broke loose of HIM?

"—and now you overslept!"

"This is good?"

"Albert never overslept."

"Oh," I said. "I see." This was going to be easy, after all. I was starting to know a few things about Mr. Personality; now all I had to do was deliberately act contrary to them, and Corrie would snap out of it. *Let's see, I could catch a fly and glue wings on it.*

She gave me another squeeze and backed off to arm's length, beaming up at me.

"Corrie, why the change of heart? Yesterday morning, you couldn't wait for your precious Albert to return to you, and now you're leading cheers for the other side. What happened? Yeah, you said last night you were scared, but. . . ."

I had expected a weird but logical answer. I hadn't expected her to go all nervy, fiddling with things and avoiding my eyes. "Like you said, I got scared. That's all. That's all — really."

Ah. Of course. I had questioned her. That meant Albert was in charge. How convenient. Wish I'd thought this one up back when my elementary school principal had called me in about who released that blue-tailed lizard in the cafeteria.

"Okay," I said. "Fine. Where's Ava?"

"I don't know. In the kitchen with Sandy, I guess. Why?"

"Never mind why."

Corrie blazed up in fury. "You leave her be!"

"I work here, Corrie. Ava works here. I'm going to have to talk to her, now and then. What do you want me to do, learn Morse code?"

Corrie's tired gray eyes filled and overflowed. "Everything's all wrong!" she said. "It's no use. You're too strong for us — I shoulda knowed that — *known* that."

Okay, yep, I was Albert. I wondered briefly if a sharp conk on the noggin might cure her.

She sank onto one of the hard wooden chairs and held her head in one hand, elbow on the rough wooden table. "I wish I could be happy about it again. Everything was going to be so wonderful when you came back." She looked up at me, eyes dull; drained of fear and hope. "Maybe I'm just not as dumb as I was when you were alive. I can pick out all the tricks and lies you used on me. I can see how you lied to everybody. Told us what we wanted to hear. You were as good as Mary at making folks believe what you said."

"Stop it!" I sat next to her and touched her arm. "I'm not him, Corrie. I'm not him! Albert Alaister was a writer. Now he's a dead writer. That's all."

Corrie's tears came again, and I folded her in my arms. Over her shoulder, I saw the kitchen door open. Ava stood in the doorway, disapproval covering her like a second apron.

Corrie's plaintive cry was muffled in my shoulder: "I want. . . ." She drew a deep breath and raised her face. "I want Ava!" She rubbed away her tears with her hand. "She used to be so good to me. Before *he* came. Her and Sandy was like another family t' me. An' he jus' took everything, you know?"

"I know," I said.

When I looked back for Ava, she was at our side.

"Mitch, go to Sandy and get Mr. Andrew's tray and take it downstairs."

Corrie gasped and sat up straight, turning away from the housekeeper.

"And you," Ava said. She grasped Corrie's shoulders and compelled her to stand. "You come here." Ava put her arms around Corrie and held her like Mrs. Brandt held us when we were hurting inside. She crooned, "Now, now, *liebling*, little one, the bad man is gone forever, the good man only is here."

"The good man"? Meaning me? Man? I smiled at Ava and went into the kitchen.

Sandy glanced up with a friendly grin and clapped the lid on a tray.

"I came for Dr. Andrew's breakfast," I said. "Am I eating with him again?"

Sandy lounged back against the sink and said, "Naw, when Ava called him, he said he was into something and couldn't stop. She figured you could have something with us, and then something when you take Miss Amelia's breakfast up to her at 9:30. That's when she always has hers. Needs her beauty rest." He winked. "Where's Ava?"

"In there." I hooked a thumb at the servants' hall. "She and Corrie are making up."

He lifted his shaggy blond eyebrows. "No kiddin'! What brought that on?"

"She heard Corrie crying for her."

"Crying for her? For Ava? She know Ava was listening?"

I was astonished at such cynicism in someone over thirty. "No," I said, "she didn't know Ava was listening. Corrie is going through some kind of change, here lately. I mean, if the way she was when I first got here is the way she usually is, she's different."

"Glad to hear it," Sandy began, but stopped when Ava came in, closing the servants' hall door behind her. Then he whispered, "What's with Corrie?"

"Corrie is washing her face," said the most practical of women. "She and I will breakfast together, when we've delivered the family's trays. Why don't you fix some of your wonderful French toast for Mitch, hmm?"

"Ava," I said, "I have to talk to you."

"Of course. What is it, Mitch?"

"Do you think I could. . . . I don't want to be any trouble, but. . . . Do you think I could . . . change to another room?"

"Another room?"

"Yes, ma'am. I'll ask Aunt Missy first, of course, but if she doesn't mind?"

"I'm sure she wouldn't mind. Why should she?" Ava asked more questions with her vivid blue eyes than she did with her voice. "Is anything wrong with the Honduras Room? Is it stuffy? Is it dusty?"

"No, the room's great. I know you went to a lot of trouble getting it ready for me; it's real clean and everything."

"Stop pulling his leg," Sandy said. "You know what it is. Corrie is about to 'Albert' the kid to death. Maybe if he's in a different room, the little freak'll give him a break."

Yes, that was my plan. Funny how simple it sounded when Sandy talked about it.

"Corrie is not a freak," Ava said sternly. To me, she said, "I'll get another room ready for you. And," she nodded briskly, "we'll hear no more from Miss Crawley about Albert." She kissed Sandy on the cheek, picked up a tray, and carried it out.

"Well, if that don't beat the Dutch," Sandy said. He shrugged. "Oh, well. If The Boss says Corrie is okay, Corrie is okay. Can't argue with The Boss, right?"

When I took Dr. Andrew's breakfast downstairs, he poked his head out of an inner room, said, "Just put it on the table," without really looking at me, and disappeared again.

It seemed like a good time to do some of the snooping that Mr. Walton had asked me to do, and I looked behind some books and opened and shut a drawer, but it gave me the heebie-jeebies and I had to quit.

I went upstairs and out the mud room door. I wanted a walk in the garden to celebrate.

Celebrate what? My new room, for one thing. Goodbye, Shrine of the Dear Departed! Corrie and Ava making up, for another thing. If Ava had been off of Corrie because of Corrie and Albert, and now they were chummy again, didn't that mean Corrie was off of Albert? Now, I ask you, didn't it? Probably?

Of course, copping out on Mr. Walton was nothing to celebrate, but I wasn't going to think about that just now.

I wished I'd brought a jacket down with me; I'd forgotten the morning chill. I fully intended to stay on the gravel paths, in the sun, soaking up what heat was available, but I found myself drawn to the even-cooler woods, to the clearing, to Albert's grave.

Five years ago, tomorrow.

A faint noise from the summerhouse caught my attention — something between a whine and a high-pitched moan.

I eased up the summerhouse steps. The latticework was overgrown with creepers, even the windows; the light was green and dim, the air clammily cool. "Who is it? I can't see you. Where are you?"

I heard a tense and tentative *woof* and a scrabble of claws.

"Wong?"

He gave a distressed grunt and ran to me. I gathered him up and almost dropped him, he was shaking so hard. I held him tight, warming him with my body and sheltering him from whatever had him so scared. He was soaked through, his usually fluffy coat plastered down. He looked like a sloth that had tangled with a bottle of hair tonic and lost.

"What are you doing out here, Crazy Boy? How'd you get so wet? Why didn't you come back to the house and bark to come in, or at least stretch out where the sun could get to you?"

He looked up at me with those big dark eyes, trembling and pressing against my chest.

I felt sick, then I got mad — at Aunt Missy. They were her dogs, after all. Why in the world didn't she take them away where they'd be safe? If she couldn't do that, if hiring me was the best she could do for them, okay. Why didn't she let me *do* it, then? Why didn't she let me keep them with me all the time, or at least why didn't she keep them close to her? How could she let Wong run around loose, begging to be snatched and who-knows-what, especially after what had happened to Chan?

I carried Wong up to my room and wrapped him in a towel and held him until he stopped shivering. When he relaxed enough to stick his tail out of the towel and wave it once or twice, I changed into a dry shirt and took him to Aunt Missy's room.

"Come in?" she said sleepily when I knocked.

The door made a satisfyingly solid sound when I shoved it closed behind me. Wong wiggled frantically, and I dumped him, wet fur, towel, and all, on Aunt Missy's bed.

"Wong, you naughty boy!" she fluttered. "Where have you been?"

"He's been in the summerhouse," I said. "I don't know how long. Maybe since sometime in the middle of the night. He's cold enough."

"Outside?" She sounded breathless. She re-wrapped Wong in the towel he'd shaken off and held him.

"See, there was a little bit of excitement in the night. Seems Miss Eleanor took a notion to visit her fiancé. The part of Miss Eleanor's fiancé is currently being played by me. While I was . . . talking to her, I heard Wong outside the door. Then I didn't. Then Mrs. Seldon-Hardesty came in. I assumed she put him in your room, but I guess she didn't."

Aunt Missy hugged Wong tighter.

I went on. "How did he get into the hall in the middle of the night? Don't you keep your door closed like everybody else in this asylum?"

"Yes!" At first, I thought the look she was giving me was little-girl petulant. Then I saw the tightness in her jaw. "But, if you'll take the trouble to notice, you'll see I don't have a lock. Mary had it taken off. She said at my age. . . . She said if anything should happen to me and I couldn't get to the door. . . . God forbid they should break the lock. I suppose an 'old person's' privacy is worth less than a piece of hardware and a bit of effort."

I looked at the door behind me. It was true: The holes had been filled and painted over, as if there had never been a lock there.

I would get her a new one. I would install it myself.

She tugged the towel higher around Wong's shoulders as if she wanted to hide him away. "Anybody could have opened the door any time during the night." She squeezed her eyes shut, refusing to weep.

I didn't want to hurt her any more than she was hurting now, but the first order of business was the animal huddling in Aunt Missy's arms.

"We've got to keep track of Wong," I said. "And Chan, when he gets back. Somebody in this house *is* after them. I don't know why, but somebody sure is. It's a miracle Chan didn't die from that fall, and whoever put Wong out this morning wasn't trying to do him any good."

I got all bustling and efficient. Maybe Ava was starting to rub off on me. "I'll put Wong on his leash and tie him to the bed while I go get your breakfast. I guess you're up, now."

"I certainly couldn't go back to sleep. Yes, fetch our tray. Meanwhile, I'll get dressed. We'll eat, and go for that walk, if you still want to."

"Sure, I want to," I said, and she gave me a weak smile. "Then," I said, and this was the hard part, "I'll take Wong with me. Where I go, he goes, except when he's tied to something and I know you'll be watching him."

She was hurt. I knew it.

"I just want to do my job," I said apologetically. "That's what you hired me for, isn't it?"

"Not," she said, "in the least."

Chapter 19

"I beg your pardon?" I said.

"I said, 'Not in the least.' I hired you because I was lonely for a face I hadn't seen grow up while I grew old. I wanted a handsome young man I could talk to whenever I wanted to. I get so bored with the same people all the time. Almost every one I ever really enjoyed here is dead."

"Now, wait just a dag-gone minute!" Those little pink hands had jerked me around just about enough. "I admit, I didn't believe you when you said the dogs needed a bodyguard. But they do. So don't try to give me any of this—"

Aunt Missy eased the still-bundled dog onto her lap and got some smoking gear from her bedside table. She clicked open her cigarette case and offered it to me.

"I don't smoke!"

"Then calm down without one!"

"I don't like people messing with my head," I grumped, sitting down.

"What a singularly unattractive figure of speech." She closed the case without taking out a cigarette for herself.

"So what's with the fast shuffle?"

"Whatever that means, I wasn't doing it. I didn't hire you because I thought the dogs were in danger. Yes, I believed someone was teasing them — or, possibly, teasing *me* — and doing it in an increasingly unpleasant way. I thought bringing someone here, ostensibly to guard the dogs, would discourage whoever it was. Instead, it seems to have provided a catalyst."

"Yes, well, I'd just as soon be inert, if it's all the same to you. Aunt Missy, I have to move."

She sighed wearily. "When will you be leaving?"

I think I jumped. "Leaving? Who said anything about leaving?" The mention of it terrified me.

"You said—"

"Move *rooms*," I said. "Move to a new *room!*"

"Oh." The relief on her face was the sweetest sight I'd ever seen.

"Ava said it was okay with her if it was okay with you."

"Of course, dear. It's probably a good idea. A *very* good idea."

"I'll tell her when I go down to get your breakfast."

"Good. Good." She tapped her fingers on the bedspread and focused her eyes on something I couldn't see.

"So, you think it'll be all right? You don't think it'll make Corrie and Eleanor worse, if I move, so long as I don't duck out altogether?"

"Hmmm? Oh, yes, I think it's the perfect solution. How clever of you to think of it. And now, if you don't mind, I'm ready for my breakfast."

I tied Wong to the bed before I left.

I came back with the breakfast tray, a screwdriver, and a slide bolt. I ate enough to be sociable and to fill up the empty spots that two hours had put in my French toast, then I got handy and installed the lock on the inside of Aunt Missy's door. Nothing had ever given me more satisfaction.

We made a date for a one o'clock lunch on the terrace, and Wong and I retired to Albert's room to pack.

Wong wasn't much help. He lay in one of the armchairs, licking his forelegs. There are few things as irritating as the steady, monotonous, thought-piercing slurp of a dog licking its leg. He seemed to be making a career out of it. This was more than a case of Aggravated Grooming.

I went over to check him out: There was a small length of string knotted tightly around each of his ankles.

I took him into my lap, holding him this time to stop my own trembling. He hadn't come back to the house after he got wet because he had been tied up and left in a dark, cold, damp old summerhouse. Or had he been tied up, held underwater until he was thoroughly wet, and then left in the summerhouse? Somehow — and it must have been difficult for a dog with no muzzle to speak of, he had managed to chew through the string, but he had been too scared to leave the shelter, or maybe he had been a little shocky by then. It was bad to think of a person who would kill a helpless little animal; it was worse to think of a person who would kill one slowly.

The string wasn't digging into his skin, but it was too tight to risk working a knife under. I picked the knots loose while Wong lay passively in my lap.

The string was common white kitchen twine; Mrs. Brandt had a ball of it in a drawer back at the Refuge. I'd seen one just like it in Sandy's catch-all drawer down in the kitchen. No clue, here.

There was a sharp rap on the door.

"Not now, Corrie!" I called.

The door opened, and Mrs. Seldon-Hardesty came in.

I stuffed the wet string into my shirt pocket and

gathered Wong into my arms.

She gave me the once-over with her iced-marble eyes and I got the impression she'd go back to her room and wash them when she was finished.

"Ava tells me you're moving."

"Just down the hall, ma'am." Don't get the wrong impression: In case you don't know, kids have a way of saying "ma'am" and "sir" where they might as well be saying, "Kiss my bottom." That was the kind of "ma'am"-ing I was doing to Mrs. Seldon Dash.

"It's the best thing you could do," she said.

"I'm glad you approve, ma'am."

"It's very unlike anything Albert would have done, and that pleases me — for Eleanor's sake."

"I'm happy to hear that, ma'am."

"It was always somewhat difficult to tell with Albert, but he probably would have carried on with his plans, undisturbed by any advice he might have been offered. Then, again, it was impossible to tell what Albert's plans were at any given moment, so perhaps moving is precisely what Albert would have done. Of course, you're not Albert."

"No, ma'am," I said, sincerely, "I'm not." It was such a nice thing to hear, I thawed slightly toward her.

"I feel that an apology is in order, after last night," she said, which thawed me even more.

Then she had to go and spoil it. "Eleanor told me that you—" she shuddered delicately, "—kissed her. You will apologize to her at once, or I shall put you out of this house like an unwanted stray."

You and whose army? Out loud, I said, "Will you, ma'am?"

She didn't acknowledge my question, but she hesitated just long enough to give it away that she had heard. "Eleanor is napping at the moment. She was quite upset by what happened last night. She had trouble getting to sleep afterward."

"Did she try walking the dog?"

Mrs. Seldon-Hardesty looked startled. "I'll . . . I'll expect you after lunch."

"I'm having lunch with Aunt Missy on the terrace at one," I said, a trace of mock-snobbishness getting into my voice in spite of my effort to repress it.

"Two, then." She checked her watch. "Perhaps you could have Sandy or Ava tell you when it's two; I will not have Eleanor kept waiting."

"I don't have any parents, ma'am," I said. "I do have a watch." I held up my wrist and showed her my Timex (another Boy 10+ Christmas present). "Two o'clock."

She turned and walked away.

Ava showed me to my new room, just one door over from Albert's, and I liked it. The colors were subdued blues and browns and the wood was a simple dark oak. It would be a lot easier to live with than that gold-and-scarlet passion pit I'd just left, but I couldn't help feeling I'd come down in the world.

I locked the door and unpacked again.

This room didn't have a writing desk, but it had a big piece of furniture, six feet high, I'd say, with lots of drawers in it and a piece that let down to make a desk. I found out later it's called a secretary. There was a big hole where an inkwell used to be, and a row of little holes where the quills or steel pens or whatever used to be. I put my comics in one of the drawers. There was a chest of drawers almost as tall as I was, but I looked at it, and I looked at my little stack of pants, t-shirts and underwear, and put my clothes in the other drawers of the secretary so my comics wouldn't get lonely.

Wong was with me, of course. If he had needed a leash before, he didn't need one now: I couldn't move without him riding on my foot. Not that I was complaining; nobody was going to throw him over a balcony or tie him up in the cold as long as he was closer to me than my socks.

I put his harness and leash on, though, when I took him with me down to Mr. Walton's office.

"My assistant," I said, when he saw the dog.

He frowned. "I don't allow them in here."

He could have fooled me: Wong hadn't hesitated at the threshold, and he sniffed around the furniture legs as if he was renewing old acquaintances.

"I can't let him out of my sight," I said. "In fact, do you mind if I close the door?"

His nod and gesture said, "Close it," so I did. He sat forward, toying with a pen.

"Have you learned anything?" he asked.

"About Dr. Andrew? No, sir."

He tossed the pen onto the desk and leaned back, swiveling to look out the window.

"He's been working non-stop," I said. "When I took his breakfast down this morning, he was closed up in his lab."

"Did you search his other rooms, while you had the chance?"

I shook my head. "I couldn't."

I braced myself for an explosion, but he only said, "I couldn't, either. Afraid of what I'd find. I'm sorry I ever asked you to. Please, forget I asked."

"I'll find out," I said. "I promise you, Mr. Walton. I'll find out, and you won't be sorry."

He managed a grim smile. "Well, let's see if we can get some work done before lunch, shall we?"

~*~

A little before one, we broke for the morning. When I told Mr. Walton I was meeting Aunt Missy on the terrace, he hardly seemed to hear. I left him sitting at his desk.

I knew better than to take Wong through the kitchen, so we went through the mud-room and out that door. I had my eyes on Wong; he was still on his leash, but I didn't want him pulling any of his cute sudden moves on me. He trotted at my side toward the terrace, then stopped and sat, like an automatic anchor.

"What is it?" I asked.

He growled, sounding more worried than threatening, then stood up and looked at me, as if I had been the one to interrupt our progress.

That was when I looked at the terrace, and saw that Aunt Missy wasn't alone.

She sat with her cheek resting on her soft clasped hands, like they pose little girls for studio pictures. The pose was one of self-effacing adoration. The guy she was gazing at would probably have that effect.

If Sandy was The Mighty Thor, this guy was Apollo. Three varieties of Hollywood heart-throb, all rolled into one, with sugar on top. He was olive-complected, fine-featured, small-boned, slender and tall. He had muted blue eyes and soft black curls and a mouth off a Greek statue.

He looked like a poet.

Chapter 20

I hadn't been standing there as long as it seemed when Mr. Dreamboat looked up and saw me.

"Who is this?" he asked. His voice was a low alto and had just a trace of an accent, which I couldn't place.

"Oh, that's Mitch," Aunt Missy said casually, and turned to not-quite-look at me. "What is your full name, dear? I've forgotten."

"Franklin," I said. "James Michener Franklin." I handed her the business end of the leash. "This animal is your dog. His name is Wong. It's 1968. Lyndon B. Johnson is our president. Will there be anything else?"

Aunt Missy flickered an annoyed look at me and said, "Mitch, this is Grant Marsch."

I almost said, "Ah, yes, the very dear friend of dear Albert's," but I restrained myself. He looked up with a smile that scared the bejeesus out of me: It was sweet and beautiful and stayed limited to his mouth. His eyes were crafty and speculative.

"Mitch is such a help to me," Aunt Missy said. "I've hired him to take care of the dogs. He's a very hard-working, conscientious boy."

All of a sudden I was a "boy" and a dog-keeper. *Whatever happened to "Dear Mitch, I need you?"* I wondered. But I didn't have to wonder very hard.

"If you don't mind, Amelia," Grant said, unfolding his

willowy frame from my chair, "I'd like very much to go in and rest after my journey."

"Of course, dear. Do you remember Albert's room? Why don't you stay there?"

The nap hadn't even come back up on the carpet and she was moving The Poet in.

"Albert's room will be perfect. It will make me feel closer to him."

I hoped it would make him feel as close as it had me. No doubt it would, especially since I'd had to get that lock for Aunt Missy's door from *somewhere*.

He kissed her hand. I gagged. Not out loud, but inside, I gagged. He inclined his head to me and went in.

Aunt Missy reached out and took my wrist. "Mitch, darling, I need you more than ever now! Please sit down."

"Oh, in the very chair? May I? It wouldn't be a desecration?"

"Don't be so silly! Sit down!"

I did.

Her eyes glittered, though she lounged in her chair and toyed with her coffee cup. "Before you joined us, I asked him what brought him back. He wouldn't say. Rather, he claimed he had been in Europe, had visited some of the places Albert had written to him about, and had been seized by an impulse to visit this final place. Tomorrow is the fifth anniversary of Albert's death, and Grant just happens to be seized by an impulse to be here?"

"People visit places on anniversaries."

"This is not gentle sentiment. Grant—"

The kitchen door opened, and Sandy came out carrying a covered tray. I jumped up to help him, but he grinned and shook his head. "I got it," he said. He unloaded coffee, cups, sugar, cream, plates, and a platter of thin, crustless sandwiches. "Eat 'til you bust," he said, with a wink at me.

Aunt Missy tut-tutted, but she smiled when she did it.

When Sandy had gone, Aunt Missy served out our coffee and sandwiches as if we had nothing more important to talk about than the weather, but she said, "You know, Grant was so close to Albert. Is it possible he held me responsible for Albert's death? Because it was I who brought Albert here? Could these attempts on my babies' lives be a warning?"

"A warning? You mean, 'You're next'? — that kind of warning?"

She nodded.

"But Chan got hurt yesterday, and Wong was dunked last night. You think he has an accomplice or something?"

Her round face was firm, but her voice fluttered as she said, "Why do you think I introduced you as a dog-keeper? Why do you think I pretended not to know your name?"

"I thought it was because that pretty-boy was here." Which sounded childish even to me.

"No. It was an instinctive defense. I didn't want him to know how close you are to me. I was afraid for you. Was I being foolish?"

"I don't know." I thought about that. Mary Seldon-Hardesty, who hadn't liked Grant Marsch while Albert was alive, was reading his poetry and asking for him by name on the fifth anniversary of Albert's death. But, for all her faults, I couldn't imagine Miss Mary being a threat to Aunt Missy's life. I couldn't imagine anybody wanting to hurt Aunt Missy. Or, for all my faults, me.

"I over-reacted, didn't I?" She looked a bit ashamed of herself.

"Yes, I think so. Sure, you did. But who could blame you? It's been a rough couple of days."

She laughed briefly and without humor. "Longer than a couple of days, dear. Longer than that."

Of course. For me, this twisty weirdness had started a couple of days ago; for her, it had been five years. Maybe it was wishful thinking, but I couldn't shake the notion that the whole thing was going to clear up and blow away by tomorrow night. I had it made up in my mind that the five year anniversary was the hinge (or un-hinge, more like it) and, once that was safely past, we could all relax.

I kept an eye on my watch. It wouldn't do to be late for my date with Eleanor, especially after I had smarted off about it.

~*~

I escorted Aunt Missy and Wong to Aunt Missy's room — the *snick* of the slide bolt as I left was music to my ears — and went looking for The Dragon Lady so I could do whatever she wanted me to do to absolve myself. I stood outside Eleanor's door, fist raised, eyes on the sweep-second hand of my watch, waiting for two o'clock to click around. Before I could knock, the door opened.

Mary raised an eyebrow and said, "You're on time."

"Yes, ma'am," I said.

She stepped aside for me, saying, "Eleanor, this young man has something he wishes to say to you."

It was a room that had been grown up in: cluttered with books and trinkets that had gravitated around until they found their places, then settled.

Eleanor looked wrong, somehow. She was in a blue quilted lounge suit with a matching robe, sitting in a rocker by the window, doing a needlepoint of a summerhouse scene, and she looked wrong. Like one of those find-the-mistakes drawings where somebody's feet are on backwards.

She glanced up over the top of her half-eye glasses with a face as blank as a hack portrait. That's what was wrong: She was calm. I had never seen her this way.

I stepped closer to her. "I wanted to apologize for taking advantage of the situation last night." Nice and vague. And slightly suggestive. Let Aunt Mary sweat that one out. "It was ungentlemanly of me." (I got that out of a book.)

"That will do nicely," Mary decided. "You must go, now, Mitch. Eleanor's becoming upset."

Inside, maybe. Her voice was smooth as she said, "Thank you." She put her needlepoint on a table beside her chair and stood, with a civil little smile. "It was my fault." She took my hand, then dropped it and pretended I'd already gone.

Miss Mary ushered me out with a dissatisfied look and I wondered what she had hoped for. Did she want Miss Eleanor to go into hysterics? Did she want me to say something only Albert would have known?

Back in my new room — with the door locked — I read the note Eleanor had slipped me with her handshake: "Meet me at the summerhouse after Sunday tea. Nell."

I just knew she didn't mean me. She wanted *Albert* to meet her at the summerhouse. I wondered if she knew there was a new man in the old room. I considered forwarding the note to him, but decided not to.

Suddenly, I missed Dr. Andrew. I told myself I needed to tell him I'd moved, in case he wanted to drop in for a chat, but I really just wanted to see him. Mr. Walton had got me feeling all creepy about the doc, and I didn't like it. I needed to be with him a while, to reassure myself that he was one of the good guys.

I went down the foyer stairs into the paneled hall. Might as well get some of my idiotic spying done; at least I'd be able to honestly answer "yes" the next time Mr. Walton asked me if I'd had a look around.

All the doors opening off the basement hallway were locked and quiet or open and empty. I worked my way around, listened at the doors of the lab, where things seemed to be humming smoothly, and knocked on Dr. Andrew's sitting room door. He didn't answer, so I knocked again, louder, and called, "Dr. Andrew? It's Mitch."

"Coming." His voice was muffled and distant. "Just a minute," he said, louder and closer. He unlocked the door and let me in.

Say, Dr. Andrew, are you a devil-worshiper, or what? And then, out loud, I said, "I came to . . . uh . . . see if I could help you in the lab like you said I could." My heart thudded as I asked, thinking of the kind of help Mr. Walton thought his son wanted from me.

He ran a hand over his limp black hair. "At the moment, I'd rather just sit and talk. I'm coming to the end of something, but I'm stumped on it. Dead stop. I need to relax, but I can't leave it just yet."

He flopped into one of his chairs and motioned me to another.

"Guess who's here," I said.

Dr. Andrew rubbed his eyes wearily. "I don't know."

"Grant Marsch, Boy Poet."

He looked up. "Oh, yes. It is Friday, isn't it? So he's here. Have you met him?"

"Brief-lah," I said, putting on the fakest accent I could invent.

Dr. Andrew grinned at me, and the dread Mr. Walton had infected me with blew away. "Don't care for poetry? Or don't care for poets? Or don't care for Grant Marsch?"

"Oh, I like the stuff. I mean, some of it. He just rubbed me the wrong way, that's all." *Doing what? How had he rubbed me the wrong way?* By letting Aunt Missy make goo-goo eyes at him? So what was he supposed to do, slap her upside the head? I wasn't being fair. "Bad first impression, I guess."

"It must have been. Unless he's changed quite a bit, I would think you'd like him. He was very genuine and pleasant when he was here before. A much nicer person than Albert, though that's damning with faint praise. And a very good poet. I have two of his volumes. Would you like to borrow them?"

"Not right now, thanks." The last thing in the world I needed, just now, was to be caught reading poetry by dear Albert's very dear friend.

"I changed my room," I said.

"Did you?" Dr. Andrew looked surprised and, I thought, pleased.

"Moved next door, into the blue-and-brown room."

"Any particular reason?"

"Well. . . . Last night. . . . I had a bad dream, and I woke up with Miss Hardesty in bed beside me."

"You mean *Eleanor*?"

"Well I don't mean your Aunt Amelia. Somebody seems to have told Miss Eleanor that I am Albert Alaister and she wanted to welcome me home. *Him* home."

"That poor, wretched girl." He swallowed hard. "After the initial shock of the accidents wore off — Albert's and the others' — Eleanor picked up the idea that Albert's funeral had been the wedding. Sometimes she talks about how nice it was. Sometimes she forgets it all, and reads bridal magazines and plans ceremonies."

So many kinds of unhappiness in the world.

"Were you frightened?" Dr. Andrew asked.

"Excuse me?"

"Last night. Eleanor. Were you frightened?"

"Let's just say I got out of there real fast. And then Mrs. Seldon-Hardesty came in."

"Oh, dear," he said, in the understatement of the decade.

"I had to apologize this afternoon, like I had *asked* Miss Eleanor to come wake me up with a heart attack."

Dr. Andrew tried to smother a laugh, but it came out anyway. Punchy, I guess. "I'm sorry," he said. "I know it isn't funny."

Truer words were never spoken, but it was good to hear him laugh, anyway. "Dr. Andrew, come see my new room. You look like you haven't been out in the light of day lately."

He sighed and said, "I can't just now. By tomorrow, I'll have come to a good place to stop."

"And then you'll take a very long nap."

"No, then I'll go into town and unwind."

He hadn't struck me as the type to go out hellin' on Saturday night. Then again, there was that red sports car and all.

A new idea fizzed in me. "What time do you think you'll be going in?"

"Some time after lunch, I suppose."

"Could I get a lift in? I could spend the night at the Refuge and hitch back out, or Billy would drive me back. Do you mind?"

"I don't mind a bit. I think it'll be good for both of us to get out of the house for a while."

I didn't know about him, but I knew it would be good for *me*.

Chapter 21

Aunt Missy was still in her room with Wong. When I told her I wanted to go into town Saturday afternoon and spend the night, then hitch back on Sunday, she cocked her head and narrowed her eyes at me.

"I know what you're thinking," I said. "You think I'm chickening out. You think I just want to be away from here on Anniversary Night. You're right."

"Do you intend to come back?"

Do I? Yeah, I have to. I live here.

"Of course," I said.

"Then you aren't chickening out." Her lips twitched. "I believe 'strategic retreat' is the operative term."

"Say, why don't you come, too? You and Wong? The Refuge isn't very fancy, but Mrs. Brandt would let Wong stay with me, and you could stay at the Logan Arms."

Aunt Missy smiled. "What a charming idea! How delicious to disappear again!"

That wasn't exactly what I had had in mind.

"But," she went on, "I wouldn't dream of missing Grant's first evening here. I can't wait to see what Mary's up to. And Wong will be safe, now that we have a lock on our door." She smiled a wicked little smile, like she knew a secret password she wasn't supposed to know.

She said, "That reminds me: Dr. Aaronson's office phoned. He's ready to release Chan. He plans to be in his office Sunday afternoon; I'd like you to stop by on your way back and pick up the poor boy. So, you see, you can't hitchhike. Besides, you're far too dear to me to risk your being run over."

While she phoned to get Billy's personal promise to drive me back (ruining my surprise entrance), I basked in the glow of being dear. I did wonder if she thought I might get run over by regular runners-over, or by Grant Marsch and his Anonymous Accomplice. Anonymous Accomplice — that's Greek for "What am I doing here?"

"I guess I'd better let Ava and Sandy know I'll be gone. And Mr. Walton."

"Ava and Sandy, yes. By all means. But you don't have to account for your time to Matthew Walton."

It was starting to needle me, her constantly digging at him. "I do kind of work for him a little. I mean, if you don't want me to, just say so, and I'll tell him I quit. But right now—"

"Oh, you're right, of course. You're right." She flapped a hand, as if shooing away her former objection. "Come to me here, before you leave, and I'll write you a check for this past week."

Oh, yeah. I had almost forgotten: All this fun, and I got paid, too.

~*~

Mr. Walton had me shut the office door and sit down before he spoke: "I saw you go downstairs. Did you find anything?"

I shook my head. "I looked in all the rooms that weren't locked, and they were all empty. So, if you've seen the lab, and I could get keys to the other rooms and there's nothing in them, either, there's nothing to worry about."

"How so?" Mr. Walton looked as if he regretted lighting on me for the job. There must be a flaw in my thinking; one I'd missed and he'd caught. But, then, he'd been thinking about it for a lot longer than I had.

"You're afraid he's a devil-worshiper, right?" I said. "Well, they have altars and black candles and robes and stuff. If we don't find any of that, he's clear."

"Mitch, I don't think so. I'd love to believe it would be that easy, but you're talking about the movies, and I'm talking about real life. You can't look for the same signs in real life that they look for in the movies. What we're talking about is warped by its very nature. It's not like The Seven Danger Signals of Cancer, you know."

That was quite a flaw.

"But it would help, wouldn't it? It would be a start, anyway."

He thought it over. "I'll get you a key. There's a passkey for all those doors somewhere. I'll have it for you tomorrow."

"Okay. I'm taking tomorrow afternoon and evening off, by the way. If that's all right. It's okay with Aunt Missy. I'm going to go to town and bring Chan back on Sunday."

He nodded. "You'll stay at the Refuge?"

"Yes, sir."

"All right. I'll have the key for you tomorrow morning. It won't prove anything, though. Unless. . . ." He made himself say it. "Unless he *does* have all those things."

I wanted to give him some comfort, but I didn't know how. "I'm sure you don't have anything to worry about," I said, feebly. "Dr. Andrew seems like such a good person."

Mr. Walton looked away. "Thank you, Mitch. I'd give

anything for you to be right. I'm afraid for him. Don't take any chances. Not the slightest risk. Do you understand?"

"Yes, sir."

"Promise me?"

"Yes, sir." Well, whaddya know — he was afraid for *me*, too.

~*~

After an hour or so of filing for my second boss, I went backstairs.

Sandy approved of a red-blooded young American boy going to town on a Saturday night. Ava frowned over it until I convinced her I'd be under the eye of one responsible adult or another all the time I was away. Well, Billy didn't exactly count as a *responsible* adult, but he was close enough for folk music.

I helped Sandy get the trays ready for the family's tea, and sat down to milk and warm pecan pie with Sandy and Ava. It was very homey. I half-expected Corrie to join us, since she and Ava had patched it up, but she didn't show. I was afraid to ask about her; I didn't want Sandy or Ava or, worst of all, Corrie, to think I had a particular interest in her.

Lydia opened the passage door just as we were finishing and leaned far enough in to say, "Mitch, one of the drawers in my dresser has come off the track. Can you fix it?"

"Sure, Miss Lydia." I rummaged in Sandy's catch-all fix-it drawer for sandpaper, graphite, and a tack hammer.

She waited for me, chatting with Ava and Sandy, and we walked upstairs together.

Lydia closed the door behind us. She kicked off her shoes and sat on the bed with her feet tucked up under her and my red American blood almost stirred. It was very nearly exciting, being in a closed room with Lydia. Pretty as she was, though, and limited as my selection here was, her do-gooder look and air were as off-putting as Corrie's Albertmania.

For a lady who was supposed to be well-brought-up, she was a slob. The room wasn't just cluttered, it was messy-cluttered; I'd have been willing to bet Ava refused to touch the place. As far as Ava was concerned, if Willowbrook had had mice, they'd have been *clean* mice.

She didn't have to show me the drawer that needed fixing: it was sticking part-way out of the bureau, tilted down at a thirty-degree angle. There was dust on the edges as thick as the dust everywhere; no telling how long it had been broken. Easy to see why it had happened. The drawer was crammed with scarves and belts. She'd have had to squash the stuff down and wiggle the drawer to get it closed. That's one good thing about not having much: even if you're sloppy, you don't make much of a mess.

I worked the drawer free and put it on the bed.

"You'll have to sort that out," I said. "It's too much junk for that drawer. No point fixing it, if you're just going to spring it again."

She giggled, as if having too much junk was cute and I'd complimented her on it. She raked everything out of the drawer and put it back neatly while I worked.

"Aunt Amelia tells us you're leaving. That you're spending the night at the Refuge."

"That's right."

"Why don't you just take one of the cars into town for Chan? Or I could pick him up."

"I'm entitled to a night off, Miss Lydia. I get paid

tomorrow; I want to go to the bank. I want to check the comics and magazines at the hotel newsstand. I want to visit with Mrs. Brandt and the kids. I miss them. Why? Is something the matter?" Silly question, but it just slipped out.

"No, nothing's wrong. But. . . ." She shrugged.

"Is this about not clinging to the past and all that?"

"Yes, it is."

"I'm coming back. I'm spending the night at the Refuge and I'm coming back on Sunday."

"All right, then." But she didn't sound convinced.

When I put the drawer in, the track groaned but held. She had taken out five or six scarves and a belt, which were still wadded up on the bed when I left.

~*~

Supper backstairs was Corrie-less. This time, Sandy filled me in: "Eleanor's cutting up rough. Corrie is helping out. I always had to give her that. She was always good at lending a hand with Eleanor."

"Corrie was always a good girl," Ava insisted. "It was just that . . . that *Albert* who influenced her in a bad way. A bad man, you know?"

"I heard," I said.

"She's over him now, thank God." Ava steepled her fingers for a second. "Now she is our sweet Corrie again."

"That's good to know," I said, hoping it was true.

I offered to help with the dishes, but Sandy ran me out of the kitchen. I sat with Aunt Missy until she left for the dining room, the newly docile Wong leashed by her side, then I went to my room.

Friday night. I wondered who was taking my place as one of the movie chaperones for our kids. I wondered if anybody would remember to let Davy Harris buy an over-twelve ticket, even though he was just ten-and-a-half, because he felt embarrassed to be so big for his age. I wondered if anybody would buy a box of Good-n-Plentys, even if they hated Good-n-Plentys, so they could trade Lauretta Barnes all their blacks for all her pinks, because she hated the pinks.

There's nothing so lonesome as watching it get dark, alone with memories of friendly times. The thought of that statue-perfect poet laughing across the gravy with people I wasn't good enough to eat around just about finished me.

I made myself turn on the lights and close the drapes, and then I felt so bad even though I felt better that I felt even worse.

I decided to go down to the TV room before the family dinner was over. With any luck, the sound of canned laughter would seep into the dining room and offend their sensibilities.

A light was on in the TV room, over by the bookcase, but nobody was sitting on the couch or in the chairs, or standing by the set, or by the shelves.

—I slammed back against the wall. A gigantic black cat with a man's face was crouched in front of the plants by the window!

Grant Marsch rose, smiling that creepy smile, and said, "I'm sorry if I startled you."

He was all got up like Hamlet: black shoes, black pants, black turtleneck, and a silver-and-malachite chain around his neck.

"I thought you were at supper," I said, feebly, feeling pretty stupid.

"Did you?" he asked, and replaced a book from the

bottom shelf and took out another.

I found a *TV Guide* and paged through it. I knew I'd never turn anything on while Mr. Literature was with me, but maybe the mere possibility would drive him off.

"How are you liking it here?" His tone sounded artificially friendly.

"Fine, sir."

"Don't call me 'sir.' Call me Grant."

"Okay, Grant."

He flipped through the book he'd pulled out, replaced it, and pulled out another. "Mitch," he said, "I have a feeling you're not just a dog-boy. I'm right, aren't I? Ava tells me you were staying in Albert's room. The way Amelia Hardesty felt about Albert, I hardly think she'd let just anyone stay there."

"She's letting *you* stay there," I said, before I could bite my tongue.

His smile touched his eyes for a moment. "I understand you've become a part of things here."

"I don't know what you mean."

"I'm told you've become a friend and even a confidant of more than one inmate of Willowbrook."

Inmate. Yeah, he's been here before. Now he was trying to pump me for some kind of information. I don't pump that easily.

He opened the book he held, cradled it in one thin hand, and pretended to be looking at it. "The family confides in you, I imagine."

"Imagination can be a wonderful thing," I said, "but we mustn't confuse it with reality. A teacher told me that, once."

He blinked slowly, lowering thick black lashes over his

baby blue eyes and lifting them to reveal a very piercing gaze.

"You never knew Albert, did you?" he asked.

"No, I didn't." It hit me — I was in the company of one of Albert Alaister's closest friends. And that was only partly scary. "I've read most of his stuff," I said. "He was a great writer."

Grant looked at me as if he were considering saying something, but he apparently decided against it. Matt Walton with curls.

"I think you were about to leave," he said.

I left.

Chapter 22

I had just sat down in my new room when somebody wanted in.

"I need a butler," I muttered, and I didn't miss by much: It was Corrie.

"You're leaving." She pushed her way past me.

She was in pretty bad repair, in an odd kind of way: well-scrubbed, and her hair under tight control, but she looked like a doll with its paint cleaned thin. Like we used to tease the little girls who spent too much time in the tub that they'd "wash all the pretty off." She looked close.

They say the best defense is a good offense. I said, "Where were you, about three in the morning? Bustling about, putting girls in my bed and dogs in the stream?"

Her color — what little she had left — drained away, leaving her skin faintly blue. Then her cheeks reddened, and she said, sharply, "I told you I didn't hurt them dogs, and I *wouldn't* hurt them dogs! They belong to Miss Amelia! Think I'd do anything to hurt Miss Amelia? Anything? I never did, and I never would! I don't know who tried to put it off onto me, and I don't know how you knew about it, but I *found* that leash under my bed. I swear to God, I found it there yesterday morning and give it back to Miss Amelia."

Gave it to Miss Amelia? So Aunt Missy had been holding out on me.

"She believed me," Corrie said. "She wouldn't tell on

me. How did you know about it?"

"I didn't know about it. I'm just trying to figure things out." No, of course Aunt Missy wouldn't tell on Corrie. So what else was going on that she wasn't telling me? What, now that I came to think about it, did she have any obligation to tell me? Just because Sandy gave me the details of everything *he* saw, heard, suspected, or thought, didn't mean Aunt Missy had to. Or ought to. After all, whether I was the dog-boy or the lad from the village brought in to lighten her hours by playing on the floor, I was still just an employee.

"Are you sure it's a good idea to leave now, Mitch?" Corrie asked. "With everything that's happening?"

"Oh, for Pete's sake, Corrie! Ever since I decided to take an evening off I've had to do more explaining than a murder suspect! I thought I was supposed to be the one who's *dead*; you don't grill the *deceased*." *Ugly thought.* "I'm just going to Faelin, not the dark side of the moon."

She licked her dry, pale lips. "I'm sorry, but this isn't a good time to leave. I really don't think it is. You know how Albert was able to take you over for hours when you never even knew him, and you were fighting him."

"Albert did not—"

With a frustrated shake of her head, she said, "I know you won't admit it, but you know it's true. Well, now there's somebody here who was very close to Albert. And you gave him Albert's room!"

"You mean The Poet?" I recalled his small, precise person smiling across the table at Aunt Missy.

"Grant Marsch, yes. If you leave, Albert will just possess Grant. And he couldn't fight him like you can, I know he can't. He might not want to. They might have even arranged this. Albert wasn't the kind of man to give up living just because he died."

"Listen, Corrie—"

"*You* listen! I talked to him."

I felt all the blood rush out of my head and heard myself, as if from far away, say, "Talked to who? Whom?"

"To Grant."

I sat down quickly. I waved Corrie to another chair, but I felt too weak and too irritated to be a gentleman and wait for her.

She didn't seem to notice how infected I'd become with Albertitis. She went on: "I asked Grant if Albert had sent for him. Albert in possession of you, I meant; you might not remember, if you'd done that. Do you know what he said?"

"That you need a keeper?"

"He said, 'Yes, he did send for me, in a way. A voice from the grave.'"

That "yes" sounded bad; "in a way" sounded good. The "voice from the grave" could seat Mr. Marsch pretty firmly in the He Is Not Dead But Sleepeth Club, or it could take him out of the picture altogether: Turns of phrase that come that close to the bone are usually made by people who haven't got the foggiest notion of how close to the bone they've come. I'm living proof. Or, the conversation might never have taken place. At any rate:

"Listen, Corrie," I said again, and lowered my voice. "I'm going into town tomorrow night. It's part of my plan. See, I figured Albert might decide to give up on me and try Grant, especially since he hasn't been able to take me over for about twelve hours."

"Oh, Mitch!" She clasped her hands as if she were praying.

"So I'm going to let him get control — partially, now,

not complete control — and take him into town with me for the Anniversary night."

I should have been ashamed. I just simply should have been ashamed of doing her like that. But when I tried to be honest and up-front with the girl, it only made her worse.

"Be careful! Be careful! He's nobody to play games with! Mitch, if he comes back. . . . You'll be gone, and he'll be free to. . . ."

I didn't want to hear it, but I asked, "To what?"

"He'll kill Mr. Matthew, and hurt Ava and Sandy, and I don't want to think about what he'll do to me and—" She practically jerked a knot in her tongue, she stopped so fast.

"You and who? Not you and Eleanor; Eleanor wants him back. You and Mary?" Wouldn't that be a trip, if The Dragon Lady turned out to be on the side of the angels?

"Mary wants him back," Corrie said. "I told her I did, too. It used to be the truth, although she never knew about Albert and me. Neither did Eleanor. Eleanor didn't know about Albert and Mary, either."

I wondered if I looked like an electrical shock victim in a Tom and Jerry cartoon, with my hair standing on end.

Corrie said, "Albert said it was part of the ritual."

"Albert *was* into devil-worship! I *haven't* been making up clues!" This took Dr. Andrew off the hook, with those books Mr. Walton had found. Maybe.

"What clues? Haven't I been telling you and telling you?"

She had. Of course she had. And I'd been so busy discounting everything she said I hadn't really listened.

Disgusted, I said, "So the rotten skunk brought all that nastiness into Aunt Missy's house, and he dragged you into it."

"And Mary," Corrie reminded me.

"And Eleanor?"

Corrie shook her head. "Mary brought her in, after Albert died, to fill the triangle."

That poor, vulnerable, heartsick woman whose body heat I could still feel along the side of my body.

Corrie said, "We read the Bible backwards, and pray to—"

"I don't want to hear about it." I thought I might throw up, but I just kept telling myself it could be worse. It could be worse.

"I don't want to talk about it. Mitch, we need you so much, to break his hold on us! You're the only one of us who didn't know him. You're the only one who can fight him!"

I knew I had a question to ask; if anybody knew anything anybody didn't want to know, it would be Corrie. So I asked, "Is Dr. Andrew in on this?"

She stiffened, and her sweet face turned harsh. "Why do you keep harping on him?"

"I just—"

"You know he isn't in on it. Why are you—" She squeaked off into a tiny, tinny sob and put a hand to her forehead as the tears started.

"I thought there was always supposed to be a man in on it," I explained.

"No! I said no! There's no man! It's just the three of us!"

"Well, you ought to be deliriously happy that I had to ask, because *Albert* wouldn't have had to!"

She grasped the arms of her chair until her fingers dug deep dents in the upholstery. "Leave him alone, Albert, for God's sake! You never cared nothing about me, really. It don't mean nothing to you."

"What don't — doesn't?" A light dawned. "Corrie, have you got yourself a man you think Albert is going to punish for beating his time with you?"

She didn't answer, but she gave me the old look-into-my-eyes goggle while she stood and backed out of the room. *Surely she's about to say something that'll come out wildly funny*. But she didn't.

If I was right — and I knew I was — that cleared up a few points for me. It explained why Corrie wasn't so gung-ho on getting Albert back any more. It explained where her affections were directed, since it wasn't toward me — or Him — or us — any more. It also explained why I'd been seeing less and less of her, and why she kept begging, "Don't leave *us*."

I wondered who the lucky man was. Some good-looking hunk from town, most likely. Or some hardware clerk who lived with his parents and thought Corrie was an angel with a broken wing. I promised myself I'd have to meet this guy. Check him out. Make sure he was the right man for her. When you have a crush as heavy as the one I'd had on Corrie, even if it only lasted for about 75 seconds, it gives you a kind of proprietary feeling.

Corrie had a fella. Well, well, well. You learn something new every day. Whether you want to or not.

Chapter 23

The next morning, I woke with a light and merry heart. In the first place, I wasn't in The Big A's room any more. In the second place, I was going home to Mrs. Brandt. Even if it was only for one night, it would be great to be back.

I took the stairs directly to the kitchen; I didn't feel ready for Corrie yet.

Ava gave me a nod and a smile. Sandy greeted me: "Heya Mitch! How's it going? Gonna have a big night out on the town, huh?"

"Yeah, supper and a bed at the orphanage. A real wild night."

"You're gonna miss the party."

It's a mark of how ordinary I felt that I said, "What party?"

"Old Albert died five years ago tonight. That's a reason to celebrate for *me*."

"Alexander Schneider!" Ava exclaimed. "Don't speak so ill of the dead."

"Why? It can't hurt him now. That bum. Anybody ever tell you how he died?"

"Sandy," Ava said sternly, "you're gossiping again."

"So what?" Sandy shrugged. "Who's going to tell Albert?"

I could have given him a list.

"So," he said, "did anybody tell you?"

"I don't much care, really."

"He drowned in that trickle they call a brook, out by the summerhouse." He mushed up his features and wiggled his fingers to indicate smallness. "Fell, hit his head on a rock, and drowned. In six inches of water."

"There aren't any rocks out there," I said. "Just pebbles."

"There was one rock out there. Miss Mary took it. Uses it for a paperweight. Shocked?"

"Not even surprised. If she used a pickled head for a paperweight, it wouldn't surprise me."

Sandy laughed; Ava made a disapproving noise.

"You are getting to be as bad as *he* is," she said, gesturing toward her husband.

When Ava went to answer a buzz, he leaned across the counter to whisper, "There's some say it was the dogs that killed him. There's some say the dogs ran around under his feet and tripped him."

"And then Chan hit him in the head with a rock and Wong held him under?"

Sandy straightened up, grinning, and went back to stirring blueberries into pancake batter. "I never took no stock in it neither."

"Who are the 'some' who said so?" This, I wanted to know.

"Miss Eleanor. She told me once, when she got loose from Miss Mary."

Motive. But why wait five years for revenge? But she hadn't waited, had she? Mr. Walton had said the dogs had been missing before, and Aunt Missy had said the attempts of the last few days were only the worst in a series. Maybe I should tell Mrs. Seldon-Hardesty, so she could. . . . So she could what? She already kept as close an eye on Eleanor as anybody possibly could without investing in a set of leg irons. And who was it who insisted on the dogs being leashed and limited? *Miss Mary.*

"Corrie is fixing your breakfast," Sandy said. "The girl's been looking bad, but she's been doing good. This morning she waltzed in, all spiffed up, and, just as normal as you please, offered to do the breakfast for all of us back here to give me a little Saturday slack."

I was stunned, and just a little apprehensive. What had brought this on? Just exuberance from making up with Ava?

"I told her I'd as soon do my own job — in a nice way, I told her — and of course I thanked her, but she looked so disappointed I said she might want to help with tea. And you know what?"

He stopped, eyebrows raised and spatula poised, until I said, "No, what?"

"She smiled at me." He concentrated his attention on flipping pancakes and said, oh, so casually, "I was sort of wondering if you and Corrie. . . . I mean, I know what lovesick looks like, and she's had all the earmarks."

If I'd had anything in my mouth then, I'd have choked on it. I said, "I think Corrie has been lovesick, but not exactly with me."

"With Albert, you mean? You're not kidding. I thought maybe you'd took over from him."

"*That's* different."

He didn't know what I meant, and I didn't tell him. I just waved him goodbye and went into the servants' hall in search of breakfast.

And there was Grey Corrie, and I couldn't believe it. Her dove-colored uniform was not only ironed, it was starched. Her hair was bright copper again, and it curled so sweetly I could have cried. She still looked worn out, but she looked like she'd recover.

While she was cooking and while we were eating, she chattered away about how nice the gardens looked, and the problems peculiar to keeping this house clean as opposed to the cracker-box she'd been born and raised in, and so on. Not that dialogue was discouraged; I chattered away, too, but it was an odd conversation. Or, rather, it wasn't odd, and that was unusual. And she seemed natural with it; the only time she looked uncomfortable was once, when I started to ask what was the deal.

I offered to do the dishes, and she let me; said it was a good opportunity to catch up on some things, and left.

I wondered what had happened. Suddenly, Corrie was stable. Suddenly, I was a friendly acquaintance. Suddenly, we were taking pride in our appearance. Could all this be the result of my moving out of the Honduras Room and The Poet moving in?

Maybe he was getting the same routines I had. Maybe Corrie thought he was Albert now, and was taking up where she'd left off with me. Or, God help her, where she'd first started.

I thought maybe I'd ask him about it, and then I thought maybe I wouldn't. Because maybe he thought he was Albert now and, if he thought it hard enough, it might as well be true. You don't have to *be* Jesse James to shoot people like Jesse James.

~*~

At 9:30 I went to Aunt Missy's room. She didn't call "come in" when I knocked, but I could hear someone crossing her floor.

Grant Marsch opened Aunt Missy's door, his eyes making a quickly-muffled inventory and value-judgment of my appearance.

"It's Mitch," he said, over his shoulder.

If she says "Mitch who," I'll kill them both.

"It's all right," she said. "He may come in. He probably wants his paycheck."

I loved that. Oh, my, yes.

The rhymester left us, pointedly not closing the door.

Pointedly, I closed it and shot the bolt.

Aunt Missy hugged Wong, using him to stifle her laughter.

"I don't think it's funny," I said.

"Oh, Mitch. . . ." She tried to stop, but she was having a giggle fit, like one of the little girls at the Refuge.

I still didn't think it was funny. "I'm going home, Miss Hardesty. I'm going back to the Refuge. I don't think I'm really ready for the family circle. I don't understand how it works."

She reached out for my hand with both of hers, but I pulled away and stood there, sullen and ashamed.

"Mitch, dear," she said, putting her hands on Wong and staring at them, "I told you why I had to treat you so coldly around Grant. I thought you understood that."

When I didn't say anything, she pulled a strip of paper from under a book and handed it to me. It was a check for eighty dollars, the biggest paycheck I'd ever had in my life.

"I would like you to leave the bulk of your things here," she said, "and reconsider your decision to leave."

I still didn't answer. My throat felt like it was packed with sand.

"If you decide to stay away, you can call here or

contact Lydia at the mission. Ava can pack for you and Lydia can drop your things off on her way to work one day. You never have to come here again, if you don't want to. Never."

I looked at her face then, and was surprised to see that, far from overflowing with maudlin tears, her eyes were like blue steel. In my head, I heard her say what I knew she would never say out loud, because I might feel guilty if she did: "I'll have to handle it myself — or try to."

I cleared my throat and said, "I did find out one thing. Did you know that Eleanor believes Albert tripped over the dogs, and that's how he fell and hit his head and drowned?"

"No, I didn't." Her voice was expressionless, but whether it was disinterested or guarded, I couldn't say.

"Well, she does. She told Sandy. I think Eleanor's the one who's been after the dogs, to punish them for killing Albert."

"Do you have any proof? Not of what she thinks, but of anything she's done?"

"No." I flushed. "But I know more about Albert Alaister than the guy who wrote his biography. He made quite an impression around here, one way or another, and Mary Seldon-Hardesty is doing more to Eleanor than cutting her meat for her. I mean, after all, since Albert and Mary—"

I stopped, and wished I had bitten my tongue off before I had let that cat out of the bag in front of Aunt Missy.

"Well," she said. "So you've heard about Albert and Mary. And under my very roof, not to mention Alain's and Eleanor's."

"You know about it?" The whole thing seemed uglier, messier, more vicious and obscene because it had forced itself onto Aunt Missy. Miss Hardesty. That lady I worked for once.

"Matthew was good enough to enlighten me," she said. "I can't think who might have told you. Corrie?"

I nodded.

"And, of course, you know about his involvement with Corrie. And Eleanor." She lit one of her pastel cigarettes. "Corrie is a sweet girl, and I've done her no good. She was much, much happier before she came to work here."

"So was I. You know what you ought to call this place? Fruitcake Acres. And you're as bad as the rest of them. You come and hire me to guard your dogs and tut over a girl no kin to you, and your own niece is being picked to pieces and you don't say a word. Miss Eleanor's the one who's in danger. Chan and Wong are just the . . . the . . . canaries in the coal mine. The stuff that's happened to them — that just shows how sick Miss Eleanor is, after five years of 'being taken care of'. How can you let Mrs. Seldon-Hardesty be in charge of Miss Eleanor? Did you ever think she might be doing Miss Eleanor more harm than good, to spite her because Albert was going to marry her?"

"The thought has never been out of my mind," Aunt Missy snapped. "But how can I speak up? I'm over seventy, and Matthew Walton is in love with the woman I'd accuse. People my age who draw the kind of attention you suggest risk commitment. I tried, Mitch, when I realized what you've realized, and earned myself a reputation for what is known in the well-to-do as 'eccentricity'. I can't do anything. What do you think I need *you* for?"

I just stood there and we looked at each other. Then I said, "Oh."

"Do go into town. Stay as long as you like. Stay

forever. But help me." She gathered her gracious dignity around her and became the lady I'd first met in Mrs. Brandt's office. "I don't want you to do anything you'd rather not. I've given you your wages for doing the job I hired you to do. We're even."

She held out a plump, soft hand. I took it and held it. She wouldn't look at me.

Chapter 24

After I left Aunt Missy, I stood in the middle of the hall and felt liberated and unobligated and lousy. I'd never had a real fight with a grown-up before. No grown-up had done me the honor of letting me fight with them. Only Aunt Missy. And I was running out on her.

As fast as my stocky little legs would carry me.

I let them carry me down to Mr. Walton's office. I had good news for him, at last.

He was pacing his office floor, working a key around in his fingers.

"I have it," he said. "He's in his room, now."

"It doesn't matter. I was right. He isn't into devil-worship, and those aren't his books."

"Whose are they, then?"

"They're—" I stopped short. What was I going to tell him? They belong to the woman you love? They belong to your niece? They belong to the maid, who's been dumped on all her life, so what's one more load? "The books were Albert's. Corrie told me. I didn't ask, she just told me." *Well, practically.*

"Albert's?"

"Absolutely. Just like him to hide his trash in Dr. Andrew's lab. He probably got a big kick out of it."

Mr. Walton gave that some thought, then smiled grimly. "That does sound like him." He took a deep breath, sucking in oxygen down to his toes, and laughed. His eyes crinkled at the corners and, when he relaxed his facial muscles, son of a gun if he didn't have lips after all! "They were Albert's," he repeated.

His gaze focused on the bookcase, and I knew which book in particular.

"Now I can burn the abominations. But first, I'll indulge myself in a good hearty gloat. They aren't Andrew's." He clapped me on the shoulder; my knees almost buckled. "Thank you, Mitch. I told you I wouldn't forget this, and I won't."

"It was no trouble to me, Mr. Walton. I always knew Dr. Andrew was innocent. I'm glad I could set your mind at ease."

"You have, you have!" He tucked the passkey into his pocket. "Enjoy your night out. I'll see you tomorrow."

"Uh, right."

I supposed he would. Even if I decided to quit out here, I still had a ride arranged with Billy; I'd pick up Chan, bring him home, and clear out. Or not clear out. Every time I thought of Aunt Missy flipping me off in front of The Poet, I knew I couldn't stay. Every time I thought of Aunt Missy before The Poet came, I knew I couldn't leave. He wouldn't be here long, and then I'd have her back. But I'd remember. And I'd never know when somebody else might come, or she might decide to fly to Laos or somewhere, and then where would I be? Then *who* would I be? Nobody from East Nowhere, not even "the good boy from the Refuge" any more.

~*~

I went to my room. Grant Marsch was at my — at *the* — secretary, flipping through my Conan the Barbarians.

"Well, howdy, Slim," I said. "Comic fan, are you?"

He stopped, straightened the comics, closed the drawer, and considered me. I had shut the door coming in, as usual, and, if I hadn't, I believe he would have closed it before he spoke.

"I was looking for something."

"That was the impression I got, when I saw you rooting through my stuff."

"I wasn't 'rooting,' but let that pass. I was going through your things. I admit it. As I said, I was looking for something; something which belongs to me. It's somewhere in this house, if it hasn't been destroyed, and I will search every room and between the walls if I have to, but I will not leave this house until I find it."

Probably his book of *Common English Words that Rhyme*.

"What makes you think I'd have something of yours? I'm no thief."

"Oh, no, no," he protested, holding up a delicate hand. "I didn't mean I thought you had stolen it. I thought perhaps you had it, not realizing what it is."

"What is it?"

He gave me one of those should-I-tell-him-or-should-I-not looks I was coming to know so well, and asked, "May I sit down?"

"Oh, go a*head*. Make yourself at *home*. This is Liberty Hall, here."

A slight frown disturbed the perfection of his forehead. Or, rather, he frowned a perfect frown. "All right, all right," he said. "I was going through your things. We've established that. But I'm not sorry. All I want is what's mine."

"I don't *have* anything of yours."

His smile was very polite, very civilized. "But I don't know that for a fact," he said, reasonably.

I am not civilized, I guess.

"Get out."

He rose and left, again leaving the door open. I closed and locked it.

What was that all about? Was Longfellow really missing something? A personal article, like a piece of clothing or a handkerchief, perhaps? Very useful in black magic, I've heard.

Now the question was: Should I warn Our Boy Byron? And the answer was: No. He being a pal of the late great Mr. A's, he probably knew all about that stuff. Or would, soon enough.

Me, I was going to town.

Laying out what clothes and gear I wanted to take wasn't much of a project. I rolled everything into a cylinder and fastened it with a belt.

There was a familiar tap at my door and I opened to a new Dr. Andrew. He looked like . . . like a man who'd shoot into town on Saturday night in a new red sports car. Black boots, black velour hip-hugger bell-bottoms, black turtleneck, red and yellow paisley vest, and black frock coat. As my Beatlemaniac friends would say, fab gear.

"Wow!" I said.

He flashed the smile that sweetened his face. This time, the smile stayed. "Ready to go?"

"I'm way ahead of you."

"Said your goodbyes?"

"Ava, Sandy, Corrie, Miss Lydia, your father, Aunt Missy, and The Poet."

He cocked an eyebrow at the end of my list, but didn't say anything about it.

He did say, "Lydia's afraid you're making a mistake, going back for a visit so soon. She says you'll 'never adjust to having a family if you're going to spend half your waking hours back at the Refuge'."

I refused to cry as I said, "I don't have a family. I wish she would straighten out her thinking on that point. I have a job. Just a job."

"Aunt Amelia tells me you may not even have that. By your choice, of course. She says you might decide to stay in town. She asked me to pick up Chan at Dr. Aaronson's so you won't be 'forced' to come back. That's how she put it."

"If it's all the same to you, I've got that arranged. I'll do it."

He searched my face, but I don't know what he could have read there, because I didn't know what I felt.

"If that's what you want," he said. He looked away from me, trailing a bony hand down the bannister. "I understand, if you hate it here, but I'm sorry. I've enjoyed your time with us."

Just what I needed. More guilt. Too bad they didn't have a dewy-eyed infant who could cling to my leg and wail.

As we left the house, I heard footsteps above us and turned. Grant Marsch walked across the head of the stairs, leaned on the railing where Chan had taken the plunge, and watched me out the door.

My roll came undone on the porch: shaving kit, clean underwear, and everything. Dr. Andrew left me to re-pack while he went around to get the car. I had just heard him start the engine when I saw Mrs. Seldon-Hardesty regarding me through the drawing-room window. It gave me, as they say, quite a turn.

The doc pulled his snazzy red car around then, and I got in. As we pulled away, I turned to wave (I thought it would be a nice touch), but she was gone.

I was headed for Faelin. A nothing little burg in itself, but it was friendly and familiar. It was simple-minded and understandable. In Faelin, if somebody called you by the wrong name, you both had a big yuk over it for the next fifteen years. Not much of a recommendation, but it suited me.

Goodbye, Fruitcake Acres.

Chapter 25

Dr. Andrew let me out on Main Street. I just stood there and looked around. Noise, cars, concrete, and not two trees together as far as the eye could see. Beautiful!

While I was going to the bank and shopping for comics, I thought. I thought about *Curse of the Strange Clouds over the Widow of Waltonhouse*, for the most part. And Sandy and Ava, and well-intentioned Lydia, and Aunt Missy, and Dr. Andrew, and Mr. Walton, and Chan and Wong. Then I thought about Corrie. I thought about Mary Seldon-Hardesty and Eleanor. I thought about Albert and Grant and all the secrets people kept ramming down my throat. I thought I'd better get some help.

Not Mrs. Brandt: She'd make it all seem harmless and commonplace and it just might not be.

Brains Brannigan. Brains is the guy I need to see. Scott Masters, ex-Refugee, the only guy in town who was in anything like the same boat I was.

~*~

Mrs. Masters told me Scott was out in the shed, so I went on back.

I rapped on the door and yelled, "Hey, Brannigan! Open up!"

He threw open the door and we punched each other in the arms to show how manly we were.

The shed was Scott's own personal lair. Mr. and Mrs.

Masters let him decorate it any way he wanted to — within limits, I would guess. The walls were covered with black-light posters, and he even had a floor lamp (a pole with four swiveling lights on it) with black-light bulbs. He had a lava lamp and a portable tape player with all kinds of cool music that Mr. Masters taped for him. It looked like a real druggie pad with just one thing missing: no dope.

It was so great, just being there again, I almost let the whole question slide, but I knew I'd regret it if I didn't at least try to come to terms with the mess I'd been wading through.

"Scott," I said, "I have a problem."

"So tell me about it."

I hardly knew where to begin. "When you were adopted, was it weird?"

"Weird how?"

"Just . . . you know . . . weird. Did Mr. and Mrs. Masters do things and say things that threw you for a loop? Crazy stuff. And then, after you'd been in the family a while, you saw that it wasn't crazy stuff at all, that it made sense, but it just seemed crazy because it was new?"

He thought about that for a while, then he said, "No."

I was afraid he'd say that.

Nothing for it but to take the plunge. "See, where I work, it's like this:" I told him The Plot Thus Far. It took some time. I expected him to interrupt with questions, but he didn't.

When I had finished, he regarded me warily, then asked, "How long did it take you to think that one up, Squire?"

I should have expected that.

"No, it's true!"

"Tell you what," he said, in an in-all-fairness tone. "I'll consider this problem as if I believed you. If it's true, there you are. If it isn't, you can't say I fell for it. Deal?"

I told you he was smart.

"Deal."

We sat on this busted-up couch covered with a blue-red-and-purple tie-died sheet while he thought. After a few minutes, he said, "You, the old aunt, and the doctor get what's-her-name — the one who got into your bed, you dog — to a good head-shrinker. Tell Mr. Walton about The Dragon Lady and have the old aunt back you up. That ought to settle The Dragon Lady's hash, all right."

"You think so?"

"Sure."

"Well, maybe." I hadn't told him the part about Mr. Walton being sweet on Mrs. Seldon-Hardesty. It wasn't just that thinking about it creeped me out. It would have felt like invading Mr. Walton's privacy.

"That'll take care of the dog thing, too: squeal on The Dragon Lady and get the crazy one some help."

"I guess." I didn't mean to sound ungrateful; that *was* a good idea. Maybe they *did* need me there. Maybe it would take an outsider like me to talk them into going against Mrs. Seldon-H. Still, it seemed too simple. It was common sense, and Mrs. Seldon-Hardesty was anything but common.

"Something else?" Scott asked.

"See," I said, after a brief silence, "there's this tune. Albert's tune, the maid calls it. I just started to whistle it since I've been at Willowbrook. This Albert guy used to whistle it all the time, and now I'm starting, and nobody whistled it or hummed it for me. I just seemed to already know it."

Scott put on his "expert" face and instructed me to run the tune by him. I was afraid either he wouldn't recognize it or it would turn out to be something as gross as most everything else about Albert.

I whistled about sixteen bars, and Scott had it.

"Are you sure you want to know?" he asked.

Well, I wasn't, but I said I was.

He threw back his head for the first note, let it out like the howl of a wolf, then straight-eyed me for the rest.

"Ohhhhhhhhhhh," he sang, "Lydia, oh Lydia, say have you met Lydia — Lydia the TA-aat-tooed lady?"

I could have kicked him — and Albert, and Corrie, and Lydia, and Groucho Marx and, most of all, myself. Of course it was "Lydia the Tattooed Lady." It hadn't been a month since we had taken the kids to see "A Night at the Opera" and "A Day at the Circus" at the vintage film fest.

"Lydia the Tattooed Lady." Funny, Albert.

But solving the Riddle of Albert's Tune did more for my morale than I would have guessed. It made everything look as simple to me as it did to Scott. For the first time in days, I really relaxed. I still didn't know if I'd go back, but I wasn't *afraid* to go, now.

I called Mrs. Brandt to tell her where I was and when to expect me, shot some basketball with Scott, and had dinner with the Masters.

Most of the kids were still up when I got to the Refuge, around nine.

Mrs. Brandt kissed me and said how glad she was I'd come back to visit so soon. She had hot chocolate on the stove and buttered toast in the oven. She sent one of the girls to wake up the little ones to come see me.

Jimmy Gassman ignored me with a sulky glower until he spotted the paper bag under my arm. He knew what that meant: new comics.

"Stop eying this package," I told him, the way I always told him. "This has got nothing whatsoever to do with you."

"Whaddja get?" He plucked at a corner of the bag.

I put the bag on the table, sat down, and put an elbow on the brown paper bundle. "A book about kissing girls and one about cutting your toe nails — you could use that one; maybe I'll let you borrow it."

"C'mon, Mitch! Whaddja get?"

A couple of the other kids said things like, "Let him alone, ya pest!" and "Can it, Gollum." It was so weird. Like I was somebody you had to keep the dog from getting hairs all over, not like somebody who'd half-raised the dog. I quit teasing and gave Jimmy the Silver Surfer Meets Dr. Doom comic I'd bought for him.

I didn't like the way things were going. I didn't like it but, when the final blow fell, it brought with it a certain sad acceptance: I was ushered into the dining room and there, at what used to be my seat, was our scrapbook, opened to the history of Squire Cornelius Cokebottle.

I remembered summer visits from my own childhood — how I'd dreamed of being the grown-up, self-sufficient, orphan-with-a-home whose visit was the occasion for a party. And here I was. Visiting.

The little ones went back to bed before long, but us older ones — and Mrs. Brandt — stayed up until three reminiscing as if I'd been gone a year instead of four days. It was obvious that I'd joined the ranks of Those Who Have

Found Places in the Outside World, that I no longer belonged in the only place I'd ever had.

You can't go to the Home again.

Sunday morning, we had sweet rolls and milk and walked down the street to Grace Lutheran Church.

It was good to be back with my regular people again, even if they were treating me like a has-been. They'd get over it in a few days, after Mrs. Brandt and I told them I was back. Back for a few months. Back until I turned eighteen, and had to leave all over again.

I could always stay in Faelin. There were lots of jobs as good as the one I'd left when Aunt Missy hired me. Better jobs. I could stay at the Refuge until I got a room or an apartment. I could call Dr. Andrew and give him Scott's advice. Whether or not he took it was *his* lookout, not mine. Wasn't it?

Pastor Meuhlnickle stepped behind the lectern and said, "The Lesson is written in the third chapter of Exodus, beginning at the ninth verse: 'Now therefore, behold, the cry of the children of Israel is come unto me: and I have also seen the oppression wherewith the Egyptians oppress them. Come now therefore, and I will send thee unto Pharaoh, that thou mayest bring forth my people the children of Israel out of Egypt.'"

I stirred uneasily.

The Psalm was the sixth, verses four through seven: "Return, O Lord, deliver my soul: oh save me for thy mercies' sake. For in death there is no remembrance of thee: in the grave who shall give thee thanks? I am weary with my groaning; all the night make I my bed to swim; I water my couch with my tears. Mine eye is consumed because of grief; it waxeth old because of all mine enemies."

A large lump of shame formed in my stomach and sat there like a stone.

"The Epistle for the day," said Pastor, "is written in the First book of Corinthians, the thirteenth chapter, the fourth through the eighth verses, also the thirteenth verse: 'Charity suffereth long, and is kind; charity envieth not; charity vaunteth not itself, is not puffed up, doth not behave itself unseemly, seeketh not her own, is not easily provoked, thinketh no evil; rejoiceth not in iniquity, but rejoiceth in the truth; beareth all things, believeth all things, hopeth all things, endureth all things. Charity never faileth. . . . And now abideth faith, hope, charity, these three; but the greatest of these is charity.'"

Charity, he pointed out, was another word for Love.

Oh, well, I've borne and believed and hoped and endured pretty close to all things this week; I haven't got far to go.

So I'd go back. Who did I think I was kidding, playing with the notion of not going back?

Pastor moved from the lectern to the pulpit, waited for us to stand, and said, "The Holy gospel is written in the twenty-fifth chapter of Matthew, beginning at the thirty-seventh verse: 'Then shall the righteous answer him, saying, Lord, when saw we thee an hungered and fed thee? or thirsty, and gave thee drink? When saw we thee a stranger, and took thee in? Or when saw we thee sick, or in prison, and came unto thee? And the King shall answer and say unto them Verily, I say unto you, Inasmuch as ye have done it unto one of the least of these my brethren, ye have done it unto me.'"

Enough! I'm going back, already!

The sermon was taken from Genesis, chapter four, verse nine: "And the Lord said unto Cain, Where is Abel thy brother? And he said, I know not. Am I my brother's keeper?"

~*~

Billy took me by Dr. Aaronson's to get Chan after a lunch of bologna sandwiches on store-bought bread, and cream soda. Comfort food, now, for me — food I used to eat when I was little. Food of the past.

At the vet's, Billy waited outside while I went in for Chan.

Dr. Aaronson handed me an envelope and said, "Here are some instructions for Chan's care. Be sure to give them to Miss Hardesty as soon as you get to Willowbrook. I'll call later, to be certain I've made them quite clear."

In other words, he'd call to make sure the dumb kid had given the brilliant doctor's precious instructions to the goofy old lady.

"Yes, *sir*," I said. And I meant it to sting.

Chan was happy and excited; he kept cracking me in the hand with his cast and slobbering all over. Billy gave him dirty looks all the way to Willowbrook, as if a little dog drool could hurt the scummy upholstery in his ratty car.

I asked Billy to pull around to the garage to drop me off, so I could carry Chan in through the mud room. I wanted Aunt Missy to be the first "inmate" I saw.

I stood in the bare little room, breathing in the smells of the house, looking out the window at the hedge-garden, and felt something I'd never felt before: How good it was to be home.

Chapter 26

I heard someone clattering down the stairs. It was Sandy and Ava's day off, I remembered. I wasn't sure I was ready for Corrie. I considered ducking through the kitchen, but I didn't move fast enough.

It wasn't Corrie, though; it was Lydia. (Lydia, the Tattooed Lady. . . .)

"I saw the car pull past," she said. "I'm so glad you came back." She gave me a sideways hug while Chan squirmed and tried to lick her face.

"I had to," I said. "I left my comics here."

We laughed.

Lydia took Chan from my arms and cooed over him.

"Are you taking him to Aunt Amelia?" she asked. "Have you had lunch?"

"Yes, Miss Lydia. Yes to both."

"She's napping. We could peek in and see if she's awake."

No, we couldn't. Not if she'd locked her door, we couldn't. The thought gave me a smug, warm glow. "Let her sleep. I'll slip a note under her door or something."

"I love how considerate you are. Aunt Amelia was very fortunate to find you."

"Yeah, yeah."

Lydia laughed and said, "Sorry. I did it again, didn't I?" She handed Chan back to me. "I was on my way to cut some flowers for the hall table. Want to come?"

Ordinarily, I would have said yes. Today, I couldn't. I hefted Chan a little and said, "I don't think this guy's up to it. I'd better keep him on a short leash for a couple more days."

"Oh, of course!" She twiddled her fingers at me, picked up a long basket open at both ends, and went out the mud-room door.

~*~

Before I took Chan to my room, I tiptoed to Aunt Missy's door and listened. Quiet. Slowly, I turned the knob, and was relieved and pleased to find the bolt was shot.

Chan whined, probably scenting his Mistress and his pal, so I hurried back to my room and closed us in.

When I heard a knock, I did something I wouldn't have thought of doing 24 hours earlier. I asked whoever it was to come in. Just like that. It's enough to make you doubt the value of R and R.

Grant Marsch entered and closed the door. He looked grim. He looked *perfectly* grim, excuse me.

Chan sniffed indifferently and curled up near my feet.

"Hi, Grant," I said. "Read any good comics lately?"

"I've been talking to Lydia."

I wondered if that was supposed to be an answer to my question. If it was, I resented it. Where did he get off, making cracks about my people?

"I was right," he continued, so it wasn't supposed to be an answer. "You aren't just a dog-boy. You're very much a part of life in this house."

"Most gratifying," I said, and bowed from the waist.

He ignored me. "I searched your room yesterday. I came back after you left, and finished."

"I noticed," I lied. "Thank you for sorting my socks."

He looked at me from under his lashes. Supposed to be charming and attractive, is my guess, but he wasn't my type.

He said, "I didn't find what I was after. That being the case, I'm sorry I searched through your things."

That was a kind of apology, so I kind of accepted it by shrugging one shoulder.

He settled himself in one of my chairs. "I've come to explain a little, to describe my property, and to ask you to help me recover it."

"Well, now, Grant," I said, reasonably, "I don't know that I want an explanation and so on." I had enough to handle with the people who lived here, I didn't need tourists coming in and asking for help.

"Albert Alaister was my best friend," Grant said, as if he were on a TV talk show and both my arms were broken so I couldn't change the channel. "I was younger than you, when I met him at an autograph day for one of his books." A small smile played over Grant's lips. "I wrote him a letter that evening, in care of his publisher, enclosing one of my poems as a sort of . . . offering. He wrote back. We corresponded regularly after that; he even stayed with my father and me whenever he was in the Chicago area about three times a year. Albert got my first volume of poetry published. He taught me how to maintain my soul in my art, in the face of failure. And of success."

I pulled one of my chairs over near where Chan was curled and sat in it. Grant followed my every movement, his eyes never leaving mine, as if he wanted to be certain I was listening to him. I was. *This* was what I had wanted, when I'd asked Corrie what Albert was like.

Grant went on: "I had just received a letter from him

when the phone rang. Albert was dead."

He stopped speaking and dropped eye contact. He was too late: I had already seen the shine of his eyes, and the sudden redness of the lower rims. I was terrified he was going to cry out loud, but he only sat silent for a moment, then spoke again.

"I put the letter somewhere. I wasn't thinking too clearly. And I packed. Packed to go to Albert's funeral. From Willowbrook, I left on a speaking tour of Europe, and I forgot all about his last letter."

I had a flash of jealousy. This man had been best friends with (in spite of everything) one of my favorite writers. He had letters from a man the New York Review of Books had called "The greatest epistler since St. Paul." I had a book of Alaister's correspondence with his publisher, among my others. Grant must have seen my collection when he searched my room; that was probably what had convinced him to confide in me. And Grant had had so many letters from Albert Alaister, he had just tossed one aside and forgotten about it.

"My father sold the house this month," Grant said. "When he was packing what used to be my room, the letter turned up between my bureau and the wall. He mailed the letter to me. It was one of Albert's vast missives; some of his letters were more like short stories. It went into detail about something Albert had mentioned in an earlier letter. A book, black and red — You've seen it?"

Had I jumped? I guess I had.

"I . . . may have."

"You have." Grant sat forward. "That book is mine. Albert had been going to send it to me under separate cover. It never came, so he must have died before he could mail it.

As I said, Albert had mentioned the book in an earlier letter; I looked for it, when I was here for the funeral, but I couldn't find it. I even stayed for the other funeral — the family's. Finally, my welcome ran out and I had to leave. Then my father sent me Albert's final letter, and I fully understood the importance of what I'd missed. I had to come back. I have to have that book. You've seen it? Please to God, do you know where it is? Have you seen it recently?"

"There were two of them," I heard myself say.

He nodded. "You've seen them. That was my primary fear, that they might have been destroyed."

". . .*burn the abominations,*" I heard Mr. Walton say again.

Suddenly, I realized I was sitting in a closed room with a friend of Albert's, who was frantic to recover two of the most evil-looking books I'd ever seen.

"Where are they?" Grant asked.

"Gee," I said, doing my best imitation of Jerry Mathers as The Beaver, "I don't know."

"You mean you won't tell. What do you want? Money?"

I could feel my face tightening up.

Grant stood. "I haven't finished. I have quite a bit of searching to do; I'd hoped you could save me some trouble. But, with your help or without it, I'll find those books. And, when I do, I rather think you'll be sorry you didn't help."

His voice held no threat, only cordial regret for my folly, and I felt just a little queasy.

Chapter 27

When my hands stopped shaking, I wrote a note to Aunt Missy, telling her I was back and had Chan with me. I slid it under her door, hoping Wong wouldn't use it for a play-toy. Then I went looking for Mr. Walton. He was the one to go to with Brannigan's advice. My certainty that I could get anyone — especially Mary's fond admirer — to listen to that advice had withered to a wisp of a hope. Still, Mr. Walton was the man to see. Maybe, when he had said he wouldn't forget my help in clearing Dr. Andrew, he had meant it. Maybe he would at least listen to me now.

Outside his office, I met Corrie.

"Mitch!" She flung her arms around my neck and hugged me with delight. Chan wheezed jealously from the floor, thinking we were all having fun and leaving him out. Corrie pulled away, the joy in her face clouded with concern. "You're all right, aren't you? You didn't. . . . He didn't . . . give you any trouble last night?"

"No, not a bit. Everything's fine, Corrie. I went to church this morning."

She clasped her hands beneath her chin and simply shone with happiness. "Oh, I'm so glad! It's perfect! Just perfect!"

"What's perfect? What's happened?"

Grant. She was Alberting with Grant, and he was stringing her along, trying to get her to help him look for those devil books. But that couldn't be it, because she'd just asked me if Albert had given me any trouble in town. She couldn't think Grant was Albert if she still thought *I* was.

"You mean what's happened here?" Corrie asked. "I don't know; I took the evening off, like you. Oh, Mitch!" She hugged herself and laughed. "You can't imagine. You just cannot imagine!"

"I'll have to imagine, if you won't tell me."

She chuckled and shook her head.

She had my curiosity going, now. I took a guess.

"Something to do with your boyfriend?"

She gasped, then tried to cover. "What makes you think I have a boyfriend? What boyfriend are you talking about? You're crazy."

Talk about the pot calling the kettle black.

"Say," I said, "what's the matter with you? I asked you a direct question, and not only are you not scared, you're standing there sassing me. What gives?"

She threw her arms around me again and squeezed me hard. "It's all because of you, you little sweetie! This place was like . . . an enchanted castle in a fairy tale. And you came along like a big old handsome prince and broke the spell."

That was really cute, but I hoped I wasn't going to be granted the standard reward; I'd rather have a glass of warm spit than the hand of any princess *this* kingdom had to offer. I'd rather kiss a toad.

"Yeah," I said. "Well, I'm glad you're in such good spirits." *You should excuse the expression.* "I'm looking for Mr. Walton. Do you know where he is?"

"I haven't seen him since before I left yesterday. Why?"

Her "Why?" wasn't suspicious or terrified, it was just a normal person's idle question. I savored it.

"I have to tell him something."

"About you? Can you tell me?"

Could I? Should I? Corrie wouldn't run and tell Mary I was trying to have her prize patient taken away from her. Corrie would probably be on my side. Still. . . . "Not about me, and I guess I can tell you. You know about it anyway, most likely. I want to tell him I know for sure the black and red notebooks he found in Dr. Andrew's room were Albert's, not Dr. Andrew's."

Corrie gaped, then laughed so loud she clapped a hand over her mouth to smother the rest of the sound. "Of course they're not Andrew's! Mr. Matthew took them? I've been so frightened!"

"I don't follow you." *But, then, when have I ever?*

"I thought. . . . Come here." She led me into the servants' hall, checked the kitchen, closed all the doors, and continued. "I thought She had them. Mary. After Albert died, I took the books and hid them for him. I was afraid somebody would destroy them, or that Mary would get them and use them for herself. I checked on them, every so often, and then they were gone. . . . What a relief!"

"Mary knows about the books? That's probably what she was looking for in Mr. Matthew's office the other day. She didn't find them."

Corrie shuddered. "Good!"

"Something else: Grant Marsch is looking for them. I caught him searching my room and he didn't even pretend he was doing anything else. He said Albert promised him the books in a letter."

"He may have. They were very close. But he can't get

ahold of those books. They've gotta be burned or something as soon as possible."

"There's no rush, is there? The Big Night came and went, and nobody's the worse for it. Are you?"

She shook her head, and her dimples showed themselves again. "You have no idea. Before you came, I never thought about anybody but him. I lived for him. But when I met you and saw how much like him you are, but how different you are. . . . When I saw how hard you fought him, when it'd be so easy to give in. . . . It changed my whole life. My whole life."

I cleared my throat. "I can't believe that I—"

"I know. I know you can't. But you just don't know."

"No, I guess I don't." She obviously wasn't going to tell me what happened on her evening off. Her privilege.

She patted my cheek. The look she gave me was affectionate, but not adoring. If I wanted to be fawned over now, I'd have to start slipping table scraps to the dogs.

Corrie said, "I do the family's tea on Sundays, since it's Sandy and Ava's day off. Come to the kitchen around four and we'll have a celebration."

"Thanks, Corrie. Whatever it is we're celebrating, congratulations."

She patted my cheek again and all but danced into the kitchen.

I went back to Mr. Walton's office and tried the door. It was locked. I knocked and called, "Mr. Walton? It's Mitch!" but there was no answer. It was Sunday, after all: Maybe he was in his bedroom having a nap, or taking a walk in the garden, or out for a drive. I'd find him, by and by. Meanwhile, the books were safely locked away and hidden.

~*~

Aunt Missy was awake when I went back upstairs. I don't know what I expected — kill the fatted calf, I guess. Instead, she cried over Chan, lifted him into her lap, let Wong climb up there, too, and not a word or a look for me.

"I'll be in my room," I said at last. "Call me, if you need help getting Chan downstairs for tea."

She looked at me, then, her eyes steely. "You might have left me."

"Yes, ma'am." I tried to read her. Was she angry?

"You very nearly did leave me, didn't you?"

"Yes, ma'am." *That's the way jobs work: You could fire me, or I could quit. The power doesn't only go one way.* Was that what was behind those metallic blue eyes?

"Why did you come back? Out of pity for a loony old lady?"

Something told me that "yes" would be the wrong answer. Something told me that the truth — *I came back because I adopted you, whether you want me or not* — would also be wrong.

"I like the job," I said. "It pays good."

Our gazes locked for a moment of silence, then she said, "Has Matthew told you that I'm irresponsible?"

I couldn't remember if it was Mr. Walton or Dr. Andrew or Sandy who had told me that, so I didn't answer.

She laid her hands on the dogs' heads and said, "I don't care for responsibility. I never accept it, if I'm asked to or required to."

I still didn't say anything.

When it was clear I wasn't going to respond, she said, "That isn't the same as being irresponsible."

I answered, then: "It'll do, until irresponsibility comes

along." I heard what she was saying: The more I wanted, the less I could expect.

"I never *accept* it," she said. "That doesn't mean I don't take it, of my own free will. As if it were a job. A job for which the pay is good."

"A job you can quit, whenever you want to?"

"I'm not a quitter, Mitch. Bear that in mind."

Lydia opened the door and peeped in. "Knock, knock! Are you decent? Hi, Mitch. I'll take over from here."

"Yes, Miss Lydia." I went back to my room, with plenty to think about.

The table was set for three when I went back to the kitchen to meet Corrie. She had spread Sandy's battered square table with a flowered tablecloth. She'd set the table with white plates, and cups and saucers so thin you could practically see the pattern of the cloth through them. A white pot and a pale blue one sat on hotpads near one end of the table, and a tray with a country scene painted on it held a sugar bowl, a creamer, a plate of lemon wedges, and a strainer.

Corrie looked so proud when she displayed the table to me, I bit back the impulse to scratch my armpit in sheer reaction.

"Three places?" That seemed safe enough, so I said it.

"Andrew is joining us."

"Oh, yeah? I dare you to call him 'Andrew' to his face."

She laughed and said, "He told me I could."

"He did, eh?" He'd told me *I* could; why shouldn't he tell Corrie? It put my nose a little out of joint, though, especially since I still didn't have the guts to drop the

"Doctor" and here Corrie was reeling off his name like she was born to it. "He's a nice guy, isn't he?"

"Pretty nice," she said, in an off-hand way that kind of steamed me. I was going to inform her that Dr. Andrew was more than just "pretty nice," but he came in and I bit the words back. Maybe later, I'd talk to her about it. Maybe not.

We had a real like-in-the-movies fancy tea with little frosted cakes with squiggles and rosebuds on them. None of the hearty, he-man stuff Sandy favored.

"Sandy makes them on Saturday for the family to have on Sunday," Corrie explained. "He made some extra for us, this week." Picking up the blue pot, she said, "I'll be Mother," and giggled. "Miss Amelia used to say that, when she taught me how to serve tea, back when I first came. Remember?" she asked Dr. Andrew.

"I remember," he said, and passed me the cakes.

Corrie poured strong tea out of the blue pot into our cups, through the strainer to catch the leaves, and hot water out of the white pot to water it down to drinkable strength. Weird looking process, but I had to admit it was good. She handed around the sugar, cream, and lemon wedges, and Dr. Andrew and I said please and thank you like little gentlemen.

It was kind of cool. Different. I enjoyed seeing Corrie having fun with the Lady stuff. I tried to catch Dr. Andrew's eye, to see if he was enjoying it, too, but he only glanced up from his cup and plate every once in a while. Thinking about his experiment, I guessed, or maybe about his night on the town.

He and Corrie practically acted like the other one wasn't there; it was almost embarrassing. Either one of them would talk to me, but they hardly said anything to each other and, every time their eyes met, they looked away.

When tea was over, Dr. Andrew started to help clear the table, but Corrie said, "You go on, now. Finish whatever it is you're working on down there."

Personally, I thought Corrie was getting a little too full of herself, but Dr. Andrew only gave me one of his sweet smiles and left.

"That's pretty nervy," I said, when he had gone. "Telling the son of the guy who owns this house to shoo, like he was a cat under your feet."

"He likes it," she said. "He isn't high-and-mighty like some people I could name. *He* doesn't think people who work for a living are just *things* to use."

Her jaw set like she was ready for battle; I wondered if she was thinking of the son of that other house — the first one she'd worked at — the one who had . . . treated her so bad. No, Dr. Andrew wasn't like that.

"He's better than 'pretty nice,' isn't he?" I asked.

"Yes," she said. "He is."

I helped her clean up, satisfied at having made my point.

Chapter 28

So tea was over, and I had a date with Miss Eleanor. Albert had a date, that is, and I was coming along, like a pesky little brother. If I spent any more time out by the summerhouse, I might as well buy a cot and a camp stove and take up residence. On second thought, maybe not.

Miss Eleanor wasn't in the clearing when I got there. I hoped she hadn't been able to get away from Mary, but her pale face swam out of the green shade in the summerhouse and she whispered, "Albert!"

"I'm out here," I said. I didn't want to leave the sunlight, even if it shone on Albert's grave as well as on me.

"Come in."

"You come out."

"Please! If Mary should catch us. . . ."

I went in. Miss Eleanor tried to kiss me, but I pushed her away. Gently, but firmly.

"Watch it," I said. "I don't want to have to apologize again."

"I know, darling." She took my hand. "I'm so sorry. I don't know what made Mary treat you that way. I don't understand her at all. While you've been away, she's been helping me talk to you." I shivered, but I don't think Eleanor caught it. "She told me you were back. I know she did! Then she said you weren't. I don't understand. But I know you're back now, and I'm so glad!" She raised my hand and kissed it.

"Has . . . uh . . . has she been helping you avenge my death?" I asked.

"I've been trying, Albert, truly I have, but I've . . . I've failed you, dearest. I'm so sorry."

Unlike Corrie, Eleanor wasn't afraid. Apparently, Albert had shown her a different face than he'd shown poor Corrie.

"That's all right, um, Nell. Just tell me what you've tried."

"Someone's coming! Mary always looks for me here!"

I heard the footsteps on one of the gravel paths, too, distant but clear in the Sunday quiet. I didn't particularly want Mary to find me with Eleanor again, but I had to know.

I grasped Eleanor's shoulders. "Nell, who do you think killed me?"

"Those dogs!" she whispered. "Those dogs of Aunt Amelia's! Mary agrees with me, but she won't let me *kill* them!"

"Not the dogs," I said. "It wasn't the dogs." I knew, as surely as if I'd been told, that Eleanor wasn't totally delusional: Albert's death hadn't been an accident. But I knew just as surely that the dogs had had nothing to do with it. So who had caused it? I remembered Dr. Andrew's face whenever he talked about Albert. Mr. Walton — Aunt Amelia had accused him of insane rages, and I had figured she was just picking at him, but what if she wasn't? I remembered Corrie's changeability, and how intense she could get. I remembered Aunt Missy telling me that Mr. Walton had made Albert hateful to her. How much strength would it have taken to drop a rock on somebody's head, supposing you tricked him into — say — kneeling down to pick something up for poor little you?

No. None of the above. I might as well suspect Sandy, because Albert had made a pass at Ava. I might as well suspect The Dragon Lady, although a crime of passion was the last thing I'd think of laying at her door. Still, they said she and Albert. . . . No, I didn't even want to *think* about that. That had to have been a false rumor. It had to have been.

"I have to go, Albert. Please!" Eleanor pulled against my hands.

"All right. Calm down, and I'll let go. But leave the vengeance to me, you promise? Don't do anything else unless I tell you to. Promise?"

"I promise."

I let go.

She pelted out of the summerhouse and ran into the woods, away from the garden path.

By that time, the footsteps had passed from crunching gravel to snapping twigs on the path to the clearing, so I thought I might as well stay in the summerhouse until I could see who it was, possibly until whoever it was had left. Between the latticework and the creepers that grew over it, I had a fair view all around with little danger of being seen.

It was Grant. He certainly did get around. He stopped when he saw Albert's grave, and approached it slowly. While I watched, not believing what I was seeing, he took a credit card out of his wallet and used it to cut into the grass of the grave.

I blasted out and down the steps, but I couldn't bring myself to go any closer.

"Get away from there!" I shouted.

Grant jerked, dropping the card, and turned a shocking shade of red. He leaped across the grave, grabbed me by both shoulders, shoved me backwards, and grabbed me again. I wouldn't have thought he'd had it in him.

"This is none of your business!" he said. "Don't you have work to do? Why don't you go do it?"

"Get away from that grave." I batted his hands from my shoulders. He had some height on me, and a lot more muscle than a poet had any right to sport, but I thought I could probably knock his block off if I put my mind to it.

"I have something to do first," he said. "Stay and watch, if you must; then run and tell, if that's your style; but I'll flatten you, if you try to stop me."

Like I said, I didn't think he could, but brawling over a grave wasn't my idea of a good way to spend a Sunday afternoon.

I had to watch him. I didn't want to, but I couldn't look away. What was he doing? What would he do to me for seeing him?

He went back to the grave and lifted off the small square of sod he'd cut. Then he reached in his pocket and pulled out a black bead necklace, small and delicate as a little girl's. The beads weren't flat black, but iridescent, and there was a pendant. It wasn't a necklace. I knew what it was, now: Jennifer Anstley, one of the Refuge kids who'd come and gone, had been a Catholic. Grant held a rosary.

He saw me staring. "Would you like to look at it? It's a beautiful thing." As I squatted across the grave from him, he said, "I had it made for him in Italy. Look." The pendant was a silver crucifix and, where the pendant met the necklace, there was an opal, just like the ones on Chan and

Wong's leashes. No, the crucifix wasn't upside-down. It was real.

Grant ran the beads through his fingers, stopping at the jewel. "Amelia Hardesty sent me this opal. She had given it to Albert and, after he died, she had it made into a pendant and sent it to me, care of my father. I've worn it, these past five years, in Albert's memory, but I want him to have it again." The rosary lay cupped in his palm. "This has been blessed by the Pope in St. Peter's Square, in Rome. Albert would have cherished it." He kissed the crucifix, dropped the beads into the hole in Albert's grave, then replaced the sod and pressed it flat.

He sat back, making the sign of the cross. Grant stared at the grave, and I stared at him. Finally, I broke the silence.

"I thought he worshiped the devil."

Grant lifted his face, and his black-lashed blue eyes showed me nothing of his thoughts. "Don't believe everything you hear. Albert was no more or less religious than most people, I suppose, but he certainly didn't worship *Satan*. You've read his books: His fiction was moral. He measured all his characters against a scale of absolute values, and he never let them get by with anything."

That was true. It was one of the reasons he was my favorite writer.

Grant said, "He claimed to be an agnostic. Although he said he had 'no quarrel with any philosophy or institution of spiritual responsibility', he didn't believe in worship."

"Spiritual responsibility? Don't make me laugh. If he wasn't into devil-worship, he sure left a pretty strong impression to the contrary."

Grant hunched his shoulders, looking down at the grave, and shivered. "That was one of Albert's ugly little jokes. He could be very cruel at times. He said occultism paved his way with women. Some women. He used what he knew or invented of the occult as he did any other facts or fancies: to gratify as much of his baser nature as possible. He felt that, by satisfying his lower self at every available opportunity, he could keep it from distracting him when his higher self was trying to create. You've read the results."

"He was one of the greatest," I said, though I told myself I'd never read him again.

Why did I believe all this? Why, after five days in a house where the only certainty was that you'd never get the same story from the same source twice running, did I believe this guy? Because it sounded like Albert. It sounded just like Albert.

Then it hit me what it meant.

"One of his ugly little jokes," I repeated. The family at Willowbrook was torn and tattered and turned against one another and in on themselves, and globe-trotting Aunt Missy had sentenced herself to five years' house arrest, and why? Because Albert was having an ugly little joke and died before he got to the punch line.

"The books you've been looking for," I said. "What were they? Props?"

And he told me. Albert's letters from Willowbrook had been about how wonderfully rich the family was in material, about the stories he'd been writing secretly, based on their reactions to his various posturings. They were about his intense admiration for Matthew Walton, who had legally looted as much of Eleanor's and Amelia's funds as possible, to keep Albert from having access to their money. They were about how genuinely grateful to Aunt Missy he was, and how fond he was of her; he said this sincerely even while he was dismantling her family and picking over the pieces. The letters were about Corrie and Mary and Eleanor, particularly about Mary. Somehow, the last letter said, she had guessed at his vampire purpose (his phrase), and was hinting for a look at the stories. She would certainly have destroyed the works if she'd read them. To camouflage the stories, Albert had written them in an "occult" Latin code, with another book of symbols and drawings taken from research and his own rich imagination as a blind. His last letter to Grant had included the code.

"The stories can be retrieved," Grant said. "Now you see why I must have those books."

"I see why you think so," which wasn't the same thing. If the stories in the black-and-red notebooks were up to Alaister's usual standard, it would be a crime to hide or destroy them. But wouldn't it be a crime to let them be published, to hold up the family — the family I loved — to ridicule?

"Where are they?" Grant asked.

"I don't know. I told you that before."

"You still don't trust me."

"It isn't that I don't trust you. It's just that there's no reason why I *should* trust you. Around here, that's enough."

"I don't understand."

"Suppose I told you that Albert's joke wasn't buried with him? Eleanor and Corrie tell me that Mary is leading them in rituals to bring Albert back from the dead. They've been creeping around at night for five years, now. They didn't know it was all in fun, see. How could they?"

"Because he didn't mean it! It wasn't real! They can't. . . !" For the first time since I'd met him, he was ugly. He had thought he was going on a treasure hunt and had ended up with a bit part in ALICE IN LOONYLAND.

"It's true," I said gently. "He didn't do these people any good. I don't know that I want to help you boost his output at their expense."

Grant swiped his palms across his face, leaving a smudge of damp earth on his left cheek. "For what it's worth," he said, unsteadily, "he would never have wanted to do such harm. Although that actually makes it all so much worse."

I couldn't have agreed with him more.

"You haven't told anybody else about Albert's little joke, have you?" I asked him.

"No."

"Not here — not anywhere?"

"No."

"You haven't showed his letters around? Sent them to his publisher?"

"No. They were private. Personal. I've never shared Albert's letters." He looked me in the eye. "I never will."

I didn't believe him, although I believed he thought he meant it. All I could hope was that the folks here would have had time to heal and recover their strength before Grant went back on his word.

"Albert's joke," I said, "stays between you and me. I'll figure out who to tell and when, so it doesn't do any more damage than it already has. Don't you tell anybody else. Not anybody here, anyway."

"No," said Grant. "My God. No."

Chapter 29

I left him contemplating the tombstone, as if he could read an expression on the marble.

It was time for backstairs supper, but I wasn't hungry. I muttered something to that effect when Corrie tried to stop me on my way past the servants' hall door. I think I told her I was sick, and I'm sure I looked it.

Sooner or later, no matter who else was kept ignorant, Aunt Missy had to know. She had asked me to help her get to the bottom of what was going on at Willowbrook, and the truth about Albert was just about as bottom as anybody was ever likely to get. The truth might hurt her, but knowing it wasn't going to hurt her more than not knowing it did.

So I went to her room and told her.

"Matthew never explained," she said weakly, when I had finished.

"He didn't know all of it."

"I mean his part of it. The money. The house. I never liked him much to begin with; I assumed the worst of him, and he never explained." She pulled the dogs into her lap and hugged them.

I doubted it would have done him much good to try, and the self-reproachful look Aunt Missy cast up at me seemed to say she was thinking the same thing.

Next item: "Eleanor told me, herself, that she's the one

who's been after the dogs," I said. "She said 'Mary' won't let her kill them."

Aunt Missy cuddled the dogs closer.

"But," I went on, "Mrs. Seldon-Hardesty's been 'helping' Miss Eleanor talk to Albert, and telling her he was coming back. She told her he *is* back, and that I'm him. This is Mary Seldon-Hardesty I'm talking about, not Corrie."

Aunt Missy shook her head, trying to deny what I was saying. She was pale; I could see that she wore rouge, lipstick, and eye shadow — all invisible when she had her natural color. I knelt beside her chair and put my arms around her, dogs and all. *I shouldn't have told her. I should have told Mr. Walton, and we could have kept it from her, somehow.*

"Damn Albert!" she growled, and my arms sprang away from her in shock. "God damn that miserable son-of-a-bitch to hell." She went on in that vein for a while, using some material that probably dated back to the twenties, and possibly some stuff that she had picked up from her father. I didn't understand everything, but it all sounded pretty ripe. *Poor dear little old lady.*

"Have you told Matthew?" she asked.

"Haven't found him. He wasn't in his office, and I don't know which room is his. Corrie says she hasn't seen him all day."

"We'll put the dogs on their leashes and then we'll find him. You tell him what you've told me; we'll get Grant to back it up, if he won't believe us. Eleanor will not stay another night under Mary's care."

We both stood up. She handed the dogs to me and snapped the leashes onto their harnesses.

"You take charge of them," she said. "I want my hands free."

Little and old she may have been, and she was certainly dear to me, but my Aunt Missy was no lady, and I hoped Mr. Walton wouldn't try to be difficult.

He wasn't in his room. We just buzzed in and buzzed out; I only got an impression of brown everything, and a portrait above the bed of a woman with Dr. Andrew's smile. His office was still locked, and there was still no answer when I rapped on the wood and called his name.

Lydia found us debating whether or not we should hunt up a key.

"You're looking for Uncle Matt? Mother told me he flew to Boston this afternoon for an emergency meeting. He won't be back until some time tomorrow. Why do you want him? Could I help?"

I wasn't sure I wanted to tell The Dragon Lady's adopted daughter (great title for a book) that we wanted to take her mother's prize "patient" away from her. I could see that Aunt Missy didn't like the idea, either.

"Thank you, dear," Aunt Missy said, "but we'll have to wait for Matthew. Um, I want to tell him I think we should give Mitch a raise."

"How nice!" Lydia beamed. "That calls for a celebration!" She winked. "Mother has driven Eleanor to Louisville for dinner and a show; they're staying overnight at the Brown." (Louisville's swankiest hotel — Trust Miss Mary for that.) "Sooo," Lydia hunched forward conspiratorially, "why don't you have dinner in the dining room, Mitch? With the family? The way we always wanted?"

She seemed to think it would be such a lovely treat for

me, I almost hated to turn her down.

"I couldn't do that. It wouldn't be right."

"What do you mean?" Lydia asked, but Aunt Missy knew.

"Mitch means Corrie is a human, as well," she said.

"Oh, you!" Lydia hugged her. Aunt Missy rolled her eyes at me. "I'll tell Corrie she's joining us, too. Mitch, you see if you can pry Andy out of that lab of his."

"What about Grant?" I asked, not nearly ready to feel chummy toward him. "How does he stand on the question of slumming with the help?"

"Oh, Mitch!" Lydia's predictable protest was squashed by Aunt Missy's reply.

"He'll like it or lump it," Aunt Missy said. "Lydia, I'll come with you. I haven't had a good heart-to-heart with Corrie in far too long. Will you take the dogs, please, Lydia?"

"Sandy doesn't like —" I began, but Aunt Missy interrupted me:

"Sandy isn't here."

Lydia laughed indulgently. Me, I planned to squeal on both of them if Thor found any dog-hairs in his kitchen.

~*~

I whistled on my way to the lab, and the tune wasn't "Lydia, the Tattooed Lady", either.

"Mitch! Come in! Come in!" Dr. Andrew's weary face was relaxed and seemed fuller, somehow. His lank hair even seemed to have more body, and his smile touched his mouth even when he wasn't smiling outright.

"Looks like whatever you're doing down here is going okay," I said.

"Splendidly!" He slapped his hands together and rubbed

his palms. "Come here; I'll show you."

I wasn't altogether sure I wanted to go into The Lab, but I followed him. No monster, no tanks of living matter. Just two tables. One, so low it was more of a metal platform, held a gizmo that looked like a satellite or something: round, with tubes and wires projecting from it. The other table was small and wooden, and held a cylinder of water, like a tall thin fish tank.

"Turbulence," Dr. Andrew said, as if this explained something. "In a jet engine, it's perfect; it's just what you want. *But*, above the wing," he lifted an eyebrow and shook a finger, and I understood that turbulence above the wing was not a good thing to have. "In a heart valve," he went on. "Even in an oil pipeline." He shook his head. "Nature is orderly. Fluids move in an orderly, patterned, predictable way. And then, suddenly, they don't. The movement shifts from order to chaos. Why? At what point? And, most important, *what happens at that point?*"

I could tell this was a very exciting question for him. I tried very hard to look intrigued, like this was a try-out for *Mr. Wizard*.

"Look at this." Dr. Andrew motioned me over to the cylinder. It was actually two cylinders, one inside the other, with water in between. "A turbulence machine. Watch." He plugged in a cord and the inner cylinder began turning. "Watch closely." He switched on the satellite. A thin, brilliant beam of light came out and illuminated the cylinder.

The inner cylinder moved faster, the water between the cylinders moved faster. In the light through the tubes, the water seemed to gather itself, to form itself into shapes, like doughnuts stacked in a pile, turning in unison. The inner cylinder spun faster; the doughnuts began to ripple. Faster; the doughnuts were gone in a mess of movement.

"Did you see it?" Dr. Andrew asked.

"I saw *something*."

"What did you see? A pattern?"

I nodded.

"And then?"

"Then no pattern."

"No!" He crowed it. "Wrong! For years, we've been trying to figure out why the pattern breaks up. Now I'm convinced that the pattern does *not* break up. What looks like random movement is a pattern. A complex pattern that we don't understand yet, but a pattern. I was looking back through the literature." He pulled a book out of a stack of papers and opened it. "You see? Lorenz' 1963 paper on deterministic chaos. Right here."

He went on to talk about three-dimensional concept space, trajectories, surfaces folding back on themselves, system dynamics, and something called a "strange attractor," that caused all these effects. It sounded very weird, and very familiar. So that's what Fruitcake Acres was: a turbulence machine. Everything's going along fine, Aunt Missy brings in a strange attractor, and WHAP! There goes order and predictability, right out the window. The dead got courted, dogs got dunked, people woke up with people they hadn't invited in bed with them. But, if Dr. Andrew was right, there was a pattern to all the chaos, if I could only see it.

It didn't matter, now, though. The worst was over. Tomorrow, Mr. Walton would be back, Grant and Aunt Missy and I would have a private conference with him, and Eleanor would finally get the healing help she needed. Mary could probably do with a little therapy, herself, but it would take a nicer person than I am to care much about that right now.

Dr. Andrew finished talking and I tried to think of something to say that wouldn't make me sound like I walked with my knuckles dragging the ground.

"What next?" I said, as if I'd followed everything up to that point and couldn't wait to hear more.

"Next. . . . Ah. . . ." Dr. Andrew stood regarding his twirling machine, then reached out and switched it off. He switched off the satellite ray-gun. He sighed and ran a hand through his hair. "Next, I give up."

"Give up?"

He shrugged, his smile shy and sad. "I haven't got the mind for this. I'm ready to admit it. Finally." He sighed again. "I thought I had a future in theory, but I can't think deeply enough, far enough ahead of the experiments and the mathematics. Other men are years ahead of me. I'm thirty-two. I should have made a major contribution to the field. *Some* contribution to the field."

"What about this turbulence stuff? Sounds pretty important to me."

"Does it?" He rested a hand on the top of the cylinder, where the water was slowing in the sudden quiet. "It's crackpot stuff, at this point, as far as the scientific community is concerned. This time, I'm too far ahead. Or I'm wrong. I could be wrong, though I don't think I am."

"See," I said, "that's the trouble with working alone. You need, like, a study partner to bounce your ideas off of."

"Yes, I do." He chuckled. "In a way, it's a relief: losing the pressure to excel. Plodders do an awful lot of useful work, you know. And I do miss the camaraderie of a group setting."

I got a picture of a roomful of physicists sitting at lunchroom tables, saying stuff like, "And the other guy says, 'Don't you know an electron when you see one?'" and slapping each other on the back with tears of laughter in their eyes.

Dr. Andrew leaned against the corner of the turbulence machine's table and smiled at me.

"Y'know," I said, "for a guy who just gave up a dream, you sure look happy."

"Do I?"

"You do. Because of losing the pressure to excel?"

"Partly that."

"Because you're sure you're right about this chaos pattern stuff?"

"Partly that."

"Because you feel so good after taking last night off?"

His grin widened. "Mostly that."

"Dr. Andrew! What did you do, out on the town in that flashy suit you wore out of here?"

He laughed. "You have no idea. No idea."

Lydia called down one of the stairways to me, and I remembered what I'd come to say.

"Your Aunt Mary is in Louisville with Eleanor tonight, and Corrie and I have been invited to eat with the Quality. Lydia seems to think it's some kind of party. Will you come?"

He laughed again. "Love to."

Since it was Sandy and Ava's day off, Corrie gave us cold shaved chicken sandwiches on Sandy's home-made bread and re-heated black bean soup that Sandy had made the day before and left in the refrigerator. Lydia helped her set the table and carry the sandwich platter and the soup tureen. The dining room was brightly lit by two electric chandeliers, and had a mural of some gold-lit countryside (Florence, Italy, I learned later) all over the walls except for the doors, and a big piece of furniture they told me was a breakfront. This breakfront deal had a shelf at about waist height, and Corrie and Lydia put the food on it and told us to help ourselves.

Lydia, Corrie, and Aunt Missy chattered away like three old friends, except that Corrie kept pulling herself up short, as if she had to guard against one particular subject, but had it too much on her mind to keep away from it. Dr. Andrew talked almost exclusively to me, and Grant turned the charm on us all.

When we had finished eating, Dr. Andrew stood up with an air of determination and tapped his glass with his spoon. When he had our attention, he said, "There's something I want you all to know."

Corrie paled and glanced around.

I felt my heart plunge: Dr. Andrew had found out about Corrie and her boyfriend, had found out something she didn't want us to know, and he was going to tell. That wasn't who I wanted Dr. Andrew to be! I knew he didn't like Corrie, but—

"Corrie and I are married," he said.

I didn't quite register that.

"We were married last night — drove to Tennessee and back. Corrie wanted to keep it a secret until things became more settled here, or until I could get a post or a position and take her away, but I can't pretend anymore. I have to acknowledge her." He put out an arm, and Corrie moved into it.

Sherlock Franklin. I must be a closet snob or something: It never occurred to me that Corrie's man was

The Young Master. I only hoped she didn't get pretensions of grandeur and hyphenate her name. I mean, Mary Seldon-Hardesty has a certain ring to it. Corina Crawley-Walton, you must agree, doesn't.

Chapter 30

Lydia pretended to fuss at Corrie for not sharing the secret about her romance with "Andy", but it was obviously one of those things girls do, and nobody believed she was really mad. Grant toasted the newlyweds with a speech so ooey-gooey it would caramelize vinegar. Aunt Missy seemed to get as much of a charge out of what Mrs. Seldon-Hardesty would think as she did out of Corrie's and Dr. Andrew's happiness.

We all helped clean up the dining room and the kitchen, even Dr. Andrew and Grant and Miss Lydia. After the dishes were put away, Grant excused himself. No doubt he planned to seize the opportunity to toss a room or two while we were occupied. After he was gone, any formality that had survived dinner fell by the wayside. We brought chairs into the servants' hall and sat around the table drinking milk and yakking until almost eleven.

It seems Dr. Andrew had fallen for Corrie when he came home in '62 but, because of her past, she was afraid of him. She was just starting to trust him when Albert — Mr. Chaos — blew in. After that, it was Albert all the way, until time and her native intelligence had started to wake her up. Then Aunt Missy dropped me into the mix. With that extra shake-up, Corrie transferred all her devotion to where it belonged: to Dr. Andrew, who'd never stopped loving her.

Romance comics are more like real life than you care to think.

~*~

When I left Aunt Missy at her room, she reached up and hugged me. I thought I was going to cry, right there in front of her. I remembered what she'd said, though, about not letting people saddle her with being responsible for them, and I managed to hold it in.

"Tomorrow," Aunt Missy said, "we lower the boom on Mary Seldon-Hardesty!" With a sigh of malicious satisfaction, she reeled in the dogs. She shivered. "I'm all keyed up," she said. "Perhaps I should have asked Andrew for something to help me sleep."

"You want me to go tell him?"

"No, dear. Thank you, though."

"Tell you what: I'll leave my door unlocked. Give me fifteen minutes to brush my teeth and get into my jammies, and then you can come in and talk if you want to. If the light's off, just flick it on."

"I wouldn't want to wake you up."

"I don't care. Come ahead on, if you want to. I probably won't be asleep, anyway. I'll probably just be lying there with my mind going a mile a minute. So feel free."

She shook her head, but she said, "Thank you, dear," as she closed the door.

~*~

I went to bed giddy and wide-eyed, certain that I would hear Aunt Missy and the dogs padding along presently, and that we'd see the sun come up together. Instead, I seemed to have dropped off to sleep as soon as I tucked myself in.

I woke with someone shaking me. Aunt Missy? No, the hands on my shoulders were strong. Dr. Andrew? One hand was removed, and the bedside lamp clicked on.

It was the Dragon Lady.

"I thought you were in Louisville," I said.

"You thought a lot of mistaken things. We drove away, then we drove back and waited for all the lights to go out. Then we waited a little longer. Now, you will get out of bed, and we will go to the summerhouse."

That didn't sound like something I wanted to do. Not even a little bit. "I don't think so," I said, too freaked out to be polite. "I think you'll get out of my room and I'll lock the door."

"You'll do as I say, or your precious 'Nell' is a dead woman."

She said the words, "precious Nell ", with more venom than I'd ever heard in a human voice, and of course it wasn't *my* precious Nell she was talking about. It *was* Miss Eleanor, though, no matter who she was precious to, so the threat had teeth, regardless.

I eased out of bed. I didn't see a weapon. I wondered if I could knock her down, or if she had that crazy-person super-strength adrenaline rush going for her. With Miss Eleanor's life at stake, I couldn't take the chance.

"How is she a dead woman?" I asked.

"You'll see. Out the door and down the kitchen stairs. Now."

"Lemme put some pants on first."

"No. Go now."

"*You're* dressed — why shouldn't I be?"

In fact, she was dressed in some kind of body-thing, black, that went from a turtleneck collar down to her wrists, and on down to her ankles. She wore black zip-up half-boots. Very trendy, very Carnaby Street; I wondered if she'd ripped it off out of Lydia's closet, or if she was a go-go girl on the weekends. I was surprised and repelled to notice that she didn't have a bad figure.

"Now," she said.

Barefoot and in blue cotton pajamas, I felt nothing like a hero, so I went. If Miss Eleanor really was in some kind of death-trap or something, my going along might be her only chance. I pulled the door almost shut, then shoved it half-open.

"Close that," Mary said, quietly.

I pulled the door closed again. She waited until she heard it latch. So much for the forlorn hope that somebody would get up for a snack and see the door open and come looking for me. Like anybody would look in the woods in the middle of the night.

Sandy and Ava were still away, visiting their married daughter in Paoli, Corrie had said. I couldn't try for help from them. If I only knew where Eleanor was, I might grab a pot from Sandy's overhead rack and ring Mary like a gong.

I heard the slithering sound of metal on wood as Mary pulled a knife from the butcher-block knife-rack. I twitched.

"Don't look around. Go on. You know the way."

The terrace was slick with dew, and cold. I thought it must be very early in the morning. I wished I had looked at the clock on my bedside table, as if it mattered what time it was.

The night was cloudless. The moon barely cleared the trees, looking bright and huge; too big to be for real.

The garden was silver, the gravel paths glittered. Pretty, but painful. Every step hurt. I was going to have stone bruises from toe to heel, not to mention the perforations. I could hear Mary's shoes crunching along behind me.

"You're really enjoying this, aren't you?" I asked. I expected the knife in the back, but she only laughed very softly.

The twigs and nut-casings on the path through the woods didn't feel any better than the gravel. I swore my way into the clearing, Mary chuckling at each oath. It was the most fun I'd ever known her to have.

"Into the summerhouse," she said.

"Where is she?"

"In the summerhouse."

I edged up the steps, afraid of what might be in the dark, but more afraid of what I knew was behind me.

"Eleanor? Nell?"

A sudden, sharp, solid pain in the side of my head was the last thing I felt before I passed out.

When I came to, the inside of the summerhouse was lit by dozens of flickering candles of all shapes and sizes; slim ones in brass candlesticks and fat ones sitting on their bottoms. At first I thought they were black, but then I saw at least some of them were dark red. None of them were ballerina pink, that was for sure.

This was the first time I'd seen the inside of the summerhouse clearly. A bench ran almost completely around the interior. No, not a bench, cupboards, with thick tops suitable for sitting on but hinged to open up. Two were open, now. I felt a little disembodied, lying there, and I thought,

You could keep blankets and paper plates and plastic forks and stuff out here and be ready for a picnic any time. That's very convenient. When I saw Miss Mary bend over one of the open cupboards and lift out a folded cloth, I thought, *See? Picnic blanket.*

No, it was a robe. She put it on over her black body-thing. She looked very impressive, especially from my vantage point of bleeding all over the floor. Liquid trickled into my hair and, when I put my hand to it, my fingers came away smeared with damp darkness. I wiped the blood off on the floorboards.

"Awake?" Mary said. "I was afraid I'd hit you too hard, this time."

"This time?" My voice was slurred and sounded unfamiliar. "You? You, Mary? *You?*"

"I was afraid you didn't know. That's one of the reasons I wanted you back. This time, you'll know." Her cool I-am-a-lady expression turned into a mask of barely-controlled rage. "I told you to stay away from my daughter. You could have had any woman you wanted. I rather enjoyed helping you to the fools. But when you had the effrontery to plan to marry into my family and then, when Lydia came home for the summer and you started talking about her . . . talking to *me* about her. . . ."

I thought I might retch, and it wasn't just from the pain and shock of the blow to my head.

"I didn't mean it," I said. "About Lydia. Mother-and-daughter acts are a bit much, even for me. It was a joke."

Mary lifted a necklace from the cupboard and fastened it around her neck, "It turned out to be a very ill-conceived joke, didn't it?" The pendant of the necklace was an inverted cross. "And you did mean to marry into my family.

That alone was unforgivable."

I was suddenly furious. "Albert Alaister is a great man! A great writer! How *dare* you consider me beneath you because of what my parents and grandparents did for their livings — because my ancestors immigrated later than yours! I was short-listed for the Nobel Prize! What has *your* family ever achieved besides a high score in polo and a knack for making tasteful flower-arrangements?" I was so dizzy, I hardly knew what I was saying. I just wanted to throw her off-balance, I guess. Buy myself time to recover.

I heard a groan, and it wasn't from me. *Eleanor!* I craned my head around, but I couldn't see her. The movement made me dizzy, so I stopped.

Mary smiled. "Your fellow participant in tonight's festival. Today's, rather. You thought you were very clever, didn't you, leaving on the anniversary of your death?" She laughed. "I never planned to do anything that night. The night of your death would be too powerful a time for you, and this ritual is under *my* control. It's for *my* benefit. I always planned it for now. Not tonight; you might have expected it to be tonight. No, this morning."

Why this morning? Sunday? No, this was Monday. Monday. The day Albert was buried. The day Jason and Joan and Mary's husband, Alain, died.

"I swore I'd make you pay for that," Mary said, as if she knew I'd followed the twist in her reasoning. "After I killed you to save Eleanor and Lydia and Alain—"

I heard myself cackle. "Alain?"

"You would have told him about us. The longer I knew you, the more certain I was of that. He was a dear, kind man."

"You had nothing good to say about him."

"He was everything I said to you, but he was dear and kind! I couldn't let you hurt him! But you did, in spite of me, didn't you? You killed him! And Joan and Jason with him! Perhaps you had that arranged before I killed you, so you could marry Eleanor's inheritance rather than waiting for it. But why Alain? Why couldn't you leave me Alain? Once you were dead, I could have cleansed myself, renewed our marriage. But you murdered him!"

With the word "murdered", she kicked me in the head, on the side opposite my previous wound. I thought my neck had snapped. I saw those stereotypical stars.

"Innocent again," I gasped. "I am many things, but never a killer."

"Liar!"

"Oh, yes; certainly that. But not a killer." I was dazed, babbling, words coming from I didn't know where. I only hoped they would be the right ones.

Mary swayed toward me, as if she were about to attack. The candle's glow played along her cheek as she tightened her jaw, forcing herself back under control. She took a ragged breath and said, "For five years, I've used Eleanor and Corrie and the things you taught me—" she waved a hand at her robe and the candles, "—to bring you back. Then Amelia brought that boy home, and Corrie saw you in him, and I knew I had succeeded!"

I laughed, but it hurt my head and I stopped. "The things I taught you! I never believed in all this claptrap! I thought you were intelligent enough to sense that. I thought it was a joke we shared, my love."

"Joke?" Mary said, uncertainly.

"Now, let's stop all this." I rolled onto my side, facing her. "Blow out those candles, and let me get my rest."

"No." She shuddered and picked up the knife. "It's too late, now. I'm going to bring you back with blood. A blood sacrifice. And guess who'll get the blame? The stray, the mongrel, Miss Amelia's dog-boy. His victim put up a fight, but the boy was merciless — a wild, mad thing. I'll do it myself, of course, then I'll knock you out again and put the bloody robe on you. Put the bloody knife in your hand. Then one of your blasphemous Satanic candles will fall over and this tinderbox will burn down around you. I hope you're conscious when I send you back to hell!"

I struggled to my knees. "Nobody would believe it. The boy is not unknown."

She laughed. "Who would stand up for him? Civil servants? Schoolteachers?"

"Who do you think is on the police force in Faelin? On the bench? On the jury? *His* peers, not yours."

Mary wavered for a moment, then her focus returned. "You can't make me doubt myself any more. I am in control! *I* am! First the blood and then the fire!"

"Nell! Nell!"

"Relax, darling," Mary said. "Your precious Nell is sound asleep in bed." She grasped my collar and jerked me around to the edge of the other opened cupboard.

I looked down into the terrified eyes of a bound and gagged Matthew Walton.

Chapter 31

"I had planned on using Corrie," Mary said, "but I couldn't find her, and Matthew kept following me all over the house, bleating about my having mourned Alain long enough. As if five years were enough to pay for what I'd done to Alain. What *you* did to him. As if a self-made, up-by-his-bootstraps shopkeeper were a fit husband for a Seldon."

"At last, Matthew," I said, "we find common ground: We've both committed the unpardonable error of considering ourselves on Mary's social level. For this, we must die."

My head felt like it had been used to crack walnuts. I could barely hear myself talk. I could see from Mr. Walton's eyes that he thought I'd gone crazier than Miss Mary.

She went on: "I had some water laced with sleeping powder that Andrew gave me for Eleanor. Matthew and I brought the bottle and two glasses out here to 'talk things out.' Matthew said his mouth always went dry when he was nervous." She laughed. "I would imagine it's dry now, wouldn't you?"

Mr. Walton had been in that cupboard, drugged and bound and gagged, since the afternoon? Had he been there, unconscious or semi-conscious, when Eleanor and I had met, and I didn't know it? Had he heard me? Tried to make a sound, to draw my attention, and I hadn't heard, or hadn't noticed?

"First the sacrifice," Mary said, "then the purification."

"No!" I said — shouted or whispered, I couldn't say which. "No! You can't!"

There was a movement in the doorway, and a smooth voice said, "He's right."

I turned my head and my mind cleared, as if a mist had lifted. My eyes focused on Grant Marsch, candle-light playing over his black clothes. "The honor belongs to me."

"Grant." Mary moved slowly toward him.

"No," Grant said. And he smiled.

Mary looked at me, then back at Grant. "Albert?"

He stepped into the summerhouse. "Why didn't you invite Grant to your little ceremony in the first place? Why did I have to wake him and call him out? I was nearly too late, too. I wouldn't have liked that."

"Albert!"

I lost all feeling in my hands and feet; even my nose felt cold. All the blood had gone into the racing of my heart. *Whaddya know,* I distantly felt myself thinking. *Corrie was right.*

"You stupid cow," Grant said, fondly. "You should have known I'd rather be Grant Marsch than some indigent mongrel. I was that in my own youth. You should have planned to give me Grant's body all along. Kill Walton, blame the boy, and burn the evidence. Then you go your way, redeeming yourself, and I go my way. As always."

"I have to kill you!" Mary said, raising the knife.

"No, you don't, my love. It isn't *my* fault you betrayed your husband. You could have told me no. Isn't that true?

Hmmm? Could a Seldon be seduced by a *nobody*, unless she consented to the seduction? No, my love, that was your decision; the sin of that was all yours."

"You killed Alain."

"*You* killed Alain. Who was driving that day? Alain. *I* certainly never told him about us; I had no desire to be thrown out on my ear. But what makes you think he didn't realize the truth without being told? What makes you think he didn't drive into that tree on purpose? Poor man. Perhaps he hoped Jason and Joan would survive; perhaps he was too unbalanced to care."

"No!"

"'Why so pale and wan, fond lover?' Where's my fierce Mary?" He crooked a finger under her chin and lifted her face so she looked him in the eye. "Where's my Dragon Lady?" He took the knife and moved, with casual grace, to my side. "We'll just get this out of the way." He put down the knife, gripped me under the arms, and pulled me to the door. With a strength I wouldn't have expected in him, he hefted me out. I rolled down onto the grass.

"No!" Mary said.

"I'll bring him back in, when the time comes. We don't need him now; his presence would only interfere. He isn't going anywhere. You've seen to that, you delicious viper."

The wet grass revived me a little, and I pulled myself back up the steps. I tried to stand. . . . Couldn't. . . .

I screamed as Grant leaned over Mr. Walton's prison. The knife disappeared from my view, Grant sawed and sawed, and Mary chanted words I didn't understand — didn't want to understand.

Mr. Walton. He killed Mr. Walton, and all I did was watch.

He left the knife in the cupboard and came back to me. He put his arms under mine and his lips right against my ear. I flinched, but he held me fast.

"How are you doing?" he murmured. "Can you stand on your own?"

In the summerhouse, Mary shrieked with fury. She stood over the cupboard, and howled a jumble of accusations and threats. Grant released me and leaped up the steps. Mary reached into the cupboard and pulled out the knife, clean and shining in the flickering light, and plunged it toward him. Grant dodged it and backed toward the door.

I leaned against the doorway and took a shaky step into the room. Maybe Mr. Walton wasn't dead. Maybe I could still help him. My head swam, but I stayed on my feet.

"I do as I please, Mary," Grant said. "I always have. Did you think you could control me?"

She stabbed at him again. He grabbed her wrist and swung her around, twisting her arm up behind her back. She cried out and dropped the knife. *Then* that strength-of-ten adrenaline kicked in, and she broke away. Grant kicked the knife to me, and I managed to push it out into the grass. Mary went for him with her nails, with her fists. Grant forgot about being a gentleman and started punching, but she just wouldn't quit.

I had the woozy impression that Grant was maybe a Good Guy, after all, but I was far from certain. At any rate, there was nothing I could do to help, short of falling down and making somebody trip over me. All I wanted to do was get past both of them and see about Mr. Walton.

I heard someone keening in the distance. *Corrie? Is Corrie crying? No, Corrie's happy.*

Grant and Mary, locked in a desperate embrace, knocked

into me and I crumpled to the floor. I went cold again, then hot, and my vision began to fade to black. The last thing I saw was Matthew Walton rising from the cupboard and clubbing his own true love in the head with a brass candle-stand.

~*~

I woke in a hospital.

I knew I'd end up in a nut-house. Or maybe I started out in a nut-house. Maybe I hallucinated the whole thing. Crazy as a tree full of hoot owls. What a relief! "And then he woke up." Corny, but—

My head hurt. I reached up and felt a bandage. *So, the padding came off my cell, and. . . .*

A nurse came in to give me a shot.

"Where am I?" *Not original, but to the point.*

"Oh, you're awake! The doctor will be so pleased. You've been out for hours."

"I'm in, now. But where am I?"

"I'll be right back."

Bureaucrat.

She wasn't gone long, and the doctor answered my question.

"You're in Faelin General Hospital."

"What ward?"

He gave me A Look and said, "Feel like visitors?"

"Depends on who they are."

He gave me another Look and left.

Aunt Missy came in alone, first. She hugged me and we both cried. We didn't say anything, but we didn't have to.

Finally, she said, "Mrs. Brandt was here for hours, but

she had to go back to the children. I promised I'd call her when you woke up."

"Did you? Call her?"

"I told the nurse to do it."

We were both silent again until I got the courage to ask, "Mr. Walton?"

"Matthew is shaken, but unharmed, thanks to you."

"I didn't do anything but pass out."

"You stalled Mary long enough for Grant to catch up to her. And he stalled her long enough for Matthew to help himself, and nearly long enough for the police to get there."

That must have been the wail I'd heard — the cop-car siren.

"Who called the fuzz?"

"I did. Grant woke me up and told me he'd seen Mary taking you into the woods and that he was going to follow. He suggested I call the police. A very sensible young man, on the whole, especially for an artistic type."

"And they came when you called?"

She sniffed. "I didn't tell them I was Amelia Hardesty, reporting her niece-by-marriage on a homicidal rampage. I told them I was calling for Matthew Walton, reporting a trespasser. Property. That's the golden key."

I knew what having to use Mr. Walton's name had cost her pride, and I expected her eyes to go all steely, but she surprised me with a twinkle. "Golden keys can be very useful, at times."

"And Mary? Eleanor?"

"Mary is in custody. In the mental ward of this facility, as a matter of fact. I doubt very much if she'll be fit to stand trial any time soon. Eleanor, as you may imagine, is extremely upset, but Corrie is explaining matters in a way only Corrie could. We are assured that Eleanor will do quite well with weekly sessions of professional therapy."

That only left one person unaccounted for.

"Did she. . . ? Is Grant. . . ?"

"Grant is waiting to see you. He seemed to think you might refuse, but he asked me to plead for him." She raised an eyebrow. "Should I send him in, or send him away?"

"In."

She left, and I heard whispers in the hall.

Grant stepped in, closed the door, and stood there, as far across the room as he could get, staring at me. I stared back.

"Something woke me up," he said. "A hand, shaking me." It took him three tries to get the next sentence out: "Nobody was there. Something urged me to the window. I looked out and saw Mary taking you into the woods at the point of a knife."

I licked my lips. "You told Aunt Missy to call the cops. Why her? Why not Dr. Andrew or Lydia? Most people think she's in the ozone. Goofy."

He cracked the edge of a smile. "You and I both know that Amelia Hardesty has more sense and more grit than the rest of that house put together."

With a smile-fragment of my own, I nodded.

"And then what happened?" I wasn't sure I wanted to know.

"*You* tell *me*. I followed you out to the summerhouse. I walked in and saw you leaning over an open box. You turned around. The next thing I knew, the police came in. It was as if . . . I had been. . . ." He swallowed so hard I could see it from across the room.

"Adrenaline rush," I said. "You went on auto-pilot." He

looked unconvinced. "You were great. I mean it. You cut Mr. Walton loose and held Mary off until the cops got there. You saved our lives, yours and mine and Mr. Walton's."

"I did?"

"Yes."

"Are you sure it was I?"

Hospital lighting isn't so great, but he probably looked worse than I did. He looked like a guy whose hair was primed to go white overnight.

"I'm sure."

"Mary says—"

"Mary's a psychopath. Never mind what Mary says. You were you. You were great. You're a hero. I'll make you a medal when I get back to shop class."

He got some color, then, and even blushed. "About Albert," he said. "I know what you must think of him. He had his flaws — enormous ones — but he . . . had a better side, too."

"I know," I said. Grant started to look worried again, and I said, "I've read his stuff, remember?"

He nodded uncertainly and left.

I had one more visitor waiting, but he had to cool his heels while a nurse took my temperature and pulse and changed my IV. That gave me some time to think.

I wished I could believe that Grant was lying about his amnesia, but I didn't. He really didn't remember what he had said and done in the summerhouse. So either I was right, and he had acted out a part on automatic, or Albert Alaister had saved my life.

Me, I liked the automatic pilot story.

Chapter 32

My last visitor was Mr. Walton. The nurse tried to tell him visiting hours were over, but he handed her a note and she left us alone.

"Special dispensation from the Chief of Staff," he explained to me.

Golden keys can be very useful, at times.

"I want to thank you," he said, poking at the edges of things on that rolling tray stand they feed you off of. "I've been hearing about some of what you've been through this week." He cleared his throat. "I'm not unaware of the fact that I added to your burden. A burden that a child should not have been asked to bear."

"Mr. Walton—"

"Hear me out." He cleared his throat again. "I know that you're almost eighteen, almost out of high school — nearly a man, in fact. But. . . . Well, I spoke to Mrs. Brandt. She thinks. . . . She believes — well, she assures me, actually, that there would be very little trouble, given your age, even though I'm no longer married. . . ."

"Mr. Walton, are you. . . ." I couldn't say it. I had thought I knew exactly how much going through the world alone meant to me, but I had simply had no idea. I hadn't even been close.

"I would like to adopt you," he said. "Send you to college — the best you can test into, and I'm betting that'll be a pretty fine one."

I felt more stunned than I had in the summerhouse. "What one did you go to?"

He shrugged and dropped his gaze. "I didn't."

"Maybe we could go together," I said, and he looked up with a startled smile. "Be roomies. Wear matching letter jackets. Sing the old school song together. Wear the old school tie. How about it, Pop?"

"'Pop'?" His lips twitched. "Well, perhaps not."

We laughed over the image, which was the idea, and we were both glad of the laugh. It kept us from blubbering all over each other, and we didn't want to do that. That wouldn't be manly.

THE END

www.ingramcontent.com/pod-product-compliance
Lightning Source LLC
Chambersburg PA
CBHW060908250626
47159CB00008B/2918